The Key to
Flambards

www.davidficklingbooks.com

OTHER BOOKS BY LINDA NEWBERY

Young adult fiction

The Shell House
(shortlisted for the Carnegie Medal)
Set in Stone
(winner of the Costa Children's Book Award)
The Damage Done
Some Other War
Sisterland
(shortlisted for the Carnegie Medal)
Flightsend

Junior Fiction

The Brockenspectre
(illustrated by Pam Smy)
Tilly's Promise
Blitz Boys
The Treasure House
At the Firefly Gate
Nevermore
The Sandfather
Catcall
Andie's Moon

Stories for Young Children

Lob
(illustrated by Pam Smy)
Barney the Boat Dog
Cat Tales
Posy

Adult fiction

Missing Rose
(Quarter Past Two on a Wednesday Afternoon)

The Key to Flambards

Linda Newbery

David Fickling Books

31 Beaumont Street
Oxford OX1 2NP, UK

The Key to Flambards
is a
DAVID FICKLING BOOK

First published in Great Britain in 2018 by
David Fickling Books,
31 Beaumont Street,
Oxford, OX1 2NP

Hardback edition published 2018
This paperback edition published 2019

978-1-78845-005-8

1 3 5 7 9 10 8 6 4 2

Papers used by David Fickling Books are from well-managed
forests and other responsible sources.

DAVID FICKLING BOOKS Reg. No. 8340307

A CIP catalogue record for this book is available from the British Library.

Typeset in 11/16 pt Sabon by Falcon Oast Graphic Art Ltd.
Printed and bound in Great Britain by Clays, Ltd., Elcograf S.p.A.

*To Kathy Peyton, of course, with love and admiration –
and thanks for lending me the key*

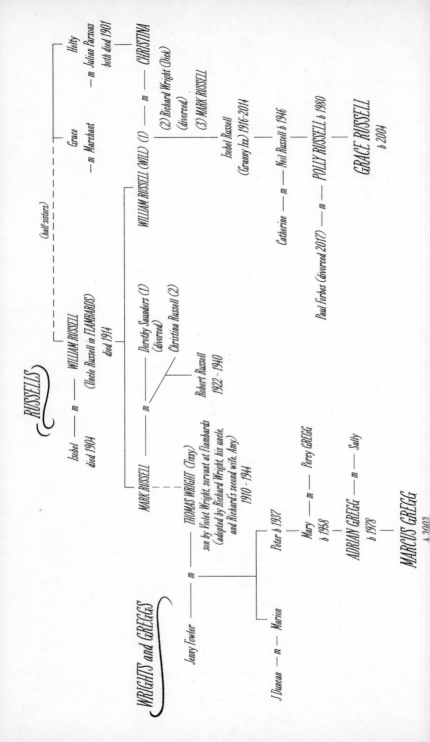

Contents

CHAPTER ONE

In Colour

It felt strange now to realize that Flambards had been there all the time. It was a real house after all, not just a memory – out in Essex, reachable by train and car in little more than an hour.

'It's in colour!'

That was the first thing Grace said when Mum showed her the website. At once she heard how silly that sounded, but Mum laughed, knowing what she meant. Until now they'd seen Flambards only in Granny Izz's old photos, in black and white. Grace had always *thought* of it in black and white too, preserved in time like a museum exhibit – the big old house standing proud and alone, walls thick with ivy, windows dark. It had an air of defiance, as if it knew it was marooned in the past, but would stand there until the modern world shoved it out of the way. In the website photo

1

it looked more cheerful; more approachable, with pots of flowers each side of the open front door and two smiling people in the porch, coming out.

Look! it said. *I'm still here!*

'It's been waiting for us,' Mum said, 'and we never knew.'

Unlike Grace, Mum had actually *been* to Flambards – just once, a month ago, after the message that had brought it so surprisingly into their lives. Now, with bags packed for the whole summer holidays, they were on their way there. Soon Grace would see it for herself, the place where Granny Izz – really her *Great*-Granny – had been born and brought up. Granny Izz had died four years ago when Grace was ten, at what everyone called the Grand Old Age of ninety-eight; if she were around now she'd be the even grander, nearly impossible, age of a hundred and two. She had always been so alert, so keenly interested in everything, even when she was frail and old, that it was still a surprise to find her gone.

Grace felt a bit sad to be going to Flambards without her to show them round. Everything they knew about the place came from her photos and memories. She'd told Grace that she loved Flambards, but had left as soon as she was old enough and never lived there again. 'London was the place for me. I had to be in London, at the heart of things. Couldn't bury myself in the country all my life.' But there had been something wistful in her voice, as if she'd left part of herself behind.

The city sprawl had thinned, giving way to fields and

woods. Through the train window Grace saw trees, grazing cattle, a busy road threading through a cut, and now and then a station stop.

'Ours next.' Mum put her book and water bottle into her bag, and soon the train slowed again.

It stopped at the smallest station Grace had ever seen, just a brick building on one side of the tracks and a footbridge to the other platform. Following Mum, she clambered down awkwardly, humping her bag behind her. They were the only people who'd got off, and there was no café or waiting room, no one checking tickets or waiting on the platform. A ticket barrier stood open and unattended.

As the train pulled away, taking its passengers and its trailings of city-ness, the silence was broken only by birds singing. Grace was used to busy streets and shops, sunlight mirrored by windscreens and windows, heat bouncing off buildings and pavements. Here the quietness was like a pressure in her ears, almost audible. They walked out into sunshine and a small road where a single car was waiting.

'Oh good.' Mum put her phone away. 'Here's our taxi.'

She'd booked it ahead; otherwise, Grace thought, looking around, they'd have been marooned in the middle of nowhere.

'Russell?' the driver called to them. 'For Flambards?'

'That's us. D'you know the way?'

The driver nodded. 'I do. Take people up there or back, most weeks.'

While he loaded their luggage into the boot, Mum opened the back door for Grace, waited for her to climb in, then got into the passenger seat. They weren't used to taxis – in London there were always buses or the Underground, and taxis were expensive – but there was no other way of getting themselves and their baggage to Flambards, a few miles from the station.

'Some kind of arty holiday place, int it?' The driver lowered himself heavily into his seat. 'You off for a holiday, then? Nice weather for it.'

'Not a holiday exactly, not for me,' Grace's mother told him. 'I've got a job there for the summer.'

'Oh yeah? What, teaching painting, or something like that?'

'No – in the office. Publicity.'

Settling herself while they chatted, moving her leg to a comfortable position, Grace looked out as the taxi pulled away.

In spite of her doubts about the weeks ahead, she felt a swell of excitement. Just a few more minutes! On the website she'd seen the gallery of photographs, the links to courses on art and history and poetry, but in her mind the two versions persisted, side by side. There was the long-ago Flambards of the photos, back in the days of floor-length skirts and horse-drawn carts and great-great-relatives whose names she muddled up; and there was this one, the real place they were heading for. Mum had said that Granny Izz would barely know the place now. The photo gallery showed sleek bathrooms and people splashing colours on to big abstract paintings, others twisting themselves into yoga poses or laughing in the glow of a campfire.

4

'Yes, it used to be my family that owned it, ages ago,' her mother was telling the taxi driver. 'The Russells at Flambards go back well over a hundred years, to Victorian times when the house was built. But it was sold before I was born.'

The Russell name, it seemed, meant nothing to the driver. 'Must have changed hands a good few times over the years, I reckon.'

'Yes, it has,' Mum agreed. 'That's why I'd never been there till last month. It was privately owned till two years ago – I didn't even know it was a retreat centre till the new manager got in touch.'

Grace saw hedges and trees; nothing but trees and hedges and fields reaching into hazy distance. The taxi slowed for a tractor carrying a load of hay, and the smell of sweet dry grassiness through the open window made her think of the school field, the running track, the excitement of sports day; limbering up ready to sprint, her legs full of running.

But that was Before, the way so many things were Before. The tractor driver, seated high in his cab, raised a hand in thanks.

'Be a bit quiet for you, won't it, out here in the sticks?' their own driver said, catching Grace's eye in the mirror. She gave a wincing smile back.

Yes, it would. That was the whole point. Curious as she was to see Flambards, Grace had baulked at Mum's idea of staying for so long. Wouldn't just a day visit have been enough?

What was she going to *do* there? She'd be cut off from Marie-Louise, cut off from everyone – even from the people she didn't especially want to see. 'For the whole summer holidays?' she had protested, when Mum told her. 'But that's weeks and *weeks*!'

Her mother had said that they could both do with a change. As if they hadn't had more than enough change already! And none of it through choice. What she meant, when Grace pressed, was that they needed a change from being at home – though they couldn't really call it home any more, with most of their things packed up in boxes.

Grace didn't like not knowing where home would be. When they'd closed the front door at Rignell Road earlier this morning, it felt like leaving for ever. Where would they go after their stay here? Mum didn't know, though she kept promising that something would be sorted out.

The taxi had reached a village street. Grace looked out at a pub and an old-fashioned shop – or was it actually a modern shop pretending to look old? – with baskets of fruit and vegetables out on the pavement and loaves of bread in the window. An old man with a whiskery grey terrier on a lead stopped to talk to a woman with a shopping trolley. She thought of texting Marie-Louise: **All ancient people round here. Wish you were here! It'd be a lot more fun.**

Marie-Louise was in Paris with her parents, having left on the first day of the holidays. When they came back, and Grace and her mother were settled in, she might be able to come and visit. Grace hoped so. Everything would be much less strange if Marie-Louise could be here to share it with her.

'Not far now,' said the driver. Beyond the church and graveyard he turned off the road into a narrow drive, bordered by trees. A large painted sign at the junction said, *FLAMBARDS – courses, retreats and workshops throughout the year*, with a website address and a colour photograph of the house. Now they entered what looked like a private road, fenced on both sides; it led slightly uphill, a wood to the right, a field on the left with sheep grazing. Grace looked out with a sense of travelling farther and farther from everything she knew. If she wanted to get out – to go down to that village shop perhaps, though it didn't look promising – she'd have to walk there and back. Was there a bus, perhaps, that might take her somewhere else? At least Mum had promised there'd be wifi, so that was something. She could hardly bear to think of six weeks without wifi.

The car turned a bend and the house came into view. There it was: Flambards, leaping into vision with a tug of familiarity, the house of her imagination made real and solid. Huge, it looked, standing square and proud, as if it were saying, *Here I am. People come and go, times change, but I'll always be here.*

The taxi pulled round in front of the house and halted with a scrunch of tyres on gravel. Grace tilted her head, looking up. The house reared tall, clad to its eaves in a dark mantle of ivy.

Mum sorted coins while Grace heaved herself out of the

back seat and the driver lifted their luggage out of the boot. A white van had followed them up the drive, not slowing as it veered round the parked taxi – barely missing the rear bumper – and went on past, spitting gravel, where the drive curved to the left of the house. Grace glimpsed the curly dark hair of the man at the wheel as he darted a scathing look their way, as if the taxi driver had done something stupid by stopping there.

The taxi man, dumping Grace's case, raised his eyebrows. 'Always in a hurry, that one.'

'You know him?' Mum asked.

The man jerked his head to one side. 'Lives in the cottage here.'

Perhaps everyone knew everyone else in a small place like this.

'Thank you.' Mum handed over the money. 'Keep the change.'

He nodded thanks in return and drove off, waving out of his open window. Grace watched him go; he seemed to have become a temporary ally, his friendliness set against the hostility of the van driver. So that man lived here? It wasn't a good first impression.

The only other people in sight were a man and a woman, both youngish, busy with sketchbooks under the shade of a tree. This tree, an immense cedar with spreading inky branches, was recognizable from Granny Izz's photographs – unchanged, as if the passing years meant nothing to a tree. Neither of the pair with heads bent over their drawings had taken any notice of the taxi's arrival and departure.

Stone steps led up to an open front door, flanked by deep bay windows. On each side of the porch stood big tubs bright with scarlet flowers, and a tabby cat lay stretched out on the doormat.

'What now?' Grace looked at Mum, whose bright smile showed that she too was anxious.

'Roger's probably in the office. He's expecting us.'

'Mum, this Roger, and the others here' – Grace edged closer and spoke quietly, though no one was close enough to hear – 'they do know about – about *me*, don't they?'

'Oh, Grace.' Mum put an arm round her. 'Yes, of *course* Roger knows. And you'll like him, I promise. It'll be fine, you'll see.'

Chapter Two

It

So much had changed in the last year and a half that Grace felt her old life had been torn into bits and fed through a shredder. First, Mum and Dad's split, after several months of will-they-won't-they, with Grace caught in the middle, not wanting to take sides but trying to take both sides at once. That had been bad enough.

And then that day – that May evening that severed Grace's life into Before and After. That day that should have been marked on the calendar with a big red WARNING sign and flashing lights.

The day of It.

Since then, she'd gone over and over the small things and ordinary decisions that had funnelled her into It, as if It was meant to happen. Without any one of them, the day would have been as unremarkable as any other Thursday, not particularly remembered. If only it had been raining, then she wouldn't have gone out for a run. If only she'd decided to go the other way to the park, through the alleyways, as she often did. If only her maths homework had been harder, taking her a few minutes longer to work through – a few minutes, *a few minutes* would have made all the difference between what happened and what so easily needn't have.

If only the Peugeot driver had taken another route. If only he'd stopped to fill up with petrol or buy chocolate. If only the traffic lights had changed to red a moment sooner. If only he'd been concentrating, not laughing with the woman in the passenger seat, singing along to loud music as he came round the corner too fast, much too fast, beating the red light.

Any of those things could have been different, but they weren't, and never would be. No matter how many times she replayed, it was always the same – herself running along the pavement, the red Peugeot turning right at the junction, the two of them pulled together as if by a powerful magnet.

The moment when the engine sound became more than that of passing traffic. The car swerving straight at her. The driver's hands wrenching the wheel, the woman passenger open-mouthed in horror.

I'm dead, Grace thought, trapped by a high wall to her right. She could still recall the instant in which she was able to think that quite calmly.

But next moment she twisted away and leaped, for a wild second thinking she'd jumped clear—

Then the impact, the sickening slam. The car bucked forward as it struck. Her head and shoulder crunched hard against the bonnet. Searing pain carried her away on a dark wave.

That was all she could remember. Letting the merciful darkness wash over her, drown her. Dying must be like that.

Afterwards, everyone said she was lucky not to have been killed. If she hadn't been pinned against the wall, she could have been flung right through the windscreen.

Lucky.

That depended how you looked at it, and she certainly didn't feel lucky.

Somehow she was still alive, but they couldn't save her leg.

She was too drugged and groggy after the emergency operation to take it in properly. It was Mum who told her in words that seemed meaningless, nothing to do with her as she floated in and out of sleep. 'You're here, that's the most important thing,' Mum kept saying, with a sob in her voice. 'And we love you, we'll always be here. We'll get through this.'

Dad was there too, she was sure he was. Did that mean they were together again?

Much later – hours or days, she couldn't tell – she was suddenly awake, staring at the ceiling. She registered that she was still in hospital. Did she live here now? Dad was slumped by her bed in a chair, making a small whistling sound as he snored. A drip thing was attached to her arm;

she felt a dull pain in her hand, and saw the bandage that held the tube in place and the bag of liquid suspended on a metal stand.

They'd said something about losing her leg, or had she only dreamed that? It was the sort of thing that happened in a nightmare and then you'd wake up, flooded with relief because you were in your own bed and everything was the same as usual. When she glanced down she saw the shape of her left leg – thigh, knee, waggle-able foot – all perfectly normal under the thin blanket; then a cagey shape over the other. So it was there, then. But she kept puzzling, knowing they wouldn't say that unless it were true. How could her leg be gone?

No. No. They couldn't chop off part of her. She needed two legs; everyone did. How would she walk? Run? How would she be herself? She tried to wiggle her toes, but only felt heaviness there. Her mind blurred in panic and disbelief.

'Dad. Dad! Wake up!'

'Hmmnn?' He pushed himself up, blinking.

'My – my leg. What's happened?'

'Oh, Gracey.' He leaned close, cuddling her. 'Sweetheart.' He could only force the words out with difficulty. 'They – they couldn't save it. It was too badly crushed. They had to amputate below the knee. You've still got your knee.'

Even though it didn't seem real, she found herself sobbing, holding him tight, smelling the clean cotton of his shirt and a faint sweatiness and soap while he rocked her.

She knew he was crying too, and trying not to. At least he didn't tell her she was lucky.

My leg, she thought, *my leg!* It seemed the most precious part of her. It'd be sports day soon – she'd need her leg back by then. How would she run the 200 metres, the 4x100 metres relay? How could they take part of her body away? What had they done with it?

One moment the truth of her situation thudded into her; next instant it skittered away, impossible to grasp.

Days followed days of hospital, rehabilitation, physiotherapy. Marie-Louise came to visit, often; so, once, did some of her other friends from school, Carrie and Jenna and Luke. She didn't know what she wanted from them. Not sympathy: 'Oh, how awful,' Carrie kept saying, her eyes filling with tears. 'I can't imagine what it must be like.' (I know, Grace wanted to say, but perhaps you could *try*?) Jenna talked only about herself, as if the whole subject of Grace's accident were best avoided; and Luke kept saying how cool it was, how Grace could be a blade runner and win medals in the Paralympics. 'Tokyo, twenty-twenty. You'll have three years to train.' And, 'What happened to your leg, after they cut it off? Did it have its own funeral?' which struck Grace as just *sick*.

Marie-Louise was the only one she really wanted to see. Marie-Louise, who wanted to be a doctor, seemed to understand that Grace didn't want tears, or sorrow, or constant questions, and they had the kind of special friendship that meant they didn't need to talk all the time. She brought

14

books and magazines, and chocolate truffles her mother had made. She talked about prosthetic limbs and how people got used to them, as if all this were quite normal. As if there were a huge but perfectly manageable job to do, and she'd be there to help, all the way.

There were times when Grace hated her body, wished she could slip out of it. It was spoiled for ever, broken, incomplete. Instead of a right shin and foot, her leg – swollen, multi-coloured with bruising – ended in a smooth stump below the knee. She could hardly bear to look, though the stump received constant attention to check that it was healing well, and had its own special shrinker sock to bring down the swelling.

Stored on her phone was a photo she couldn't help looking at, though it felt like being kicked in the stomach. It had been taken by Marie-Louise at the start of term, on the running track in the school field. There stood Grace – the old Grace, as she couldn't help thinking of herself now – lined up with three others, eager, smiling into the sun. She wore a vest and Lycra shorts; her legs were long and slim.

Legs. Both of them. Two; a pair. Ready to run. How fantastic it had been to have two fully functioning legs. She thought now that she should have been grateful for that, every single one of those days when she'd never given it a thought.

When she remembered running, lived it, *felt* it with all her senses – she wanted to wail and howl. How could that have been taken away from her? The very worst thing she could have lost. Running was more than just running. It was who she was.

This is me. Running.

Now? *That* was *me. That was the real me, not this wreck of a person. How can I get the old me back?*

Looking at the photograph through a mist of tears, she poised her thumb to delete it, but couldn't. To do that would be to lose herself, her self. Fit, athletic Grace. Where was she now?

I can't let go of her. Can't give in. That would make it real.

'It's all right, it's all right to cry,' said Nurse Liz, Grace's favourite, with her corkscrew curls that sprang out from a tight ponytail and her big smile that could quickly turn to seriousness. When Grace sobbed, 'It's not fair, it's not fair!' Nurse Liz agreed that no, it wasn't fair at all.

There were greater unfairnesses in the world, Grace knew; no one had any special right to go through life untroubled, undamaged. But that knowledge couldn't cut through her grief.

'You were just unlucky. In the wrong place at the wrong time.' She lost count of the number of people who told her that. It was the *just* that got her, that sneaky little word that crept in everywhere. Too bad, it meant. Put up with it. There's no choice.

In her dreams she had two legs again; she could run, swim, dance. She was anchor in the relay team, sprinting across the line with energy to spare while her team-mates

16

yelled from the trackside. Reality and dream must have switched places; she would wake up, laugh off her disturbing nightmare and go for a run. Her mind was a betrayer, a cruel tease.

At home the mantelpiece and windowsill were lined with the cards people had sent. *Get well soon*, some of them said, as if she could grow a new leg, or had nothing more lasting than measles. Looking at them from the sofa, Grace felt that she'd died, that these sympathy cards had been sent to the girl she used to be.

Tuesday's child is full of grace. Now the idea of being graceful was a sick joke.

She progressed from a wheelchair to crutches, and consultations about a prosthetic limb once the shrinker sock had done its work – a temporary one at first, then endless fittings and tweakings and learning how to walk on her own new leg. It was weird that she had to learn that, how to step forward, how to balance on her new foot like a toddler finding its feet.

Finding your feet. That was one of those sayings she'd never taken notice of before, but now kept hearing in everyday conversation. *Stand on your own two feet. Put your best foot forward.*

It had taken a year for the case to reach court, the trial coinciding with the first anniversary of the accident. Grace's parents attended each day, and Grace herself was interviewed via a video link to the courtroom. It was a new ordeal for all of them, and now it was over: Gavin Haynes, aged twenty-eight, had been found guilty of dangerous driving and given a ten-year prison sentence.

'Ten years!' Grace's mother had raged. 'Ten years, and I bet he'll be out in five!'

Sometimes Grace thought of him, in prison. He had wept in court and said that he was sorry, over and over again. 'Sorry! A lot of use that is!' Mum kept muttering.

In a corner of her mind Grace thought that both of them, Gavin Haynes and herself, were serving a sentence. She was surprised to feel a flicker of sympathy because he'd done something awful that he could never change, or put right, and he'd have to live with that for ever.

'Huh! Don't waste your pity,' Marie-Louise said, when Grace explained this. 'He pleaded Not Guilty, didn't he? Otherwise there'd have been no court case and you and your parents wouldn't have had to go through all that.'

Now the house in Rignell Road, Grace's home all her life, was up for sale because of the divorce. The proceeds would be split between Mum and Dad when eventually the sale went through, and Dad was buying a brand new house with Chloe, who had money of her own. It seemed to Grace that he'd moved on far too quickly, making this whole other life for himself, while she and her mother scraped together the leftover bits of their old one. She had thought, in her post-operative daze, that the shock of the accident had jolted her parents back together, but no. It was too late for that, and the divorce had gone through soon after.

Now she and Mum needed to find a flat for themselves, and soon. There was no way they could afford a whole house without Dad's salary. Although Mum got plenty of work doing marketing and publicity, it was freelance, so she didn't get regular earnings or holidays or sick pay. They'd need to stay in Hackney, near enough for Grace to continue at Westfields High, but – ideally – far enough from the fateful road junction for her not to pass it every time she went out, whether walking or on a bus. Mum said she felt sick whenever she saw the place – the rebuilt wall with its clean new bricks, the bollards, the traffic lights. What Grace felt was a thrill of revulsion that set her heart pounding and all those stupid *what ifs* clamouring again, pointless but insistent.

Grace's mother had only just started flat-hunting when she received a message from Roger Clark, who till then she'd never heard of. 'Oh!' she exclaimed, staring at her phone, and 'Oh!' and 'Well!' It was a few moments before Grace could get any sense out of her.

Roger was the new manager at Flambards. Researching the Russell family for a First World War project, he'd found Mum's name – Polly Russell – at first on an ancestry website and then on LinkedIn. 'This is probably a long shot,' he had written, 'but I wonder if you might be related to the Russells who lived at Flambards in Essex in the 1900s?'

Yes, Mum was.

They had talked, agreed to meet; Mum had liked Roger, visited Flambards – 'Oh, Gracey, it's just as I've always imagined!' – and learned that it was now a centre for residential courses. Roger had plenty of good ideas, Mum said after her visit, but they were struggling to get enough bookings to keep going, and needed an urgent boost in publicity.

One thing soon led to another. The Trustees, who made all the decisions, had a meeting – Roger was one of them – and they agreed to take Grace's mother on until the beginning of September, to see if she could make a difference.

Grace was at first intrigued, then doubtful. 'You mean *stay* there? But how can we find a flat if we're stuck out in the middle of nowhere?'

'It's not that far from London,' her mother said, and showed Grace on Google Maps. 'I might even get myself a car.'

So here they were: Mum with a job to do, and Grace with little idea of how she'd spend six long weeks.

Chapter Three

Just Christina

'Welcome to Flambards! Though it doesn't seem the right way round, me welcoming you two Russells.'

Roger was tall and slim, about the age of Grace's dad or perhaps a little older, with a ready smile, and longish hair streaked with grey. He asked about their journey, then said, 'I'll take you straight round to the stable yard, so you can see where you'll be living. The tour can wait till after lunch. Here, let me take one of those cases.'

There was a moment's pause. He looked at Grace; she made a point of grasping the handle of her own wheeled case, to show that she could manage by herself. Instead Roger took Mum's case, as she had a hefty bag as well, and they turned past the house frontage along a drive that curved round to the left. The wheels of the cases jolted and scraped on gravel.

'We've got a group in, till Friday morning,' Roger explained. 'Landscape painting – you'll see them at lunch. Then another lot arriving that same evening.'

Grace felt his hesitation as he glanced sidelong to check that she could keep up; yes, she could. It had taken hours of physiotherapy and exercises at home to walk without lurching, so that when she wore jeans and trainers no one would notice anything unusual, unless they looked more closely than most people did.

The drive passed underneath a brick arch, and now they were in a square yard flanked by buildings on three sides. A clock above the archway chimed the half-hour with a slightly mournful sound.

'The stable yard!' Mum said, looking around. 'Just imagine, Grace – Granny Izz learned to ride a pony here, almost before she could walk.'

Imagine this being *home*, Grace thought. Living in a huge house that stood all alone. Walking round to a yard full of horses to ride. It must have seemed quite normal to Granny Izz, as if everyone lived like that.

'No horses here now,' Roger said. 'The old stables have all been turned into guest rooms. When your Russell relations lived here there'd have been eight or more horses, grooms to look after them, a coach house.'

'Oh, I know,' Mum said. 'Granny Izz used to say that the horses were looked after better than the people. They got the best food, hours of grooming, warm rugs in winter – they lived in complete luxury.'

22

The guest rooms had doors that opened in two halves, like stables, and there was a large stone block in the middle of one row, topped by a pot of scarlet flowers. Grace imagined horse heads looking over their half-doors, and a stable boy wheeling a barrow of hay, whistling as he worked.

'At one time, before your grandmother, Isobel, was born, this used to be the local hunt kennels,' Roger was saying. 'The William Russell who owned Flambards before the First World War – now, how was he related to you? – your grandmother's grandfather, so however many greats that is. Anyway, he *lived* for hunting, it seems, till he was crippled in a riding accident.'

The word *crippled* reverberated into an abrupt embarrassed silence. Grace stood numbly. Mum shuffled her feet on the gravel and Roger looked stricken, as if only now realizing what had come out of his mouth, but with no way of snatching it back.

Crippled. No one said that any more, but Grace knew what it meant. She felt a flash of sympathy for this William Russell, then withdrew it as she thought of the fox-hunting. *Crippled*. It suggested someone hunched up small, moving about with difficulty on gnarled, painful limbs, like an illustration in a Victorian novel. For an excruciating moment she thought Roger was going to apologize, which would only make things worse.

'Think of Granny Izz's mother coming here from London, Gracey, when she was only twelve!' Mum put on an air of determined cheeriness, to cover the awkward moment.

'Christina. All on her own, having to learn how to fit in.'

'Oh, yes.' Roger sounded relieved.

'Christina was my great-grandmother. Grace's great-*great*-grandmother,' Mum explained.

Roger nodded; clearly he knew that. 'Yes, orphaned when she was only five. And she certainly did fit in. Ended up owning the place.'

'I can just about remember her from when I was small,' said Mum. 'But Flambards had been sold by then – she moved away for her last few years, when it all got too much.'

'She seems to have been quite a wealthy lady,' Roger said. 'I gather she inherited her parents' money when she was twenty-one, and that gave her enough to take on Flambards.'

'Mm. I've no idea where all that money went,' said Grace's mother. 'The house must have swallowed it up, I suppose. Or the horses did. Imagine owning a house the size of Flambards, Gracey, and all the land that goes with it! It sounds like you know more about the Russells than we do,' she added to Roger.

'Hardly! But I am a bit obsessed, because of the First World War stuff. We're having a special weekend here in November, for the hundredth anniversary of the Armistice, and an exhibition. So Christina and the other Russells will be part of that. And I've got a family connection of my own, but I'll save that for later. So, come and see your flat. It's upstairs – the converted hayloft. This way, next to what used to be the harness room.'

A separate door, labelled *The Hayloft*, opened to a narrow flight of stairs that led to another door at the top. Roger and Grace heaved the cases up; he produced a key with a flourish, and opened up.

'Here we are. All yours for the summer.'

Mum and Grace followed him in, and Mum exclaimed, 'Oh, this is lovely!'

They were in a light, airy main room. One wall was the kitchen – sink, fridge, cooker – and there was a round dining table, a sofa, armchair and flat-screen TV. Roger put down Mum's case in the middle of the floor, and Grace lugged hers across to join it.

'Bedroom, bedroom, bathroom,' said Roger, opening doors to show them. 'Airing cupboard here – towels etcetera. I think you've got everything you need, but let me know if not. I'll leave you to settle in, shall I? Lunch is at one – see you over at the house.'

He clumped down the stairs, and Grace and her mother looked at each other.

'We'll be happy here, won't we?' Mum said, and there was a kind of pleading in her look, as if it were up to Grace, as if you could *decide* to be happy.

'Mm.'

'Roger's nice, isn't he? I told you.'

Grace shrugged. 'He's all right.'

But she did feel inclined to like him, in spite of his blunder. Possibly even *because* of it – he'd obviously felt awful the moment he heard what he'd said.

'Which bedroom would you like, Gracey? I don't mind. They're both gorgeous, aren't they?'

Grace chose the smaller of the two, which had a sloping ceiling and a dormer window. Her mother had at first been disappointed that they wouldn't be living in the main house, but Grace thought this was better, with its wood floors and rag rugs and print curtains, everything clean and new. The big house would be full of people; over here she could get away from everyone when she wanted to.

Her window, like the ones in the main room, looked out to another yard, behind the stables, where a number of cars were parked, among them the white van that had arrived in such haste. On one side was a brick cottage with its own fenced garden, next to a greenhouse and vegetable beds; on the other, a huge barn. Beyond all that she could see fields and trees, and a distant mauvey-blue horizon.

'The shower's a walk-in one,' Mum said, coming out of the bathroom, 'so it's fine for you – I did check. We've got plenty of wardrobe space. And our own kitchen, so we can cook for ourselves here if we want.'

'Where's the wifi code?'

Grace ignored what Mum had said about the shower. She thought of Mum asking Roger about it, explaining that she had a disabled daughter. Disabled. Grace still had trouble accepting that word in relation to herself. *Disabled* had always meant other people, not her. It meant wheelchairs and handrails and ramps for people who couldn't do the simple, ordinary things everyone else did without even thinking.

Mum picked up a folder that lay on the table. 'Look, there's the hub, and here's the code. Let's make a start on unpacking before lunch.'

Grace took three photos and sent them to Marie-Louise: **It's going to be really boring here. What are you doing?**

Unpacking could wait. She looked at Instagram, followed a couple of links, but her attention wandered to what Mum had said about Christina. Grace knew from Granny Izz how Christina had come from London at the age of twelve, all by herself, knowing nothing about her relations here or about horses or the countryside. And she was staying for much longer than six weeks – she'd come to *live* here, whether she wanted to or not. That must have been just like this, only worse.

Grace hadn't taken a great deal of notice of all that family stuff; it had been too long ago to mean much, and she'd been too young to find it interesting. Coming to Flambards, though, and standing in the stable yard where Christina and then Granny Izz had learned to ride, had brought it into focus. And there was the inside of the house still to see. One of those windows high in the ivy must have been the one Christina looked out of when she woke up after spending her very first night here.

Great-great-grandmother – that was too many *greats* to get hold of. Just Christina was enough. That way Christina stayed forever young, not getting old, old, older, like Granny Izz. Christina was that much further in the past, out of reach, whereas Grace remembered Granny Izz as a frail old lady, slowly getting smaller, a grey wisp of her earlier self.

A reply pinged back on her phone: **Cruise on the Seine then ice cream and film. More soon. M-Lx**

Grace sighed, her thoughts still half with Christina and now pulled in two directions. Had Christina been parted from a best friend she'd left behind in London? If so, she'd have had to write letters and go down to the village to post them, and wait days for a postman to bring the reply. At least Grace could message Marie-Louise and expect an answer within minutes. Even if it made her think she'd rather be eating ice cream by the river Seine.

CHAPTER FOUR

A Line of Russells

Looking around the dining room, Grace could see only one person who might be under twenty-five: a dark pretty girl in an apron who was speeding in and out through the door to the kitchen. Wasn't there *anyone* her own age here? Hadn't Mum said that there would be? An older woman in an apron glanced through the doorway a couple of times, assessing the buffet table; she smiled at Roger but darted back out of sight before he could call her over.

'That's Pam, our cook,' Roger told Grace and her mother. 'We'll go and say hello properly after lunch.'

While he and Mum talked about the forthcoming courses, Grace gave her attention to the food. At least that was good, and there was lots of it – salads and dips, quiches and cold meat, with bread warm from the oven, laid out on a long table for everyone to help themselves. The three of them sat at a table in one corner, from where she saw people filtering in, in twos and threes, through doors open to the terrace and the cedar-tree lawn. Most were grand-parent sort of age, with only a few younger ones, and even they must have been as old as Mum. A man with a ponytail came over and introduced himself as Frank, the tutor for this week's course, before taking a seat with his group.

'Thanks, Irina,' Roger said, as the dark girl put down a jug of water on their table. Irina's smile took in Grace and her mother before she whirled away. Grace glimpsed slim legs in cut-off jeans and the fine bones of tanned feet in ballet pumps.

Before It, she'd never thought much about feet, but now she gave them close attention, reluctant but fascinated, whenever they were on display. Tanned feet, strong feet, painted toenails in sandals, the graceful turn of an ankle: she'd never realized before that feet could be so beautiful, so expressive. She had to push away the feeling that all these feet and ankles were there to taunt her, which was just ridi-culous. What did she expect – everyone to go around in Ugg boots, out of sympathy, in the middle of summer?

Roger turned to her. 'Irina's from Leipzig, on a gap year from uni – she helps out in the office as well as in the kitchen. It'll be a younger group at the weekend. Contemporary dance. And you'll probably meet Jamie this afternoon – my nephew. He spends a lot of time here, and there's Marcus too – Sally, his mum, is our gardener. Jamie and Marcus are great friends. So you won't be entirely surrounded by oldies, Grace.'

'I don't mind,' Grace mumbled, prodding at her slice of quiche. That wasn't exactly true, but now she felt daunted at the thought of meeting two boys who she gathered, as Mum asked questions, were both fifteen, a year older than her. They might look at her. They might know. Or they might *not* know, and find out. Which would be worse?

The dining room must have once been grand. Grace pictured Christina, a newcomer like herself, eating her dinner at a long polished table like the one that now held the buffet. The high ceiling and chandelier and elaborate tiled fireplace must have been here then – they were as old as the house, Roger had said – but there were modern touches too: bright abstract paintings on the walls and gauzy curtains at the open doors to the garden.

When lunch was over and the art students had drifted off again, Roger showed Grace and Mum the rest of the ground floor. There was a smaller, cosier room furnished with sofas, armchairs and bookshelves; next to that was the book-lined library she'd seen from outside. There was a sort of class-room, and overlooking the front drive was the office, where Mum would work with Roger and sometimes Irina. From the entrance hall a stone-flagged corridor led to the kitchen, where four people – Irina, Pam and two others – were clearing up from lunch, stacking a dishwasher and cleaning the work surfaces.

'I can't show you the upstairs rooms,' Roger said, back

31

in the entrance hall. 'It's all guest accommodation up there.'

Looking up the wide staircase, Grace saw a half-landing with a stained-glass window, and felt perversely annoyed at not being allowed to go up. She wanted to see Christina's room – if anyone knew which one it was.

'Do you live here?' she asked Roger.

'Not yet,' Roger said. 'The plan is, I'll move into the upstairs flat when it's ready. The decorators are busy there now. But that depends on whether we manage to keep the place going. For now I'm staying with my brother and his family a couple of miles away. The other staff live out, apart from Sally. She and her family are in the cottage you can see from your windows, behind the stable yard.'

Grace glanced at Mum. Presumably the impatient van man was the husband of this Sally.

'It's impressive, this entrance,' Grace's mother said. 'Those are original tiles, aren't they?'

'Yes, they are. It's a lovely house altogether, but costs a fortune to maintain – that's part of our problem. Let's go back to the office. I want to show you the family tree I've been working on. *Your* family tree.' Roger paused, looking at them both. 'I can't get over having two real-live Russells here. Does it feel like coming home?'

Mum laughed. 'I don't know about that. It'll take a while.'

'Well, to me it seems right,' Roger said, and Grace found herself adding, 'Me, too,' rather to her own surprise.

'If only you'd started four years earlier.' Mum followed him into the office, with Grace behind. 'You could have met Granny Isobel. She was born and brought up here.'

'Oh yes – born during the war; 1916,' Roger said promptly. 'I wish I *could* have met her. But now I'm meeting you. The next best thing.'

'I've brought a few of her photographs. There's an old album at home too,' said Mum. 'I'll bring that when I've got my car.'

Having talked vaguely about getting a car for a while, she had now bought one second-hand, and would collect it tomorrow. On the day she chose it and put down the deposit, she came home looking proud. 'My very own car! I'll feel so independent!' Before, she and Grace's dad had shared one.

The office must once have been a sitting room, with shelves flanking the fireplace and a bay window that looked out on to the drive. There were three desks, two of them piled with files and folders and papers. The third was bare apart from a computer and an empty tray.

'I need a good sort-out.' Roger stood by his messy desk, both hands raised to his head in a hopeless gesture. 'But first, let me show you this.'

He took a box file down from a shelf and spread a large sheet of paper on the desk that would be Mum's, the only uncluttered space.

'Here you all are. The Russells of Flambards, as far as I've got. Maybe you can help fill in a few more.'

Grace's eyes took in the branching lines, the handwritten names with dates of births and deaths, the confusing repetitions of Williams and Jameses. Following Roger's pointing

33

finger she homed in on Mum's name: Polly Ann Russell, b. 1980, and the *m* for married: *m* Paul John Forbes 2002, *d* 2017. The *d*, Grace realized after a startled moment, meant divorced, not dead. That bit had been added in pencil, whereas the rest was written in ink. Roger must have added those details after getting them from Mum when she visited the first time.

'Is that your writing?' Grace asked, and Roger nodded. It was distinctive, artistic: italic, in black ink, with swooping downstrokes. Not somehow the handwriting she'd have expected him to have.

Underneath her parents was her own name: Grace Alice Forbes-Russell, b. 2004.

It was just Russell now. Mum hadn't changed her name when she married, and at school Grace had been Grace Forbes, as they all agreed that Forbes-Russell was too posh-sounding for everyday use. After the separation she'd gone back to Russell, to be the same as Mum – which put her immediately after Marie-Louise, whose surname was Rénard, in their form's register.

Roger's pointing finger went up the page, a generation at a time: from Grace to Mum to Neil Robert Russell (Grand-dad), Isobel Grace Russell (Granny Izz), then Christina, who had been Christina Parsons until she married William, one of her Russell cousins.

'And there's Christina's three husbands,' Mum said, lean-ing over to look at the three lines and close writing. 'William first, then Richard Wright – then Mark, William's brother.'

'She married *both* her cousins, didn't she?' Grace said, looking at Roger. 'There can't be many people who've done that. I didn't know it was even allowed, to marry your cousin.'

'It's not actually illegal. But in fact Christina and the two Russell sons were *half*-cousins, look. There was a second marriage in the generation before, so Christina's mother was only half-sister to their father, the first William. What *was* illegal, till after the war, was marrying your brother-in-law. That changed in 1921 and Christina married Mark soon after.'

'Granny Izz used to say that local people thought Christina was scandalous, being married three times,' Mum told him. 'All while she was still quite young. And Gran would have shocked them too – having a son without being married, in an age when that was seen as disgraceful.'

'I'm glad she didn't marry,' Roger said. 'If she had, your name wouldn't be Russell, and I wouldn't have found you. It's a piece of luck, as you've descended mainly through the female line.'

'She didn't see the point of getting married,' Mum said. 'That must have taken some strength of character, in her day. I think all the Russells must have been strong-minded, in their different ways.'

Grace was remembering some of the things Granny Izz had told her about Christina. She'd flown across the Channel with Will in his tiny aeroplane in the early days of flying, and had been a brilliant rider as well, never afraid. She had run the Flambards farm while most of the men were away at war; she carried on hunting until well into her sixties, Granny Izz had said, and even had a go at motor-racing, at a time when few women drove cars.

I'm a Russell too, Grace thought with a sense of pride that was quickly overtaken by loss. *I'd have done those things if I had the chance*. Well, not the hunting. But the flying, the boldness, the willingness to have a go – Christina must have been brave, adventurous, with nothing to dent her confidence. As always, Grace felt the sense of resentment rise like a lump in her throat – bitter, inescapable – for the loss of her own chances. It would always be there.

'I've brought these to show you.' Mum took three black-and-white photographs out of an envelope and laid them out on the desk for Roger to see, and there *was* Christina. Grace had seen them before, but it felt different now, because she was at Flambards – in Christina's house. She studied them with new interest.

In all three, Christina was older than Grace, but still young, eighteen or nineteen, perhaps, and beautiful in an unshowy way. One picture showed her in a white dress in the garden, holding a bunch of flowers; in another she was mounted on a horse, sidesaddle; for the third she was posing next to a rickety-looking aeroplane with a thin-faced, smiling young man, almost a boy still.

'That's William,' Mum told Roger. 'My great-grandfather. Grace's great-*great*-grandfather. Only he was killed before he even knew he'd fathered a child. It makes our whole existence seem a bit chancey, doesn't it?'

'I suppose everyone's is, one way or another,' Roger said, his eyes on the picture. 'What a photograph! Christina's lovely, and I like the look of William too – the way he's caught there. He looks clever but humorous, as if he could laugh at himself.'

Grace glanced at him sidelong, surprised by this.

'And so *young*,' her mother said. She turned the picture over to show some faint pencilled words on the back. 'June 1914. He only had two more years to live.'

Roger nodded slowly. Grace knew the story: Will's aircraft had been shot down while he was flying on reconnaissance over the German lines in France. He was killed, and Christina returned to Flambards to grieve, only later discovering that she was pregnant. So Granny Izz had known her father only from a few photographs and what Christina had told her about him.

'I know he joined the Royal Flying Corps as soon as war broke out,' Roger said. 'So that would have been barely a month after this picture was taken. He was already an experienced amateur flyer. But losses were enormous at that time. The odds were well stacked against him.'

They were all silent for a moment.

'Poor Will. Poor Christina,' Mum said. 'And look – we know her second marriage, to Richard Wright, ended in divorce. But her third marriage didn't last long, either.' She placed a finger on the dates of Christina's third husband, Mark Russell.

With a jolt Grace saw that the date of Mark's death

followed soon after the marriage. She had known that, of course, from Granny Izz, who had spent most of her childhood without either father or stepfather, but it was still a shock to see the dates written there so starkly.

'Poor Christina!' Mum said again. 'She may have had wealth and looks and this lovely home, but she was terribly unlucky. Twice a widow, within the space of a few years. She was still only in her twenties when Mark died.'

It was another link. Grace felt perversely pleased that Christina, who had so much, had had her share of bad luck too. But there was more: Roger was saying, '*And* she lost her son, Robert – her son and Mark's. In 1940, in the Battle of Britain. He was just eighteen.'

'Awful.' Mum shook her head. 'That must have been devastating.'

Roger's finger was tracing the line again. 'So your Granny Isobel was Christina's only surviving child.'

'Yes,' Mum said. 'She used to talk about Flambards, a lot, but she never lived here again once she left for London.'

Grace could still hear Granny Izz's voice, sometimes, and remember things she'd said; that was comforting. In her mind, loud and clear, Granny Izz told her: 'It wasn't that I didn't like Flambards. I did – I loved it. But there was Hitler's war, and my work took me to London, and there was so much to do, always something I had to work for. I couldn't go back and bury myself in the country.'

'I can give you a few more names,' Mum said, pointing at the diagram to show where. 'My dad's – Neil's

38

– two half-sisters, and their children. But none of those are Russells.'

So it's down to us, Grace thought, with a tremor of importance. *Me.* For the Russells of Flambards to reach into the future, she would one day have to have children of her own. How would that happen? Who would ever – but no, she didn't want to start thinking that way.

'When you get a chance,' Roger said, 'have a look at the war memorial in the churchyard. There's a whole list of surnames, some of them of families who are still living here. And your William Russell's on there, of course, though his grave's in France.'

'We'll go and see, won't we, Grace?' Mum said.

'My relations are there too,' Roger said after a moment. 'And there's a link to your William and the Royal Flying Corps. My great-grandfather was in it, and he was shot down too. Badly burned.'

'Killed?' asked Grace, her interest caught by this more than by war memorials.

Roger shook his head. 'No; he was lucky to survive. Though it can't have felt like that at the time – he had a terrible disfigurement, half his face burned away. Later he had facial reconstruction. That was an important development after the war, with so many people needing it.'

'Poor man!' said Mum, while Grace thought of something Jenna had come out with, in hospital: *At least nothing's happened to your face. You still look the same.* Nothing, that was, apart from cuts and bruises that had soon healed.

Imagine if your face was terribly changed, and that was the first thing people saw when they met you. The old Grace had barely given a thought to disabilities or disfigurement. Now reminders seemed to pop up everywhere. It was like being a new member of a club she hadn't asked to join.

Roger looked at his watch. 'Let's have a quick look at the barn. Then, Polly, I'll introduce you to the wonders of our office systems.'

As they left the house by the front door, Grace saw a wheelbarrow and a canvas bag of tools on the far side of the lawn, but no gardener. Roger said that Sally would be around somewhere, and led them in the direction of the stables, taking a track that forked off just before the brick arch and led to the big yard area Grace had seen from her bedroom window. The large barn on the far side had double doors open at the front; two women leaned on the outside wall, one of them smoking, while inside several other people were busy at their easels or talking to Frank.

'This is our biggest working space,' Roger said, as they went in. 'We use it for the larger groups, and it's great for dance and yoga and things like that, with a sprung floor.'

A smiley-faced lady flattened herself in front of her easel so that they could see only glimpses of the pencil and wash behind. 'Oh, don't look at mine. It's awful. Joan's is much better.'

'No, really no good at all,' said the woman next to her, but stood back for them to look. 'Not compared to Keith's. But I do try.'

Her mother and Roger found nice things to say, rather dutifully. Grace thought the two women were funny, trying to outdo each other in modesty, when anyone could tell that they both thought they were quite good.

Back in the stable yard, Roger pointed out the woods and fields that belonged to Flambards. A gate opened on to a grass meadow with a path mown through it, leading down a gentle slope towards a stile at the woodland edge. 'There's a lake down there, in the trees. Do go down and explore. There are good paths and a bird-watching hide.'

Uneven ground, Grace saw, where once she'd have set off running without a thought. A stile to climb. But she was determined to go and see for herself, liking the idea of a lake and a hide, a place to get away from everyone.

Someone was coming up from the wood: a tall figure, easily vaulting the stile and walking quickly towards them.

'Good. Here's Jamie.' Roger waved, and the boy raised a hand in return. 'He's always around, holiday times and weekends.'

The boy came up to the gateway, his boots brushing through the grass. Grace saw straight sandy hair, a sunburnt nose, and a serious expression that broke into a wide smile for his uncle. She had been wishing for people her own age, but now felt shy of this purposeful newcomer. A camera was slung round his neck, and a small pair of binoculars. It was a proper camera, a big one with a protruding lens; he cradled it in one hand as if it were precious.

'Hi, Uncle Rodge,' he said, coming through. 'The grebe was there again.'

'That's good.' Roger put a hand on his shoulder. 'Jamie, this is Polly and Grace. Polly and Grace *Russell*, that is!'

'Pleased to meet you, Jamie,' said Mum, while Grace and Jamie just said hi, briefly meeting each other's eyes.

'Are you looking for Marcus?' Roger asked. 'I haven't seen him today.'

'I'll see if he's over at the farm.' Jamie was already walking on. 'See you later.'

'We ought to go back to the office,' Roger said to Mum. 'There's a few things I want us to go through before the Trustees' meeting tomorrow. D'you want to come too, Grace, or—'

Grace shook her head. 'I'll be fine.'

While Roger and her mother turned back through the stable yard, she opened the gate and went into the field. Becoming aware of the high burbling song of a bird overhead, she looked up and saw it, climbing, almost tumbling upwards, scaling the air. A skylark? She wasn't sure she'd ever seen one before.

With the sun striking hot on her face and bare arms, the woods looked tempting, a path winding in. She reached the stile, paused with one hand on the top rail, then climbed it, swinging her right leg over and cautiously placing the foot on the crosspiece.

In the welcome shade of the trees she was faced with a choice of three ways to go. The tracks were bare earth, well-trodden, with woody roots threading across.

'Hey!'

She turned, thinking for a moment that she'd been caught out doing something wrong. It was Jamie, jogging across the field she'd just crossed so laboriously.

So much for being by herself. Where she'd had to stop and assess the stile, and climb it in careful stages, he vaulted over again in that maddeningly easy way.

'What?' she said, as he caught up. 'Roger said I could come down here!'

'Yeah, course you can. Want to go to the lake? I'll take you there if you like.'

His smile was open and friendly – but why would he want to bother with her? Assuming that Roger had asked him to follow her and show her the way, she grudgingly agreed.

'It's nice down here,' he told her. 'I come nearly every day.'

A bramble snagged her T-shirt as she let him pass on the narrow track.

'Weren't you looking for your friend?' she asked. 'Wasn't he there?'

'No, but I saw Sally. His mum. Marc's helping his dad today.'

'His dad is the one who drives the white van?'

'Yes, Adrian. Marc works with him a few days a week, when thing are OK.'

'Why wouldn't things be OK?'

'Well . . . his dad can be a bit difficult. I expect you'll see.'

Grace wondered if she already had. She followed in silence. Jamie obviously knew all the woodland paths, veering off the clearly marked one they were on to step across a small stream. He held a low branch aside for Grace to pass underneath, and she saw the wary, concerned look on his face. He *does* know, she thought, stepping across to the firm ground on the other side; Roger must have told him. She hated the thought of them talking about her, but at least there was no need to explain.

Ahead she saw the glimmer of sunlight on water, closely hemmed in by trees. There were reeds, a sandy bank and two scrubby islands; a low wooden building on the far side must be the bird hide Roger had mentioned.

She noticed a post by the water's edge with a lifebelt. 'Is it deep?'

'Over this side it is. There used to be a gravel pit here, before they filled it in. It's shallower over where the hide is. That side's best for waders.'

'Waders?' Grace imagined paddling.

'Wading birds. Like sandpipers and egrets and snipe. We get those here. Sometimes a water-rail.'

Grace had no idea what any of those birds looked like. 'Is this what you do, then? Bird-watching? Taking photos?' She indicated the camera and binoculars slung round Jamie's neck.

'Yeah. You can call me a geek if you like. Some people do.'

'I wouldn't call that geeky! I mean, I like birds too. Not

that I know much about them. But I watch on TV some-times. *Springwatch*, Chris Thingy and Michaela. Mum and I both like that.'

'Packham,' Jamie said promptly. 'I want to *be* Chris Packham.' His face flushed, as if he'd confessed something private. 'I mean I want to do what he does. Be an expert. Go places. Campaign for wildlife. Make sure people know about birds and animals, so they'll want to protect them.' He turned and pushed on through bracken. 'Let's go in the hide. I see a kingfisher here quite often. If we're lucky . . .'

They sat on the wooden benches in the hide, and Jamie lowered the flap so that they could see out, and they waited. He said nothing, looking out with his binoculars, and Grace understood that this was what you had to do: just watch and wait. No kingfisher appeared; there was only the loud *prukk* of what he said was a coot, but she found something companionable in the silence and the watchful sitting. For a short while, anyway. She wondered if he planned to sit here all afternoon.

'A black-necked grebe's been around for the last few days,' he said, after what seemed like ages. 'That was a good one to see.'

Again, this meant little to Grace.

Jamie added, 'I could show you on my phone, only there's no signal here.' He got to his feet and shut the flap. 'It's not brilliant just now, but we can come again tomorrow, if you like. Maybe we'll see the kingfisher then, or the grebe.'

She noticed the *tomorrow* and *we*; he seemed to assume

they were friends now. She felt partly grateful, partly resistant.

They walked back a different way, winding through silver birches and holly to a different stile. This time Jamie climbed it instead of vaulting, and waited for her without comment.

The sun beat down fiercely when they were out in the open again, following a path that looped round to the field gate where they'd started. She stood for a moment getting her bearings.

'Which way's home for you?'

He pointed back the way they'd come. 'Marsh House. You go through the woods, over the hill and down past Spinney Farm, and on about a mile till you get to our lane.' Jamie looked at his watch. 'I'm not going home yet, though. I'm going up to see Uncle Rodge. There's cake about this time, whenever they've got a course on. Pam usually has some spare in the kitchen.'

As they reached the stable yard Grace saw a straggle of people, the art students, slowly making their way from the barn towards the house. She wasn't hungry yet, but thought she might as well go with Jamie.

A black-and-white collie ran fast from the direction of the barn and cottages, dodging round the slower-moving students. A boy of about Jamie's age strode after it, head down; Grace saw untidy black hair, dark eyebrows. His shoulders were hunched, face set in a scowl. She saw his intense energy and anger; she could almost sense heat radiating from him.

'Marc!' Jamie called.

The boy threw them a quick glance, paused for a moment, then marched on.

'I'd better see what's wrong,' Jamie told Grace. 'See you later.'

He sprinted after the other boy, who, it appeared, didn't want to talk – when Jamie caught up he shook his head rapidly and walked all the faster. Jamie kept pace, and the two were soon out of sight round the bend in the drive. Grace was left standing, looking after them.

CHAPTER FIVE

Snobby + Rude

'So you like Jamie?' Mum asked.

She and Grace were on their way over to the house for breakfast. From tomorrow they'd make their own breakfast in the flat, but for now they had no food in the cupboards or fridge.

'Yes. He's really nice. Kind,' Grace said: even though Jamie had abandoned her the moment he saw Marcus. She felt sure that Marcus would complicate things. From that brief sighting yesterday, she couldn't imagine he'd want to be bothered with her.

She didn't see either of the boys that morning. Mum was busy with the Trustees' meeting, and Grace considered going down to the barn – Frank had asked if she liked drawing and painting, and she'd said yes, she did; it was her favourite subject at school. Next to PE, that was. Or rather how she remembered PE, in the days before it had to be customized for her.

For a while she stayed in the flat, messaging Marie-Louise, to and fro, exchanging photos. Marie-Louise said that she and her mother were being tourists in Paris while her father was working; they'd been up the Eiffel Tower – the Tour Eiffel, to Marie-Louise – and to a flea market. She sent a photograph of herself on the steps at Montmartre, then said that her mother was getting impatient and they were going out.

But you must come and do all these things too, she finished. **Missing you!**

Miss you too, Grace texted, feeling it as an ache.

Restless now, she wandered around outside. There was a whole area beyond the cedar lawn that she hadn't investigated yet. On the far, dining-room, side of the house she found a garden laid out with wide borders, stone paths and a trellis arch smothered with pale roses. It was the sort of garden Grace's mother liked, everything a bit wild, shrubs and flowers and grasses reaching higher than she was tall, and spilling over on to the paths.

In one of the borders, a woman in a blue checked shirt was busy with a fork, prising apart a clump of sturdy vegetation. When she saw Grace she stepped out onto the path, brushed an earthy hand on her jeans and introduced herself as Sally.

'And you must be Grace. I hope you'll like it here. You'll meet my son, Marcus, if you haven't already. He'll be glad of the company, him and Jamie.'

49

'Is he here now?' Grace asked warily, but Sally shook her head.

'No. He's helping his dad, over at the farm.'

'Does he do that every day, then, in the holidays?'

'A few days each week. When there's a job on.'

Grace would have thought there was always work to be done on a farm. Tractor-driving, or harvesting, or milking cows – she was vague, but surely farmers didn't sit around waiting for work.

'Are you at a loose end? Give me a hand if you like,' Sally said, but not as if she really meant it. She didn't look in the least like Marcus, from Grace's quick impression of him; she had kind hazel eyes, light brown hair tied back untidily in a ponytail and a face that looked as if its natural expression was cheerfulness.

'I think I'll go down to the lake,' Grace said, hoping to find Jamie there.

In the grass meadow two of the art students had settled themselves with their easels, facing the woodland edge. Returning their waves of greeting, Grace walked down the path she had taken yesterday and climbed the stile into the shade of the trees. Here, out of anyone's sight, she felt the novelty of being completely alone in these wild surroundings – the almost tingling silence that seemed to brush against her skin, gradually not silence at all but the gentle stirring of leaves and distant birdsong. As she went farther in, another song burst out from the dense cover of leaves, a sound she had surely never heard before: a loud, throbbing song that made her stop and listen, made up of churring sounds and snatches of melody and long low whistles. It sounded close. Maybe she'd stumbled across something exotic. Her eyes scanned leaves and branches for some brilliantly coloured bird of paradise, but she saw nothing.

At the lake the bird hide was closed up. She went in, opened the flap and sat watching for a few minutes, hoping she might see a kingfisher and be able to impress Jamie. After a while she saw a ripple in the reeds at the nearest edge and a brown bird swam into view, like a duck but smaller and rounder. Suddenly it seemed to pull into itself and rear up a little before diving underwater. It stayed under for so long that she feared it had entangled itself and drowned, but eventually bobbed up like a bath toy, some yards away from the spot she'd been watching. She laughed aloud, surprising herself in the quietness.

Leaving the hide she took a different track from yesterday's, winding through trees for some distance before emerging at another stile. Beyond the wood was a cornfield, already harvested, with huge round bales left standing at intervals and a path leading up a gentle hill towards a skyline with a cluster of buildings amid tall trees. She must have come out on the far side. There were maps in the library for people who wanted to go out walking, but without one she thought she'd go on for another couple of fields then turn back before she got lost.

At the top of the cornfield she stopped in doubt. There was another stile, and a footpath sign through a grass meadow

– she could see the trodden path leading across – but the way was blocked by cows, a whole group of them that turned to stare, some moving closer. She had never realized how *big* cows were. They shuffled and snorted; she saw their huge eyes, damp noses and swinging udders, and smelled crushed grass and the sweet, dungy smell of their droppings.

She wasn't brave enough to push her way through. They were only being curious, but they could easily knock her over and she'd be down among those trampling hooves, unable to get up quickly.

She was annoyed with herself for being so fearful; irritated by the caution that dragged at everything she might want to do. I'm not scared, she told herself, just careful. But she'd have to give in. She made her way along the hedge boundary until she came to a gap, and went through into another big field of grass. There was so much land, so many fields, stretching out as far as she could see. Now, turning, she saw the Flambards woods some way behind her, and the roof of the house beyond. It looked farther than she'd realized, and she was flagging, unused to walking on uneven ground, her right hip aching from the effort.

Maybe it was time to go back.

Then her attention was caught by movement. A horse was cantering up the side of the field she'd crossed into, ridden by a girl – Grace saw fair hair flying out from under a helmet in rhythm with the horse's stride. The horse was bright rusty brown, big and powerful, and as she heard the drumming hooves on turf she almost *felt* the sound too, through her standing foot. She had an urge to duck out of sight, but at the same time was held mesmerized.

As the horse came nearer, up the brow of the slope, she briefly saw the mass of its chest, its legs reaching forward as if to eat up the ground, eyes eager and nostrils flared. Neither horse nor rider had seen her and she thought they'd carry on past as if she were invisible. Then suddenly the horse snorted and leapt sideways, throwing the rider off-balance. Grace heard the girl's exclamation as she lurched to one side; quickly she regained her balance, tightened her hold on the reins and wheeled the horse round. At this closer range Grace saw that the girl was maybe four or five years older than her; below the black dome of the helmet her face was oval and delicate, with features that were very likely pretty, but were at the moment drawn into a fierce glare.

'What the—? You nearly had me on the ground!' She looked down from a height, poised and upright while the horse sidled and fidgeted, wanting to gallop on. 'What d'you think you're doing?'

'What does it look like?' Grace matched the girl's stroppy tone. 'Just walking.'

'Well, you're trespassing. The footpath's up there – the sign's pretty obvious.'

It must be easy to look haughty when you were perched up there on a magnificent horse, snooting down at someone who was afraid of cows.

'I didn't mean to trespass. I haven't got a map.'

'Then you *ought* to have one. And that doesn't mean you can barge onto people's private land.'

Grace lifted her chin. 'I wasn't doing anything wrong!'

'Yes, you were,' the girl said. 'Trespassing, like I said. Where are you going?'

'Back to Flambards. It's all right, I know the way.'

'Oh – you're from *Flambards*.' Realization changed the girl's expression as she looked at Grace more closely, her gaze sweeping down her body to her feet, resting there for a moment, then up again to her face. 'You must be—'

'I'm Grace.'

She *hated* it when people checked her over like that, knowing just one thing about her, as if it was all there was to know. As if she were an exhibit. There was nothing to see; her artificial foot in its trainer looking no different from the other. Perhaps this girl had expected her to have a wooden leg sticking out from cut-off jeans, like a pirate in a panto-mime, or a running blade like a Paralympian.

'Yes, that's right. I'm an amputee,' she said, surprising herself by coming straight out with it. 'But you can't tell just by looking.'

'Oh!' The girl was gratifyingly startled, her hands on the reins holding the horse in check. 'I didn't mean to . . .'

At that moment a voice from farther down the field called out, 'Charlie!'

The girl swung round in her saddle. Looking in the same direction, Grace saw Jamie jogging up the slope by the trees.

'My brother,' the girl said, a little shamefaced now. 'We live at Marsh House. Jamie told us about meeting you yesterday. Were you coming over to see him? Sorry if I was a bit . . .'

Grace only nodded, unsmiling, because she didn't believe that the girl – Charlie – was really sorry, only embarrassed at being caught out. She was probably used to behaving like that, ordering people off her land, or her parents' land. This was all new to Grace, meeting people who owned horses and land and behaved as if it was their right.

For Jamie's sake she didn't want to quarrel with his sister. She turned her attention to the horse, not looking at Charlie. She'd never been so close to a horse before, and this one was a beauty, standing now with neck arched and eyes so big and shining that she could see her own reflection in them. It might have been a creature from legend that had dropped down from the sky.

'It's OK, he won't bite or anything.' Charlie was all friendliness now. 'His name's Sirius.'

'Serious?' Grace said, deliberately mishearing.

'Sirius. It's the name of a star. And he's going to *be* a star. He's lovely, but a bit spooky sometimes.'

Grace didn't know what that meant, but raised a hand to stroke the horse's glossy neck. His coat was silky and fine, fox-coloured, gleaming with health and grooming. 'Is he yours?' she asked, though it didn't seem right for such an animal to belong to anyone but himself.

'Yes.' Charlie was clearly proud, warming to Grace's

interest. 'I've had him nearly a year. I'll be competing with him soon.'

Now Jamie was here, with his binoculars and camera round his neck as before.

'What's going on?' He came right up to Sirius, leaning against his neck, and the horse nuzzled his shoulder.

'Sirius spooked, coming up the field. So then I stopped to say hello to Grace.'

To behave like a snotty cow, you mean.

'Anyway, I'd better get going,' Charlie said, gathering her reins. 'I'm due over at Badstocks for a lesson. See you later. Bye, Grace.'

The horse bounded forward, through the gap in the hedge and on up the hedgerow at a canter. Grace watched how Charlie sat in the saddle, perfectly balanced, hands light and back straight.

'She has lessons?' Grace said, watching them go, as she and Jamie stood on the edge of the cornfield.

'Riding's one of those things you never really stop learning. Like football, or playing the piano. You never know it all. Badstocks is a training centre for eventers. She goes there twice a week at the moment, getting ready for competitions in the autumn.'

'Can you ride too?'

'I can, but only for fun. Or transport. I'm not horse-mad like Charlie is. She hardly thinks about anything else. D'you want to go to the lake? Look for the kingfisher?'

Grace felt something shutting down: the side of herself

that could be friendly, and open, and agreeable. He was probably only being nice because his Uncle Roger had told him to.

'I'd better go back now,' she heard herself say. 'I'm going with Mum to collect the car and more of our stuff.'

There would have been time. But now everything was tainted with a mood she had become used to, a mood in which everything looked and tasted sour, her mind closing in on one simple, thumping injustice: *it's not fair.*

She started trudging back up the field edge.

It was the galloping horse that had done it, and the arrogance of the girl who sat him so easily, enjoying the speed and freedom, the open spaces laid out for her pleasure. Grace thought of how it used to feel to run, to race: revelling in her own speed and energy, the breeze in her face, legs pumping, carrying her forward.

Now . . . far from being able to run, she had walked too far. The distance, on uneven ground, was too great, where once she could have run with ease. She felt her armpits prickling with sweat; she felt her lopsidedness and the uncomfortable heat of her leg – what remained of her leg – encased in its sock, and the fibreglass and metal of the prosthesis. She looked down at her feet, walking: her real one that could flex and feel, and the artificial one that looked just the same, but couldn't.

Real Grace might as well have died that day. What was left was just a . . . a *cripple.*

Jamie was puzzled; she saw it in his walk. He was heading

the same way, towards the stile that led into the wood. At first he slowed his pace to hers, till – in a mood to resent that – she said crossly, 'Don't wait for me. I know you want to go faster.'

He was being as considerate today as he'd been yesterday, but now it rankled. This was for always. People would be kind, and she'd have to smile and be grateful while seething inside, because she hadn't chosen this.

Jamie hesitated, then said, 'OK. See you later,' and set off, jogging.

She watched him go. Always she was watching people go.

At times like this she needed Marie-Louise, who never had to say much for Grace to feel that she understood. Marie-Louise was the only one who could get her out of her blackest moods; often by doing something daft, like making a mournful sad-clown face. Even when Grace was deter-mined not to, she could never quite stay miserable when Marie-Louise did that.

But Marie-Louise wasn't here. Grace was on her own.

There was no phone signal out in the fields, but when she got back to the flat she found a text message: **Hi, hope you're having fun exploring. Have you met anyone to be friends with? M-Lx**

No, Grace replied. **Only Boy 1, geeky. Girl, snobby + rude. Boy 2, moody. That's it so far. Gx**

Geeky was unfair to Jamie and not even what she thought, but it suited her sour mood. Waiting for a reply she flopped down on her bed and lay looking up at the sloped ceiling.

Six weeks of this. Six *weeks*.

'It's like you're following Christina, coming here from London,' Mum had said last night.

Even though Grace had already been thinking this, she preferred to keep her thoughts to herself, to examine in private. Now she wondered whether Christina had lain on her bed like this, in her first days, and stared at the ceiling, wondering how on earth she'd survive here and what she was supposed to do with her time. She couldn't have known then that she'd fly the Channel in an aeroplane that looked as flimsy as a model made by a child, or fall in love three times, or gallop across fields on a headstrong horse and jump huge hedges and ditches.

In spite of her mood, Grace quite liked this train of thought. It made the years slip away, as if she and Christina had just arrived here together, from their different times and in their different clothes, and might pass each other in the yard. It made her feel less alone, thinking of Christina.

Irina, talking on the phone in the office, waved at Grace through the window while she stood outside with her mother, waiting for Roger to drive round from the car park. He was taking them to Chelmsford to pick up the car Mum was buying.

'It's not red, is it?' Grace asked her mother. She didn't think she could get into a red car, ever.

Mum didn't get it at first; then she did. 'Oh, Gracey, no! It's yellow. A nice cheerful yellow.'

Roger's car was dark green. As they got in and fastened their seat belts, Mum asked Roger about Marsh House – what it was like, and how long his brother had lived there.

'It's been in our family since the 1920s,' Roger told her. 'So we'd be sorry to part with it, though my father could only afford to keep it by dividing it in two and renting out half. My great-grandfather – Fergus, the one who had the terrible facial burns – set up his business there, after the war. He seems to have been pretty successful. Eventually he bought the place.'

'What sort of business?'

'Restoring and repairing cars – this was when cars were fairly new on the scene. He must have been quite go-ahead. Now Ian lives there with his wife Gail, and' – Roger wasn't going to ignore Grace in the back seat while he chatted to Mum, the way some adults would have done; he glanced round to include her in the conversation – 'Charlie and Jamie, my niece and nephew. You'll probably see Charlie around, on her horse – she often rides in the Flambards woods.'

Grace didn't let on that she and Charlie had already met.

'She's got a horse of her own?' Mum was asking.

'Yes – horse-mad, like your Russell ancestors. She gets that from her mum – Gail used to ride a lot, not so much now. There's a stable and a paddock next to the house. With Jamie it's wildlife, always has been. He's set on being a wildlife photographer. He's already very knowledgeable.'

'He seems such a nice boy. Doesn't he, Grace?'

'Mmn,' Grace mumbled, feeling bad about the way they'd parted and her text to Marie-Louise.

'So – where were *you* living?' Mum asked Roger. 'Before you got the job here?'

'In Colchester. I was working there and about to buy a house, but things didn't work out.'

'Oh?'

'It was complicated,' Roger said. Grace saw his sideways look at Mum, his smile that was part grimace. *Don't ask*, was what he clearly meant. For a moment Grace thought her mother was on the brink of asking more, but then she thought better of it, and was quiet.

Driving into Chelmsford felt like re-entering the normal world, with busy traffic and streets full of shops and buses and pedestrian crossings. Roger dropped them at the car dealer's, and Mum checked and signed paperwork and produced her bank card, and the little yellow Fiat was theirs.

Mum looked pleased with herself as they drove away. 'Isn't it lovely? I feel attached to it already. Home, next. Look, we've got satnav!'

A fast country road, a brief stretch on the motorway, and back into north London slowness and congestion; then home to Rignell Road, though it no longer seemed like home. Planted in the pocket-handkerchief garden that fronted the house was an estate agent's board saying SALE AGREED. Everything should be completed in about a month, Mum said.

'But our stuff's still here. What'll we do with it all?' Grace asked.

'There's still some of your dad's things here, and he'll take his share of the furniture. I hope we'll have found a flat by then. If there's more than we can fit in, we'll have to put the rest into storage.'

It all sounded so uncertain. For now, they packed more clothes and belongings into holdalls and bin bags, and stowed them in the car. What to take, what to leave behind? Grace chose some of her books, another pair of jeans, two sweaters and five tops, and then – ridiculously, she knew – a fluffy black cat toy Dad had bought for her on a work trip a few years ago.

Black cat for luck.

In the slow hospital time after the accident, Grace had thought that maybe – *maybe* – the shock to them all would be enough to bring her parents back together. Not that she'd have willingly made such a bargain, but still, something might have been salvaged from the wreckage. Now she knew how naive that hope had been – things had gone too far, Dad was already living with Chloe. They had their own lives that couldn't be swerved off course even by her own disaster. Plans had been made, divorce proceedings already started, before It happened. Mum-and-Dad were finished, and it was time she got used to it.

Mum locked up and they drove away. Quite possibly, Grace thought, she'd never see 14 Rignell Road again.

'Shopping, next,' Mum said. They took a longer route than necessary to the supermarket, through side streets, to avoid the fateful junction.

Flambards welcomed them back. There it was, calm and unchanging, overlooking its lawn and garden and fields, used to people coming and going. Mum drove the car along the avenue of chestnut trees that flanked the drive, and parked behind the stableyard. When Grace looked back, the yellow Fiat was a splash of sunshine yellow against the duller colours of the other cars parked there.

She and her mother lugged their bags up to the Hayloft. Taking the stuffed black cat into her bedroom, Grace was surprised to find a real cat sprawled on her bed, yawning widely and throwing her a casual glance as if it had every right to be there. It was the tabby cat she'd seen yesterday; it must have come in through the open window.

Later, over at the house for supper, she told Roger.

'Who does it belong to?'

'Oh, that's Cat Siggy. He turned up here a couple of months ago, and I started feeding him and he stayed around. Now he's decided to live here.'

'Siggy?'

'Yes. Short for Siegfried.'

'Why did you call him that?'

'Oh . . .' Roger looked a little embarrassed. 'I named him after Siegfried Sassoon. See, I told you I was obsessed by the First World War. Do you know about him? He wrote some of the best-known poems about the war. Criticizing it, criticizing the waste of lives.'

'But he sounds German? Was he on the other side?'

'No – you'd think so from his name, but he was English. He was given a medal for bravery, but he chucked it away in disgust. I've got his books packed up somewhere.'

When Grace went back later, Cat Siggy was gone, leaving only the imprint of his body on her duvet cover. She hoped he'd come back. It had made the flat feel like a home, having a cat visitor.

CHAPTER SIX

Plum

Next morning Grace came face to face with Marcus.

It was the dog she saw first. The black-and-white collie loped up to her, smiley-faced, wagging not just its tail, but its whole back end.

'Hello! What's your name?'

She bent to stroke it, and when she straightened Marcus was standing a few yards away, probably thinking she was idiotic to talk to a dog like that, as if actually expecting an answer. The dog ran to him and sat at his feet, wriggling with pleasure.

'Flash,' he said. 'He's called Flash.'

So close, she saw a younger version of the stroppy van man, good looking in a careless way. *I bet lots of girls fancy him*, she thought. His hair was very dark and so were his eyes, under thick brows; he had a guarded expression and she recalled his anger the other day, wondering if he was often moody, and what made him like that. He just stood looking at her, one hand resting on the dog's head. It seemed he wasn't going to say any more, so she said, 'I'm Grace.'

'I know. I'm Marcus.'

'Is he yours?'

He nodded, and even smiled – but at the dog, not at her. 'He's a working collie. I'm training him. Come on, then,' he said to Flash. 'Let's get going.' He turned away, and as the dog bounded ahead he threw an abrupt, 'See you,' over his shoulder.

After yesterday's stop for supermarket shopping, there was food in the Hayloft's fridge and cupboards. Grace and her mother made sandwiches for lunch, taking them round to the garden terrace as it was too lovely a day to sit indoors. They sat on a bench, Grace throwing breadcrumbs to a group of sparrows who kept close watch. Sally the gardener had been busy; the lawn was newly mown, the air smelling of cut grass and roses. The doors to the dining room were open, but no one was eating lunch there today. The landscape painters had left after breakfast, loading luggage into cars or lingering by the porch to wait for taxis, hugging each other and exclaiming about how marvellous it had been. Without them it was quiet, the only sound the cheeping of sparrows and the occasional baaing of a sheep. A new group would arrive this afternoon.

Mum seemed preoccupied, not saying much. When

Grace asked what she was doing today she answered, 'Planning, with Roger.' Grace noticed the downward turn of her mouth. She hadn't said anything about yesterday's meeting, and Grace assumed it was just dull business stuff.

'Isn't it going well?'

Mum sighed. 'It's just . . . Flambards isn't making money. Not enough, anyway.'

'But you already knew that. Isn't that why you're here?'

'Yes – but it's worse than I thought. The Trustees run the place, but one of them's the main sponsor, Mr Naylor. If he decides to pull out, it's all over. He was here this morning. I didn't like him much, even if it's thanks to him that the Flambards Trust even exists. He owns a local building company, and he's invested a lot – hundreds of thousands of pounds – to modernize Flambards, convert the rooms, put in bathrooms, all that sort of thing.'

'Can't they get another sponsor?'

'It's not that easy. And Mr Naylor expects a return on his money, he made that clear. He and the Trustees have agreed to give it three years, but we're already well into the second, and things haven't really taken off. If we can't get more guests here, more take-up for the courses, he'll call it a day.'

'Then what?'

Mum shrugged. 'Flambards would have to be sold. Someone might take it on as a hotel, or turn it into a luxury health club.'

67

'No! That wouldn't be right!' Grace said fiercely. What about Christina? It would be as if she'd never existed.

'It's not a question of what's right, Gracey. Sadly. It's a question of what brings money in.'

They both gazed at the ground for a few moments, where two sparrows squabbled over a piece of crust.

'But Flambards doesn't *belong* to this Naylor man, does it?' Grace asked.

'No, it belongs to the Trust. The Trustees committee votes on any decisions. Roger's one of them. He and the others don't want it to fail, or to be sold – Roger especially. He's dead set on saving it. But they can't carry on without Mr Naylor. They might have to agree to the halfway measure he's suggested – selling off some of the land for building. That means *he'd* buy it, for his company. That would raise enough to keep going.'

'Wouldn't that be a dodgy deal? Trying to make *sure* Flambards fails, so that he can buy the land and make money from it?'

'I don't think he's doing that. He started out with the best intentions, Roger said, but things haven't gone as well as expected, and he's a businessman after all.'

'So how much land would he want?' Grace asked, thinking that there was an awful lot of it round here. Maybe Mr Naylor could build his houses in a small field somewhere out of sight.

But her mother said, 'Long Meadow. The field between the stable yard and the wood. There's space for twenty or more houses. That could bring him a small fortune, I imagine.'

'But not there!' Grace's eyes swung in that direction, though the corner of the house and the rose arch were in the way. 'That's about the worst possible place!'

She thought of Jamie, and of the wood: the almost holy quiet of the trees, the green canopy overhead and cool space beneath. It wouldn't be the same with a housing estate butting up to the edges.

Mum wiped her fingers on a piece of kitchen towel and passed Grace an apple. 'People need to live somewhere, Gracey.'

'I know. But not here! Not in smart new houses. It would spoil it all. What would Christina think?'

'Christina?' Her mother looked at her sideways.

'I just meant . . .' Grace mumbled. 'It wouldn't be the same. I mean, there are changes already, but it can't be all *that* different from how Christina would have known it. And Granny Izz.'

'I know. But it can't be kept in mothballs. It has to pay for itself.'

'But what about all those arty people?' Grace asked. 'There were loads of them, and I heard some of them say they'll come back next year. How many more do you need on the courses?'

'This week was one of the successes,' Mum told her. 'Quite a few other courses have been cancelled – there weren't enough takers. We're having a good look at the programme to see how we can improve it. So you see, I'm a kind of gamble. Mr Naylor made that clear this morning. They can't really afford another member of staff, but they've taken me on for six weeks to work on marketing and publicity, and see if I can make a difference.'

That sounded like a big responsibility. Grace knew that her mother had a good reputation for her freelance work, but usually that was for small restaurants and hotels, a few days' work here and there. She hadn't done anything on this scale.

'*Can* you make a difference?'

'Only wish I knew. I've got some ideas. I'd better get back to the office. What are you doing this afternoon?'

'I'll probably go down to the lake.'

Grace had been reading for most of the morning, one of the novels she'd borrowed from Marie-Louise. They did a lot of book-swapping and sharing. Last year they'd read everything they could find by Catherine Johnson and Anne Cassidy; more recently it had been Elizabeth Wein, Mal Peet and Patrick Ness.

But she'd had enough of reading for now, and was restless. She wondered if Jamie would avoid her after her sulk yesterday. She couldn't blame him if he did.

As she came round to the stable yard, taking the back way through the garden, she heard the sound of hooves on gravel. Not wanting another encounter with uppity Charlie, she slowed her pace, but saw that the horse that had just come through the gate was a good bit smaller, a pony, with Jamie on its back. He saw her and waved.

'Hello!' he called. 'I was coming to look for you.'

She went over. The pony, dark brown with a thick black mane and tail, turned its head as she approached. It had a pretty face, with a diamond-shaped white star on its fore-head and bright eyes that looked at her in a friendly way from under a bushy forelock. Jamie's legs were long against its sides.

'This is Plum.' He patted her neck.

'*Plum!*'

'Her proper name's Victoria Plum.'

Grace laughed. All these animals – Plum, Sirius, Flash and Cat Siggy – each had a name that meant something to the person who had chosen it, each with its own personality and presence. She'd never had much to do with animals before, only seeing them on TV. And there *was* something a bit plummy about the pony; her plump rounded sides, and the colour of her coat – not glinting chestnut like Sirius's, but a glossy darker shade with a sheen on it like a ripe fruit ready for eating.

'Whose is she, then? Not yours?'

'Well, ours.' Jamie swung one leg over the pony's neck and dropped down to stand beside her. 'She was Charlie's, her first pony. Then Charlie got too tall for her and wanted to do competition stuff, and she needed a bigger horse for that and got Sirius. But we've had Plum for ages and it wouldn't seem right to sell her.'

'No!' Grace agreed.

'Charlie doesn't ride her any more, but I do, now and

then. Otherwise she just stays out in the field and keeps Sirius company. On a pony you can sometimes get closer to deer and badgers and things than when you're walking. Anyway, I've brought her over so you can have a go.'

'*Me?* At riding?'

'She's just the right size for you, and she's very well-behaved. I thought, you know' – he flushed slightly– 'with your leg. People do ride, I mean people like you. It won't be a problem, once you get used to it.'

People like you. Disabled people. But he hadn't actually said it. Sometimes people didn't know *what* to say: whether it was best to say nothing at all, or risk coming out with the wrong thing. By now Grace was used to that.

'But I've never been on a horse.' She wondered if someone else had suggested this; Roger, probably. Surely not Charlie.

'No problem. I can teach you. I mean, I'm no expert, but I can get you started. You can see if you like it.'

'OK then. Thanks!' At once Grace was eager; she could be like Christina, learn to ride. 'How do I get on?'

'You'd better wear this.' Jamie took off the helmet he was wearing and helped her to fasten the chin-strap; then he demonstrated how to mount: left foot in the stirrup, left hands holding the reins in front of the saddle, a light hop up. He made it look so easy, but for Grace, without a flexible right foot and ankle to spring from, it proved to be a clumsy scramble, while Plum stood patiently.

'Oh . . .' Grace felt herself clenching up in frustration:

72

thwarted by something that would have been so simple, before.

'It might be easier getting up from the other side. Or you could even use the mounting-block. But you're on now.' Jamie helped her adjust the stirrups to a comfortable length, and showed her how to hold the reins. Then he opened the field gate and the pony followed him through.

Although Plum wasn't a tall pony, Grace felt high up, though quite secure in the comfortably padded saddle. Plum walked alongside Jamie, obedient as a dog.

'Relax your hands – there's no need to grip the reins tightly. She's not going to gallop off. That's better.'

Anxious and tense at first, Grace realized that there was little to do other than move gently with the pony's stride. They reached the fence at the far end, and Jamie said that she could ride back by herself, while he walked a few paces behind.

She was actually riding! On her own! The pony stepping out beneath her, the bushy mane in front, little curved ears pricked alertly – she began to thrill to the new experience, already wanting more.

'Oh, aren't you lovely!' Stopping at the gate she leaned forward, full of gratitude, inhaling the warm horsey smell.

'Cool!' said Jamie, coming alongside. 'You're doing fine. Now we'll try a trot. You need to squeeze with your legs to make her go faster – a squeeze, not a kick. Do you know what I mean by rising trot?'

She didn't. Jamie explained, and made her practise at

73

a standstill, rising in her stirrups, then sitting lightly; up, down. This was harder, making her feel lopsided. She saw that the idea was to let the weight drop into her heel – easy enough on the left side, impossible on the right, where her foot kept slipping out of the stirrup and she had to look down to fumble it in again. She found a way of pressing down with her knee in an effort to stop that from happening.

'We'll give it a try, anyway,' Jamie said. 'Hang on to her mane if it helps you balance, and shout if you want to stop. Right. Let's go.'

Grace's left leg closed in to the warmth of the pony's side, while her right leg was rigid and unfeeling, but Plum, encouraged by Jamie, moved into a smooth trot.

Rise and sit. Rise, sit. She concentrated hard, Jamie jogging alongside.

'Nearly – keep going . . .'

'Oops . . .' She lost it, bumped, clutched the pony's mane, then found the rhythm again. For the next few strides it felt almost easy.

'That's it – you've got it – great!' Jamie slowed, bringing Plum back to a walk. 'Not bad! It takes some people much longer than that to get rising trot. It'll be easier next time.'

Next time! Grace liked the sound of that.

'We'll just walk a bit more now,' Jamie said. 'We can take her into the woods if we go round by the bridge.'

Brown butterflies fluttered up from the long grass as Jamie's feet and the pony's hooves brushed through. Grace thought of what Mum had told her earlier, and thought of diggers moving in, churning everything up, to build houses and roads and garages – noise and uproar destroying this peaceful meadow. No! That surely couldn't happen, not here, where the house had looked over its quiet fields and woods for more than a hundred years. Those earlier Russells, the riding and hunting Russells of Christina's day, must have ridden over this same field more times than could be counted. She almost said something to Jamie, then thought better of it; this was his special place, and he'd hate the idea more than she did.

They had come to an earth bridge over the slow-running stream that flowed into the woods. Jamie lifted a chain from the gate on the other side, and she had to concentrate on ducking underneath low branches.

When they reached the hide Jamie showed her how to dismount, and tied Plum's reins to a slender tree trunk. 'You shouldn't really tie a horse up by the reins – a nervous one might pull back and break them. But Plum doesn't mind.'

There seemed to be a proper way of doing everything. The dismounting was different from the casual way he'd done it earlier; instead she had to lean forward and swing her right leg over the pony's back. It felt awkward, but easier than getting on, at least.

The small brown diving bird Grace had seen was busy on the lake again today; Jamie was pleased, and identified it as a little grebe. 'I haven't got my binoculars, or you could have a better look.'

She remembered the unseen bird that had sung so impressively, and told him about it. 'So loud! It seemed to fill up the whole wood.'

'A nightingale!' he said at once, delighted. 'Must have been. We get them here sometimes, but not that often.'

'I thought nightingales only sang at night?'

'That's what a lot of people think. They do, but in the daytime too. It's just that not many birds sing in the dark, so people notice them then. But they're not very common. Perhaps it's still around.'

When they went back to Plum, Jamie said he'd lead her as far as the bridge and then ride home. 'If you're OK walking back. It's hardly worth you getting back on, for such a short way.'

Grace felt a little disappointed that she wouldn't be doing any more riding today. 'OK.'

At the gate Jamie vaulted into the saddle and lengthened the stirrups for his long legs. 'I'll bring her over again tomorrow, if you want?'

'Thank you! That was lovely!'

Grace walked back across the field, marvelling at the unexpected turn the afternoon had taken. She sure wasn't how she felt about having to be grateful to Charlie, but she wasn't going to let that spoil the pleasure of finding something she could do. And do well? She would certainly try her hardest.

The dance group arrived. There were twelve of them: some in a minibus, others in their own cars, calling to each other as they unloaded their bags in the car park. They were in their late teens or early twenties, mainly female, a few young men. Intrigued, Grace watched them, noticing their clothes – leggings or loose pants, slouchy tops sliding off shoulders, wide headbands – and their graceful way of carrying themselves. They might have been a rare, exotic species. Coming in to dinner some of them smiled in her direction, and one girl said hi. Otherwise they were absorbed in conversation. At one point, a beautiful black girl stood up to demonstrate a dance move between the tables; she crouched low, then rose on one planted foot, the other leg, long and slender, sweeping up and out behind, an arm scooping over to catch the raised foot – impossible, and so easy. Grace looked down at her plate then back at the group, fascinated, envious.

In the morning she saw them drifting over to the studio; she heard the same girl's infectious laugh and saw her perform a few twirling steps as she walked. It seemed that she could never quite stop dancing. Grace itched to watch them warm up and practise, knowing that it would only fill her with sadness and loss. It wasn't that she had ever wanted to be a dancer. It was just another choice she didn't have now: to be perfect, agile, beautiful to watch; drawing people's gaze to her, as this girl did.

But now there was riding. Today she would ride Plum again.

For a moment, last night, she'd thought Mum was going to spoil that.

'I wish you'd told me first. What if something happened?'

Because of your leg, she meant.

'But it didn't. Won't. Don't worry, Mum! Plum's really good, and Jamie was there. And I wore a proper hard helmet.'

'All the same, I'm not sure about it. Don't take chances. And we'll mention it to Zainab, next time we go.'

Zainab was Grace's physiotherapist – lovely, kind, generous with praise and encouragement to Grace for doing her exercises so thoroughly. Grace always looked forward to her visits. Oh, Zainab just *had* to think riding was a good idea!

Today she managed rising trot with only one lost stirrup and a little bumping. Again Jamie said she was doing well, and told her to ride all the way round the field by herself while he waited at the gate. The pony was so amenable that all Grace needed was a little pressure on the rein to turn, a light squeeze of leg to go faster. Almost, Plum seemed to know what to do before Grace had given the smallest signal.

She asked Jamie to take photos with her mobile phone. Later, looking at them, she saw herself smiling and confident in the saddle. I look like a proper rider, she thought, surprised.

She sent the photos to Marie-Louise and also to her dad, with whom she had a Skype chat next morning. Weekends were usually her time for seeing Dad, but he'd had to miss this one to go with Chloe to a cousin's wedding. Next Sunday, he said, he'd take her out for the day.

'I knew it,' he said, about the photo. 'They'll turn you into one of those hard-riding, fox-hunting Russell women.'

He was joking, but Grace felt pleased at the idea that something was stirring in her blood, something to link her to the brave and enterprising Christina. She felt as if Christina was sending a secret message of encouragement.

CHAPTER SEVEN

Those Magnificent Men in their Flying Machines

'Here it is,' Roger said, in the driver's seat. 'Marsh House. It's not too far to walk across the fields like Jamie does, but I'm usually pressed for time and do it the lazy way.'

There was a high wall, with tall iron gates standing open. The house was square and neat, built of brick and perfectly symmetrical, with steps leading up to a green front door, and a drive that swept round and out again. Like Flambards the house stood alone and self-contained.

Roger led them down a path to one side. The garden, long and narrow with an orchard beyond, was nowhere near as well-maintained as the one at Flambards. A large barn formed one edge, and a barbecue had been set up on the grass, with assorted garden chairs and tables nearby. A wooden fence split the space in half lengthways, and Grace remembered Roger saying that the house was divided into two as well. From this angle Marsh House looked less grand than she'd thought at first sight. She glimpsed Plum grazing in the orchard; she'd go and see her later if the adult conversation got too boring.

Roger's brother, Ian – they were rather alike, except that Roger was taller and slimmer and Ian's hair gingery and short – came to meet them, and introduced his wife, Gail, who was busy carrying dishes of food out of the house and setting them on the tables. She wore jeans and a loose shirt and plimsolls, making Grace think that Mum, in a summer dress and her new sandals, looked over-dressed.

'You've met Jamie, of course,' Ian was saying. 'He's here somewhere, and Charlie's on her way. I hear you've been giving our Plum a bit of exercise?'

'Yes! Thank you.'

'No, you're doing us a favour. Plum spends too long standing about in the field, otherwise. It's good for her to be ridden.'

Gail ladled fruit punch into glasses, and handed round bowls of crisps and cashews.

'Sally and Adrian are coming over too, with Marcus. Have you met Marcus?' Ian asked Grace.

'Sort of. I saw him with his dog.'

'Flash. Yes, you hardly ever see Marcus without him.'

Grace wondered how the cheerful Sally coped with such a difficult husband and son. Yesterday she had glimpsed Marcus's dad – stocky, dark-haired, with the air of bearing a permanent grudge against the world – getting into the white van parked in the yard. He had never yet come into the dining room for lunch or a coffee break, the way Sally sometimes did; presumably he spent most of his time at the farm.

She sipped the light fruity drink and listened to the grown-ups talking. Jamie's parents, she gathered, were teachers at the local comprehensive school, which both Marcus and Jamie attended; Charlie too, in the sixth form. Gail taught geography there, while Ian was head of art. He said that he'd be over at Flambards each Friday from now until the end of the school holidays, to teach a weekly class.

'Art is Grace's favourite subject,' Mum told him. 'She's really quite talented.'

'I'm really not.' Grace heard how sulky her voice sounded. PE's my favourite subject, Mum, she was thinking. *Used* to be. And she wished her mother wouldn't *do* that: praising her, making her sound special. 'I like art, but that's mainly cos I'm not much good at anything else.'

Ian and Gail both laughed, obviously thinking she was being modest.

'If you're at a loose end you're welcome to come and join us this Friday,' Ian said. 'Ten o'clock, two hours, with a break in the middle.'

The coming week would be a quiet one at Flambards, Roger was saying: a course on local architecture had been cancelled because of low numbers. That didn't sound good; Grace saw her mother's grimace.

'Crime writing next weekend,' Roger went on. 'We'll be

82

inundated by people talking about poisons and asking about the best way to dispose of a dead body.'

Gail laughed, and said, 'It's never dull, is it? All these people coming and going with their different interests and obsessions.'

'You said your family's owned this house for a few generations?' Grace's mother asked Roger.

'Yes, from the 1920s. Before that it was owned by an interesting character called Dermot who was keen on flying, like your Will.' For the benefit of Ian and Gail, he added, 'William Russell, that is – Polly's great-grandfather. Dermot had that barn built' – he nodded towards it – 'to house a light aircraft he was making. Eventually he killed himself flying it. Out there in the fields.'

Mum looked astonished. 'How did you find that out?'

'It was in the local paper – I came across it in the archives in Colchester. 1913. I made a copy – I can show you. He must have been a bit old for capers like that. But very brave. It was a risky business.'

'So there was quite a bit of flying going on around here at that time,' Mum said. 'I wonder if Will and this Mr Dermot knew each other? Otherwise it'd be an odd coincidence for *two* amateur pilots to live just a couple of miles apart.'

'I don't know of any airfields close to here, but it might have been different back then,' Ian said. 'Exciting times! I gather there was quite a craze in the early years of the twentieth century, for flying the Channel and looping the loop and suchlike.'

'There was a film, *Those Magnificent Men in their Flying Machines*,' Gail said. 'I remember seeing it as a child. Men with handlebar moustaches and women in floaty dresses, all very dashing.'

A movement beyond the garden, in the orchard where Plum was grazing, caught Grace's attention. Charlie led Sirius through the open gate from the stable, patted his neck and released him. The horse walked on, head lowered, then all his legs seemed to buckle and next moment he was rolling on his back, hooves waving in the air.

'Oh!' Grace was alarmed, thinking he must be ill.

Gail turned to look. 'It's all right – he always does that when he's pleased to have his saddle off and be out in the field. He loves it.'

With a snort, the horse finished rolling and sat up like a dog for a moment with forelegs braced before lurching to his feet and giving himself a vigorous shake that sent dust flying. Then he walked slowly over to join Plum, pausing to snatch a mouthful of grass. Beside him, Plum looked small and rather tubby. Charlie walked up through the garden to join the group there, and at the same moment Jamie came out of the house.

Introductions were made; while Jamie fiddled with the barbecue Charlie said she was going indoors for a quick wash, and reappeared a few minutes later, helping herself to punch. Smiling briefly at Grace she settled herself in the chair next to Mum, who asked about her horse.

'He looks beautiful. Roger says you're getting him fit for competitions?'

'Yes, for a couple of events in October. And for hunting, as soon as it starts in the autumn.'

'Oh! I didn't realize there was still hunting round here.'

'Well, course,' Charlie said in her *don't-you-know-anything* way. 'It's part of country life.'

'I thought it was against the law now?'

'No. We don't do anything illegal. We follow a trail, not a fox.'

'So it's not fox-hunting, then?' Grace asked.

'Well, sometimes hounds pick up the scent of a fox. It's hard to stop them. Either way, hunting's brilliant fun. Sirius loves it.'

'But if they . . .'

Grace stopped there on receiving a look from her mother that said *best keep quiet*.

'It's kind of you to let Grace ride your pony,' Mum said, and Grace added, 'Yes – thank you! She's lovely.'

She knew that she should have thanked Charlie without being prompted. Yes, Charlie had been obnoxious the first time they met, but learning to ride Plum was the best thing that had happened since she'd arrived at Flambards. Still, that was down to Jamie, not his sister. From what Jamie said, Charlie was merely letting her ride a pony she had no use for.

Charlie smiled. 'Good old Plum. Sounds like you weren't too bad, considering.'

Considering! Grace bristled at that, but Charlie added, 'Considering you'd never been on a horse before. Jamie said you did really well.'

'Did he?' That was better. 'But I haven't done much yet.'

'Sometimes you can tell though, straight away. Some people look all wrong in the saddle, and you know they'll never be any good. Others have a feel for it – the way they sit, the way they respond to the horse. Marcus is like that.'

'Marcus? Does he ride too?'

'Only now and then. It's a waste. Jamie only sees horses as transport when he wants it, but Marcus is a natural.' A pause, then as if regretting being so generous, Charlie added, 'Jamie's no expert. I'll give you a lesson myself when you've done a bit more. Then we'll see.'

With a whisking rush of black and white, Flash the collie was among them, whuffing and smiling as he dashed from one person to another.

'Ah, here they are,' Gail said, and everyone looked round as Marcus and his mother, Sally, approached. There was something hesitant in Sally's smile, and Marcus was looking at no one.

Ian got to his feet. 'Oh – what, no Adrian?'

'He couldn't make it after all,' Sally said, with a brightness that surely everyone could see was fake. Marcus, after a brief and reluctant look at the group, gave his attention to Flash, calling him to heel, telling him to sit.

Grace guessed from the briskness of Gail and Ian's response – 'Sit down, anyway, and relax. Let me get you a drink' – that this wasn't altogether unexpected. Otherwise, surely, they'd have been all concern: 'Oh dear, what a shame – is he ill?' But no one was asking any questions at all. And she had caught Charlie's reaction: upward eye roll, smirky smile. No surprise there, either.

Sally sat next to Mum and started talking quickly about the weather and the garden. Marcus took a can of Coke from Gail and sprawled on the grass beside Jamie; Grace saw them exchange a few muttered remarks, then Marcus flipped open the can and they sat in silence.

Jamie seemed different here, Grace thought. Apart from a quick 'hi' he'd barely looked in her direction. After a while the two boys got up and went down to the bottom of the garden, where the grass was left rough and unmown, and began kicking a football to each other. Roger had gone indoors to find the newspaper cutting for Grace's mother, who was deep in conversation with Sally. Charlie was looking at her iPhone (Mum would have frowned at Grace if *she* did that in company), while Ian and Gail lit the barbecue and lined up sausages and chicken pieces on the grill.

Grace went down to the orchard fence, past the boys, to look at the horses. They were grazing side by side now, and the air was so still that she could hear them steadily tearing grass with their teeth. Jamie and Marcus occasionally called to each other, and she heard Jamie laugh. Before, she'd have wanted to join in; she used to love playing football. But now her leg made her awkward and clumsy, and she could tell that the boys didn't want her with them. She watched them unnoticed, taking in their different styles. Jamie was playful, making little dribbling runs and jinks and feints; Marcus played with more serious purpose, every now and then giving the ball a powerful kick that sent it smashing into the hedge past Jamie's flailing arms.

Marcus is good looking but quite rude, she would text to Marie-Louise later. **Wish you could be here. What are you doing?**

There was something wondrous about the summer dusk: the sky in the west turning a hazy pink, then a colder blue as darkness crept over the fields and trees. Lights were appearing in the garden – candles, lanterns, the glow of the barbecue coals – and she smelled the drift of lighter fuel and smoke and, soon, of slightly charred meat. The stars slowly revealed themselves in patterns and individual dots of light. The familiar shape of the Plough was tilted over to one side, the Pole Star glittering remote and high. They were there all the time, Grace realized; but why should that feel surprising? Of course they were, the same stars that had shone through the centuries of people on Earth and long, long before that. It was dizzying to think like that, making herself and her feelings completely unimportant.

She had seen beautiful sunsets and starry nights in London, the sky streaked brilliant gold as the sun dropped below houses and flats, but there the expanse was chopped up by high buildings, the stars outshone by fluorescent lights. Here she imagined she could feel the land breathing, and creatures stirring. Down beyond the orchard she heard a harsh cry, and she saw Jamie stop in mid-dribble to listen. An owl, was it? If you lived here it would be easy to be interested in wildlife.

'Food's ready,' Gail called. 'Come on, you lot.'

You lot. She was trying to include Grace with the boys, even if they weren't.

'What was all that about?' Grace asked. 'Marcus's dad not coming, and everyone not talking about it? Did Sally tell you?'

They were back in the flat, turning on lamps, about to get ready for bed.

'It's a bit difficult,' Mum said carefully. *'He's* apparently a bit difficult. Well, more than a bit. Moody.'

'You don't say.'

Difficult seemed to be what everyone said about Marcus's father. Grace waited for more, and after a moment Mum provided it.

'He used to be in the Army, till he was invalided out. He was in Afghanistan, in a tank regiment. This was a few years ago now, but Sally says he hasn't been the same since. And he won't accept help. Won't even admit there's anything wrong. Typical man,' Mum said with fervour, making Grace think of Dad, and the arguments he and Mum used to have while she strained her ears from her bedroom and pretended not to know or care.

'So now he's a farmer?'

'No – but he works over there, at Home Farm. He rents a couple of farm units, his workshop. He's a carpenter. He makes doors.'

'Doors? Is that all?'

'Well, he can make other things too, I expect. But mainly doors. He made all the doors here, Sally said, for the conversion. He made those stable doors in the yard that open in two halves.'

Grace had never thought of doors being specially made. She thought doors were just there.

'And Sally thinks it's not good for him to spend so much time alone, in his workshop. But Adrian won't listen to her. Or to anyone else.'

'But Marcus works with him, doesn't he?'

'Yes, in the school holidays. And Sally worries about *him* too. He broods, takes it all to heart. She's so glad he's friends with Jamie. Jamie's such a good-natured boy, isn't he?'

Grace began to understand. Yes, Jamie was kind enough to spend time with her, and to be friendly whenever they were together. But Marcus came first. Marcus *needed* him, it seemed.

'Have you even met him?' she asked. 'The dad?'

'Only to say hello, in the yard the other day.' Mum hesitated. 'I was wondering whether to invite them for a meal with us, in the flat. I'd like to get to know Sally better.'

'All of them? Marcus too?'

'Yes, course.'

'*Mu-um.*' Grace was dismayed. Mum wasn't much good at cooking; she was unsure of herself and easily flustered. Grace foresaw disasters, apologies and awkward silences. 'That's a seriously bad idea. Why would you want to invite two really grumpy people?'

CHAPTER EIGHT

Something Wrong, Something Bad

'Oh, sorry!'

Opening the door at the bottom of the Hayloft stairs, Grace had almost collided with a man walking fast down the yard.

Adrian.

Always in a hurry, the taxi driver had said. He had been, but now he'd swerved and stopped dead, his eyes fixed on her face. He seemed to do a double take, and stared again before looking away, turning his head with a deliberate effort as if it pained him.

Close up for the first time, she saw the strong resemblance to Marcus. Adrian was a more worn and weathered version, with the same crisply curling black hair, dark eyes and strongly marked eyebrows as his son. And the same air of being intensely preoccupied.

He didn't so much speak as gather words together in his throat and force them out.

'Uh. Huh. You all right there?'

'Yes. Er – thanks.'

And that was the limit of their conversation. He stared at her for a moment longer, nodded as if something was understood, and turned away, walking on towards the field gate. Grace stood for a moment, puzzled, gazing after him. What had he seen that made him react with that look of fascinated horror? She turned her head in case he'd been staring past her at something else, but there was only the empty stairway.

From what she'd heard of him from Jamie and her mother, she'd been imagining Marcus's father as some kind of ogre: brutish, bad-tempered, demanding. Instead, what she'd glimpsed in him just now looked more like dismay. But he's an ex-soldier, she thought, a fighter, and I'm just a girl.

He saw something wrong when he looked at me. Something bad.

But that was just stupid! How could he have? She walked slowly towards the house, trying to push the troubling thought away.

Later, in the cool, long-shadowed evening, Roger walked with Grace and her mother down to the village churchyard to find their Russell relations.

On the way, they passed a big signboard facing the road from a grass meadow where cows were grazing. The notice said: *NAYLOR HOMES – Coming soon, COWSLIP*

CLOSE – *an exclusive development of three- and four-bedroom houses*, with website details and a red logo.

'Naylor Homes!' exclaimed Grace's mother. 'That's—'

'Rex Naylor. Yes,' said Roger.

'Cowslip Close! It's a bit twee.'

'I know. Let's hope some of the cowslips survive the diggers.'

'The other day,' Grace reminded her, 'you said *people have got to live somewhere*.'

'I know. But it does seem awful, building on green fields. And *exclusive development* – that's not exactly the affordable housing that's most needed.'

The church was behind a row of cottages. It had a squat bell tower where jackdaws gathered, clacking. A blackbird sang from the yew tree, leaning and gnarled, that dominated the graveyard. This tree was hundreds of years old, Roger said, like many churchyard yews.

'Here they are.' He stopped by a row of gravestones in mown grass.

Mark William Russell, 1894–1925. The carved name was encrusted with yellow lichen, but still legible. Grace's eyes went straight to the inscription below, in sharper, more recent letters: *and his beloved wife, Christina Mary, 1896–1985.*

Here she was. Christina.

But not here. Grace thought of her as the lively girl back at Flambards, not as someone who'd lain here dead for – wait – thirty-three years. She couldn't think of her as a beloved wife, either – especially not as Mark's beloved wife.

Christina had been William's wife first, and that mattered more to Grace because Will was *theirs*. Direct family. If Christina and Will hadn't got married and had a baby, neither Grace nor her mother would exist.

Grace had seen old-lady photographs of Christina in colour, but much preferred the lovely girl of the older black-and-white images: the bold rider, the Channel flyer. The girl who had learned to ride at Flambards, who had ridden through these same fields and woods. Christina would have looked up at the same stars and moon, and listened to the song of birds that might be the ancestors of the birds that lived and bred here now.

Again, Grace had that sense of the long line of Russells, their loves and desires and pairings leading to her own self, the simple fact that she was standing here like a marker-post between past and future. The generations marched back, back, back, while in the other direction all the possibilities of the future reached out, spinning off beyond imagining.

'So, Gracey,' Mum said, 'Christina's husband, Mark, is your great-great-uncle.'

That made him sound ancient. William and Christina were nearer to her own age, she thought, knowing that was a stupid thing to think. She thought of them standing together in the photograph, gazing back at her with confident smiles as if they expected the future to hold nothing but good. They didn't know then that the war was coming, or that it would so soon take Will's life.

'But what about our William?' her mother was asking. 'He's not here, is he?'

'No, Polly. Will's grave is in France,' Roger said. 'I found it on the Commonwealth War Graves website. But his name's here on the war memorial.'

He showed them: there it was, low down on a long list on the memorial cross beside the path. *Captain William Russell, RFC.* Below that Grace saw a shorter list of names under the heading *1939–1945*. That was the other war, the one still referred to by older people as *the* war. But she was becoming more attuned to the first one, Will's war, the one she'd sometimes heard called the Great War.

'RFC?' Grace queried.

'He was in the Royal Flying Corps,' Roger said. 'Same as my great-grandfather. There was no RAF till 1918 – the Royal Flying Corps was part of the Army.'

'I wonder if they knew each other?'

'It's possible, I suppose. But your William was killed in 1916, and my great-grandfather didn't come to Marsh House till later, when the war was over.'

'So,' Mum asked, 'are there graves from your family here too?'

'Yes, over here.'

Roger led the way round to the back of the church along a path that passed under the ancient yew. *Fergus Charles Ashley-Clark* was there, and his wife *Helen Rosemary*; nearby, their son *Christopher Fergus Ashley-Clark* – 'My grandfather,' Roger said, and moved along the row to a much newer headstone with fresh flowers laid on the grave. Grace read *Roy Christopher Clark, 1946–2016*, and Mum exclaimed, 'Oh! This must be your father!'

'Yes, that's Dad. The *Ashley* got dropped somewhere along the way. We've just had the two-year anniversary. He died in July.'

'I'm sorry,' Mum said.

Grace wondered if Roger had put the flowers there, or perhaps it was Ian or Gail.

'My mother died quite young, and Dad never remarried,' Roger said. 'He stayed on at Marsh House till it got too much for him, then he moved to sheltered accommodation in Chelmsford for the last few years, and Ian and Gail took over the house. But a lot of his stuff's still in the attic there. I've started sorting through, to see if he kept any papers or photos that belonged to Fergus. Anything to do with the war, or flying, or his facial reconstruction. There might be photos, log books, that sort of thing.'

Not specially interested in the Clark family, Grace went back to the grassy mound of Mark and Christina's grave and looked again at *beloved wife*. It wouldn't say anything on William's war grave about his wife, would it? And that didn't seem right. Christina had loved William first, and – presumably – would have stayed married to him if he hadn't been killed. No one would know that, from these carved letters.

Roger was looking at another grave, two rows back. 'Here's Richard Wright, Christina's middle husband, and his second wife, Amy. There are still Wrights in the village, two or three families. Adrian's one of them. His surname's Gregg, but his mother was a Wright before she married.'

Grace thought of this morning's encounter, of Adrian's strange reaction to meeting her. She hadn't mentioned it to her mother, feeling unaccountably ashamed.

So if Adrian was a Wright, that meant Marcus was too. This was confusing: so many Wrights and Russells.

'But these Wrights wouldn't be blood relations of the Russells, would they?' her mother asked.

'No,' Roger said. 'Christina's marriage to Richard Wright didn't last long, and there were no children. From the records it looks as if Richard and Amy adopted a son later. Maybe they couldn't have children of their own.'

'I wonder why Christina got divorced from Richard?' Grace asked.

She knew only too well how marriages could fall apart – how her parents, once so solid and permanent in her life, had become two warring individuals who could hardly bear to be in the same room. Perhaps it had been like that with Christina and this middle husband.

'I don't know,' Mum said, with a little laugh. 'It seems she was meant to be a Russell.'

There were older Russells too; Roger pointed out the older William, the hunting-mad father of Mark and William, and his wife, Isobel, their mother, who'd died young. Granny Izz wasn't here, though; she had moved away, and in any case would have *no truck*, as she put it, with churches

97

or religion. 'A woodland burial for me,' she had specified. 'No God stuff. A cardboard coffin. Biodegradable. You can all draw pictures on it.' And Grace had, with Mum, crying at first but then making it a happy project, a last gift. With felt-tips and pencils and paintbrushes they had drawn and coloured all the things Granny Izz liked: cats, and bars of music, and a giraffe with a surprised expression, and an ice-cream cornet with a chocolate flake sticking out.

Grace liked the churchyard, although not for what Granny Izz had called the God stuff; she liked the ancient yew whose long dark boughs swooped almost to the ground, making a shady green tent, and the swathes of long grass and wild flowers beyond the mown areas. She liked the sense that the church had stood here for hundreds of years and looked ready to stand for hundreds more.

'We'll bring flowers for Christina, shall we, next time?' Mum said.

Grace rode Plum each afternoon that week, except on Tuesday when Mum drove her to hospital for her regular clinic appointment. The prosthetist was pleased with Grace's progress and showed her pictures of the athletic limb she could be fitted with soon, lighter and springier-footed than the leg Grace had now. She said that the riding was an excellent idea, and recommended asking for extra exercises to stop her knee and hip stiffening up next time she had a physio appointment with Zainab.

It didn't take long for her to feel confident with rising

trot, and soon Jamie said she was ready to canter, which – to her surprise – was easier than trotting, with its rocking-horse motion. She found that she could sit to the movement quite comfortably, and learned to soften her hands so that she didn't accidentally tug at Plum's mouth.

'When can I really gallop?'

Jamie grinned, patting Plum's neck; she was already puffing from the canter. 'She's not exactly a racehorse. Try another steady canter.'

I can do this! Grace exulted as she rode away from him. I can ride! On a pony I'm almost the same as anyone else. She relished the freedom, the regular beat of Plum's hooves on the grass, the energy she could control or release as she chose.

'You could ride around on your own now. You don't need me,' Jamie said, after she'd cantered in a wide circuit round the field and pulled up breathless and triumphant. 'But if you want to learn more, you'd better have lessons with Charlie. She'll teach you better than I can, about impulsion and collected trot and the stuff she goes on about. And jumping.'

'I'd like to learn to jump.' Grace wasn't sure, though, about being taught by Charlie. She enjoyed these leisurely afternoons, with Jamie helping and encouraging. Charlie, she was sure, would be far bossier.

Next morning Jamie arrived on foot, in a hurry, meeting Grace on her way to the office to help her mother.

'Come down to the lake! Something to show you. If we're lucky.'

'What?'

He wouldn't tell her, instead leading the way through the meadow to the stile, and on through the shaded woodland paths. At one point he stopped, listening, and looked up.

'Nuthatch! There it is.'

Following his pointing finger, Grace saw a sleek blue-grey bird poised for a moment on a tree trunk, head down, before it flew off.

'How did you know?' she asked, impressed.

'Heard it! Like this.' He gave a series of shrill upward whistles – a sound she realized she'd heard in the background without noticing, the way he did. 'But that's not what we've come for.'

His pace slowed as they neared the lake's edge, and he turned to shush her, though she wasn't speaking. 'We might see from here, but we'll have to creep. I hope they're still there.'

Through a screen of leaves, Grace saw the shine and flicker of light on water where the stream flowed into the lake. She couldn't see what Jamie was after, but when she looked at him in puzzlement he put a finger to his lips and crept forward, crouching. She expected kingfishers, but by the stream's edge she heard the rustle of vegetation and then splashing. Leaning forward, she saw a dark, fluid shape slip into the water, followed by a second, much smaller one. She caught her breath. There was an excited yipping as both animals rolled and twisted in the water as if in play.

'Beavers?' she whispered. She had only seen them on television.

She saw Jamie's suppressed smile, while he kept his eyes fixed on them. 'Not beavers! Otters.'

Of course they were; Grace felt silly. Hadn't she watched enough wildlife programmes to know that? After a few moments the two creatures slipped away smoothly into the lake, and she saw their flat heads, and ripples fanning out from their strong swimming. Soon they disappeared into undergrowth on the farthest shore, and were gone.

'They must have bred here!' Jamie's delight was evident. 'That's a female and her cub. I knew there were otters in Essex, but it's the first time I've seen them here.'

'When?'

'Yesterday, and again this morning, early.'

'Thanks for showing me. That was amazing!'

For those few moments the sense of watching wild animals doing what they instinctively did, freely and joyfully and without fear, had been magical. She began to understand why Jamie felt about the fields and woods the way he did.

He shrugged. 'Well, I had to show someone. If it was just me I'd think I only dreamed it.'

They waited to see if the otters would come back, but there was no sign. Jamie thought they might have returned to a hole in the bank where the female had made her nest. Holt, he called it.

On their way back to the field gate, Jamie said that he wouldn't be able to bring Plum for her to ride this afternoon, as he was going out with Marcus. 'Anyway, Charlie says I shouldn't keep bringing her over.'

'Oh!' Grace felt herself droop with disappointment. 'No more riding?'

'Not that! She says you can go over to ours. Starting today, if you like. She wants to give you a lesson, like I said. She doesn't trust me to teach you properly.'

Grace's mother drove her round to Marsh House after lunch. Going down through the garden with a sense of trepidation, she found Charlie leading Plum into the stable.

'I need to show you a few things. Then you can come over and ride whenever you like, on your own, unless Jamie wants Plum, which isn't very often.'

'Can I really?' Grace liked the idea of that: a kind companion for exploring, the pony's four sturdy legs better than her own one-and-a-bit.

'Sure. But you'll have to learn how to bring her in from the field, and groom her and pick out her feet, and put on the saddle and bridle.'

These mysteries were briskly demonstrated. When Plum was ready, Grace mounted, under Charlie's critical eye, and they went down to a corner of the orchard where an area was marked out with letters on posts. Tracks of worn-bare grass made ovals and circles and straight diagonal lines.

Today Charlie was wearing a red vest top with black leggings and knee-high riding boots, an outfit that gave her the appearance of a circus ringmaster as she stood in the centre. Watching Grace closely all the time, she called out instructions: 'Walk to A. Circle that end. Diagonal to K. Push on into rising trot.'

It was very different from the relaxed lessons with Jamie, and Grace wasn't sure she liked it. Luckily Plum – dear, sweet Plum! – seemed to know exactly what was expected, so that Grace couldn't tell if it was her own suggestions or Charlie's voice the pony was obeying as she walked and trotted on command. At one point Charlie made Grace trot without stirrups, which was bumpy and precarious, but Charlie said very necessary.

'You've got a lot to learn,' Charlie said, when Plum came to a smooth halt at the end. She produced a piece of carrot from her pocket and the pony crunched it loudly. 'But you haven't made a bad start. You sit well, that's the main thing. And your leg isn't too much of a problem. On another horse it might be, but Plum's pretty unflappable.'

'She's so good. Thanks for letting me ride her.'

'No probs. Next time I'll ride Sirius and we'll go out over the fields. Now I'll show you how to take her tack off, and she can have a feed.'

Grace quite liked the way Charlie had just come out with the remark about her leg, not hedging around it. She brushed Plum down, feeling that she'd made good – if bumpy – progress.

CHAPTER NINE

No Plan C

On Friday, waking to a wet, dismal morning, Grace went to Ian's art class in the barn, feeling self-conscious as the only young – even young*ish* – person there. With no clear idea of what she'd do, she found herself sketching dancers: at first tentative, then warming to it, covering sheet after sheet with quick sketches of fluid, graceful poses. Long limbs, flying hair. Strong, supple feet.

Ian paused at her easel and looked at her drawings for a few moments before saying, 'Interesting. Where does this come from?'

He seemed different here: quieter and more serious than he'd been at the barbecue. Grace explained that she'd been intrigued by the dancers last weekend, though she'd only glimpsed them. He nodded, and although he said nothing she sensed that he understood. Later on he said, 'You might try crayon if you want to carry on with those. It'd encourage you to be freer, less fussy.'

A stylish Indian lady at the next easel had been looking at Grace's work with interest. She introduced herself as Sushila, and said that she was a regular in Ian's classes. 'I love this place. I come whenever I can.' She was the kind of elegant older woman who didn't seem old at all, with iron-grey hair caught up in a jewelled comb and dark brown eyes in a lively face. She wore a long tunic over jeans, and beaded sandals that showed slim brown feet. Her painting was of Flambards in bright sunshine: the house with its coat of glossy ivy and the big cedar tree casting shade, in bold acrylic colours that were larger than life but somehow right. 'I'd be outside if it wasn't pouring with rain,' she told Grace. 'But tell me about this. Are you a dancer?'

Grace shook her head.

'Art student, then?'

'I'm only in Year Nine – I mean Ten, now. But art's one of my options for GCSE.'

'So I should hope.' Sushila nodded at the sketches that now filled Grace's sheet of paper.

Grace felt encouraged – but, in the way she was beginning to see was a habit, she immediately damped down the spark by remembering Mum, the other night at the barbecue. 'She's really quite talented,' Mum had said. And what Grace had *heard* was: *Why not concentrate on painting and drawing, now that you're disabled?* She knew it wasn't fair to Mum, thinking that. But she seemed to have developed extra-sensitive antennae, acute at detecting sympathy or pity. Or, in less well-meaning people, condescension. She had to remind herself that Sushila couldn't possibly know about her leg, or she wouldn't have asked about being a dancer.

At the end of the class Sushila shrugged herself into a raincoat and said that she'd see Grace next week. Grace had enjoyed the session, and left the barn with her mind full of plans for what she might draw next. Rain was falling steadily, dripping from the chestnut trees and puddling the yard. As she mounted the stairs to the Hayloft, she heard her mother speaking. She paused at the open door, wondering who Mum was talking to, and heard distinctly: 'Maybe it was a big mistake, coming here.'

What? Grace stood on the landing, still as a waxwork.

'For yourself, or for Grace?' It was another female voice – Sally's – that answered.

A sigh. 'Well, for both of us. It'll be heartbreaking if Plan A goes ahead, and Plan B's bad enough. I'm beginning to wish I hadn't got involved. Just couldn't resist, but I should have made it a short visit, at most.'

'But you will stay, won't you, till the end of the holidays? You're not thinking of giving up, going back to London?'

'No, only for house-clearing and flat-hunting. The sale should go through in a couple of weeks.' Her chair grated on the floor as she pushed it back. 'I'll make coffee.'

Grace heard running water at the sink, a cupboard being opened, the clink of mugs. She tramped her feet on the landing and went in. Sally was at the table with her lunch box, Mum filling the kettle. They had fallen into the habit of having lunch together most days, in the garden if it were fine, sometimes joined by Roger too. Now Grace looked at them with suspicion.

'Hi, Gracey. Good class?' Mum said, as if nothing was the matter.

'I'm feeling a bit *homeless*, that's the problem,' Mum said later, when Grace confronted her. 'It's August already, and term starts in a month's time. I need to get a move on and find a flat to suit us. I've registered with a couple of agencies and I'll take a day off next week to go down for some viewings. I need to be on the spot. Any decent flats get snapped up as soon as they're advertised.'

'Can't we stay at Nan and Grandad's?'

'We could have done, but they've let their house while they're in New Zealand. Besides, it's too far to school for you, from theirs.'

Grace didn't want to start thinking about the new term – not while a whole month of summer holidays still stretched ahead. It was like going into the supermarket and seeing BACK TO SCHOOL signs everywhere, and special offers on uniform and pencil cases. Why did shops have to *do* that?

'I know! You could stay on here and I'll stay with Marie-Louise. They've got a spare bedroom, or I could share hers.'

Mum only laughed. 'That might be nice for a week or so. But you couldn't dump yourself on them for more than that – it wouldn't be fair. Anyway, I'd miss you! We've got to be together.'

It did feel strange, having cut themselves off from home, with no way back. But the thought of leaving Flambards was unwelcome too. That would mean leaving Plum, and the freedom of riding, and the birds and the space and the sky, and even the dead Russells in the churchyard. That day would come, as the start of term approached. But not yet.

'It was more than that, though, wasn't it?' she said. 'I heard you telling Sally about Plan A and Plan B. Saying it was a mistake to come.'

'Grace, you really shouldn't eavesdrop! It's a bit sneaky.'

'It wasn't my fault! The door was open – how could I help hearing?'

'OK.' Mum sighed. 'Well. It's a bit like trying to stop the *Titanic* from hitting the iceberg. Too late.'

'Saving Flambards, you mean?' Plan A must be selling off the whole place, Grace remembered, and Plan B was to sell off some of the land – the meadow – for building. 'Can't you think of Plan C? Isn't that why you're here?'

'The planning side isn't really my job. I'm here to do better publicity for the courses. I really don't know how Flambards can be saved. If there's an easy way of making it pay for itself, no one's thought of it yet.'

'Haven't you got any ideas?'

'Yes, of course – but it might be too little, too late. I'm worried that the Trustees have wasted their money, employing me. And soon enough that's what they'll decide.'

'Then what? You'll have no job *and* nowhere to live.'

'Something'll turn up, I expect,' Mum said, but vaguely, not as if she really believed it. 'I knew this was only temporary. I've still got my other clients, even if I'm neglecting them at the moment.'

There was a miaow at the open door. Cat Siggy came in, twining himself around Grace's legs. Legs. If he noticed that one of them wasn't warm and bendy like other people's legs, he didn't seem to care.

'Don't encourage him to come in, Gracey.' Mum was looking into the small mirror she kept in her bag, tweaking her fringe, getting ready to go back to the office. 'He'll start to think he lives here.'

'But I like him.' Grace bent to scoop him up, and cuddled him close. 'When we go, we could take him with us.'

'I don't think so.' Mum closed the mirror with a snap. 'He's Roger's cat now, isn't he? Besides, a lot of rented places don't allow pets.'

On Sunday, Grace's dad and Chloe took her to the seaside.

'I used to come here as a boy,' Dad said, scanning the seafront for somewhere to park. 'Years and years ago now. I thought it'd be nice to have a traditional seaside day. Fish and chips for lunch. Donkey rides. Buckets and spades on the beach.'

He must be joking – Grace couldn't see any donkeys, and surely he and Chloe hadn't brought buckets and spades. But the beach was crowded; there was no free parking space, and Dad drove farther along the coast road, saying there must be a car park along here somewhere. They ended up on a quiet headland, looking down on a river estuary where birds gathered and roosted on shining mud flats. Squinting at them, Grace wished Jamie were here to tell her what they were. To Dad and probably Chloe they were just gulls, but she could make out the slimmer, darker shapes of other birds among them. Without Jamie's influence she wouldn't have looked closely enough to notice.

When Dad had first introduced Chloe, a few weeks before It, Grace was wary, though she soon thawed in the warmth of Chloe's radiant smiles and keen attention. But Chloe was *too* friendly, too eager to be liked, too relentlessly sunny. Today, as usual, she beamed at Grace like a heat-lamp, asking her opinion of everything, enthusiastically agreeing. She wanted to know all about Flambards and how Grace was spending her time there.

'Riding! How exciting! I've always wished I could ride.'

Besides being a good bit younger than Mum, she was – Grace grudgingly admitted – prettier, with smokily made-up grey eyes, and thick blonde hair caught up in a top-knot, wispy tendrils straying attractively. There was something lush and glossy about her. She had the sort of fair skin that flushed easily, and in the fish-and-chip cafe they found for lunch she coloured up hotly when Dad took her hand and said, 'We've got news for you, Grace. A surprise. Haven't we, darling?'

Had he ever called Mum darling? If he had, Grace hadn't heard.

'Go on, you tell,' he said, smiling, his face close to Chloe's.

'No, you.'

'You're going to have a baby.' Grace plonked the words down, putting an end to this.

'Yes! Yes!' Chloe's smile widened. 'Oh, clever Grace!'

Really, did they think she was five years old?

Dad took over, smiling broadly. 'Isn't it exciting? We're both thrilled.'

Well, hurrah for you, Grace thought.

'And we hope you'll like being a big sister.'

Grace considered. Another big thing to get used to. Another change.

'Boy or girl?' she asked. As if she cared either way. Neither Dad nor Chloe seemed to notice that she wasn't exactly bouncing up and down with excitement.

'We don't know yet.' Chloe laid a protective hand on her belly. 'Maybe at the next scan. He or she's due in January.'

Grace looked at Dad. 'Does Mum know?'

'Yes. I told her on the phone.'

She felt indignant, as if they'd all been plotting behind her back. 'She didn't say!'

'No, I asked her not to. I wanted to tell you myself.'

At first, after the split, Dad used to take Grace out on his own. Now she rarely saw him without Chloe there too: it was Dad-and-Chloe now. And soon it would be Dad-and-Chloe-and-child.

A child that would be with them all the time, not just for odd days.

A child with two legs. A child without a flaw. A child who could run and jump, race into the sea and swim. A child who didn't have to take off a prosthetic leg every night before getting into bed and then hop or use crutches.

But this new child wouldn't be a Russell; there'd be no Russell blood in his or her veins. That was her one consolation.

'Anyway, can we lure you away from Flambards for a bit?' Dad squeezed the tomato sauce bottle, producing a farting sound that made Chloe giggle and Grace roll her eyes. 'You know we're having a holiday in the Lake District later this month? If you're getting bored, stuck out there in the middle of nowhere, you could come with us.'

'Oh, *do* come!' Chloe urged. 'We're renting a lovely cottage near Derwentwater. There'd be plenty of room for you.' She made it sound as if having Grace with them would be the one thing to make her holiday perfect.

Grace hesitated. Walking in the hills. Up high on the sheep tracks, looking at craggy summits. Another activity she'd have loved, before. Still, there were lakes, and boats, and things she could do. But wouldn't Dad and Chloe prefer to be on their own, gushing adoringly at each other without restraint? And . . . wouldn't it feel like abandoning Mum? And Flambards?

'Thanks,' she said. 'Can I think about it?'

*

During the drive back, a new fear struck her.

What if *Mum* had another baby too? She wasn't too old, was she? Of course she'd have to meet a suitable man first, and since Dad left she hadn't so much as been out on a date, as far as Grace knew. What if she did meet someone, though? Then there'd be two new families, with herself suspended in the middle, a damaged remnant of the life both parents had left behind.

Back in the flat, she broached the subject.

'How long have you known about Dad and Chloe's baby?'

Mum was setting out the ironing board. 'Oh – a week or so. He asked me not to tell you.'

'So you didn't. Like you owe him any favours. You could have given me a bit of warning! But – what do you think?'

'Lovely for them,' Mum said.

'Oh, come on, Mum!' Grace flashed back. 'You're nice, but not *that* nice – what do you *really* think? Aren't you a bit—'

'A bit what?'

Grace considered. Not jealous – that wasn't what she meant. She settled for, 'A bit thrown?'

'Maybe. Yes, OK. But what difference does it make, what I think?'

'I know that. But still.' Grace stopped, unsure where she wanted the conversation to go. Yes, she decided – she wanted Mum to be angry, resentful, jealous. Surely it wasn't quite truthful to say *how lovely*, as if other people's happiness was the only thing that mattered.

What about me? What about us? We're the leftovers.

'And you?' Mum asked carefully. 'Do you like the idea of being a big sister?'

Grace pictured Chloe cooing over a swaddled bundle, handing it over to be held and admired; Dad gazing proudly at his new, flawless child. A perfect family. She couldn't imagine herself as part of it. Babies could be sweet, but on balance, she decided, she preferred animals.

'Not sure. Maybe. It's not like it's *you* having another baby, that would live with us all the time.' She hesitated, remembering her thoughts on the way back. 'Would you like that?'

'Me?' Mum gave a little laugh. 'How could that happen?'

'Well, if you met someone, obviously. You might.' Hunting in the cupboard for biscuits, she added, 'There's online dating if you wanted to give it a try. Jenna's mum's always finding men that way.'

'Grace!' Mum looked up from the sleeve she was pressing. 'I *don't* want another baby, I can tell you that for sure. And I'm not looking for another man, either. I'm quite happy with the two of us. Aren't you?'

CHAPTER TEN

Full Gallop

'Shorter reins,' Charlie shouted from Sirius's saddle. She and Grace were riding along the road that led from Marsh House towards the harvested cornfields and the Flambards woods, and she was just as particular as she'd been in the schooling ring. 'Keep her together. You mustn't let her slop along. Be a rider, not a passenger.'

Grace would have preferred Jamie's company. Far from slopping, Plum was having to walk briskly to keep up with Sirius's longer stride, occasionally breaking into a jog-trot, which Charlie said not to allow. Grace nurtured a secret delight that soon she'd be allowed to do this all on her own, without Charlie – then there'd be just her and Plum, the pony's four legs to carry her, the woods and the fields stretching as far as she could see. She'd been thinking about that in bed, early this morning: how she could pretend to be

Christina, riding out on her own horse. It was impossible to pretend that now, with the constant flow of instructions from Charlie. Still, it'd be worth putting up with this to earn the freedom she longed for.

'Keep over to the left. Don't let her drift to the middle. Cars sometimes come round this bend too fast.'

As if to prove Charlie's point, one immediately did – slowing only at the last moment. Plum took no notice at all, but Sirius danced sideways while Charlie raised a hand to the driver in grudging thanks because he had at least braked. Grace was relieved when they turned off the road on to a broad uphill stretch of track.

'We'll canter here,' Charlie called out.

Sirius set off at his easy, ground-eating pace, Plum eager in his wake. Grace leaned forward in balance, her hands light on the reins. Oh, this was brilliant! – the pounding of hooves, clods of grass flying from Sirius's hooves, the breeze in her face making her eyes blur. Plum's ears were pricked keenly in her efforts to keep up with the bigger horse ahead.

At the top of the field Charlie wheeled round in front of a gate that led into woodland, and Grace slowed Plum to a trot.

'OK?' Charlie said, grinning. 'You're still here, anyway!'

'Fantastic!'

Charlie was leaning over to unhook the gate, which swung open. 'There are some log jumps in the wood, low ones. I think you're ready to have a go.'

'Great!' Confident from the fast canter, Grace felt ready to try anything.

'It's easy, like a bigger canter stride. Just lean forward and go with her. Grab her mane if you feel unsteady.'

Being surrounded by slender tree trunks on both sides emphasized the speed. Grace wasn't at all sure she was in control as Plum followed Sirius along the track, neatly jumping the logs and branches that crossed the path. Grace wobbled a little and lost her left stirrup over the second one, but regained her balance with the help of a handful of mane, and was sitting upright, panting, by the time she and Plum caught up with Sirius in a glade at the end.

I did it! Rode over jumps!

She was exhilarated. Christina, she was sure, had soared over gates and thorny hedges on a big horse like Sirius and would hardly have seen these small obstacles as jumps at all, but this was a start.

'All right with that?' Charlie was making Sirius wait, holding him with difficulty; he was full of go, sidling and almost barging into Plum as she drew level. 'They're only little, but it gives you the idea. We can canter on again along this bit – no jumps. Then we'll go all the way round and come back over the logs.'

This time Sirius gave a great plunge forward, caught up by Charlie's hands firm on the reins, and they were off. Grace heard Charlie's voice: 'Slow *down*, idiot horse . . .' He seemed such a double handful that Grace was thankful for good, reliable Plum. Straining to keep up, the pony swerved around a branch that jutted out into the ride, and again Grace was unbalanced, clinging on, jolted, hardly able to see clearly through the muddle of leaves and twigs and flying tail ahead of her.

Then, abruptly, everything was thrown into confusion. With a rattling screech, a pheasant whirred into flight from under Sirius's nose – Grace glimpsed copper plumage, a clumsy flail of wings, long tail trailing. Sirius veered to one side, reared and pirouetted round. Charlie was thrown over his shoulder, suspended momentarily between horse and ground before landing heavily with a cry of pain.

Following hard behind, Plum had to swerve to avoid her, while Grace clung on, sure for a split second that she'd fall off too.

Sirius paused, nostrils flared and neck arched as he faced Plum. Sensing unaccustomed freedom he jinked away, high-stepping, soon breaking into a gallop and disappearing among the trees.

'Oh, f—' Charlie was half-sitting up, clutching one arm, then collapsing to the ground. 'Catch him, Grace, for God's sake . . .'

'What?' Now Grace was having to restrain Plum, who was a compressed spring beneath her, wanting to go after her companion.

'The road. If he gets to the road . . .' Charlie was grimacing in pain.

'What about you?'

'I can't – something broken . . . Catch him if you can,

118

then get help from home . . .' Propping herself up with difficulty, she looked about to pass out.

What am I supposed to do? Grace thought of her phone, uselessly back in her rucksack at Marsh House. Surely Charlie shouldn't be left? And how on earth could she catch a powerful horse in full gallop? But following him was easy enough, simply by relaxing her hold on the reins, at which Plum shot off at a fast canter. Grace wasn't even sure which way Marsh House was now, after the twists and turns of the woodland paths, but she trusted that Plum and Sirius would both head for home.

The gate. Wouldn't Sirius stop at the gate? Or would he jump? Her heart pounded as she clung to Plum's mane with both hands. What if Plum tried to jump it too? She'd be thrown off, for sure . . . She was relieved when there was no sign of Sirius round the next bend or at the closed gate, but farther along a track led straight out into the next open field – there he was, on the horizon, galloping fast with mane and tail streaming. Which way was the road? If he careered into the path of a speeding car he could be horribly injured, or could cause a crash and kill someone . . .

Grace felt sick.

'Come on, Plum!'

The pony gamely gathered speed, and Grace felt the bunching and release beneath her, the lengthening of stride. She was galloping, actually galloping, and if it hadn't been for the urgency of her mission she would have shouted for joy at the thrill of it. Ahead, a line of sapling trees marked

119

the lane, and there was a five-barred iron gate, high enough to make Sirius waver and skid to a halt, reins and stirrups flying. Then he threw up his head and began pacing along the hedge one way and then the other, trying to get through, tossing his head in frustration.

Now Grace would have to try to catch his reins and lead him home. How to manage that, she had no idea. Approaching, she sat back, her hands firm on the reins to make Plum slow down. She was bouncing in the saddle far more than was right, just about managing to hang on.

'Whoa, whoa, Plum, good pony,' she panted. 'Sirius, good boy, good boy – come here, *please* . . .'

Should she dismount? But approaching Sirius on foot would be more alarming than trying to reach him from the saddle. And clearly he didn't want to be caught – he ducked his head, plunged and skittered aside in a way that looked almost playful, teasing her. *Can't catch me!* His reins were broken, trailing on the ground.

Someone was coming along the lane, concealed behind the hedge; she heard the whirr of bike tyres. Perhaps it was someone who could help, someone who could manage horses and would know what to do . . .

A black-and-white collie appeared in the gateway; then the cyclist, who stopped to take in the scene.

Flash. And Marcus. Grace felt giddy with relief.

'Hey – what happened?' Marcus was off his bike at once, propping it in the hedge. 'Where's Charlie?'

Grace explained, pointing back at the woods. 'She

couldn't get up – her arm's broken, I think . . .'

Marcus assessed the situation with quick understanding. He told Flash to sit and stay, came into the field and spoke calmly to Sirius, who was still keeping himself out of reach. Gradually the big horse stood more quietly: wary, snorting, but slowly allowing Marcus to approach him, take hold of the trailing reins and pat his shoulder. It was clear that Marcus knew how to handle horses, and Grace remembered that Charlie had called him a natural.

'You go on to Marsh House and get help,' he told Grace, when they were all through the gate – luckily it wasn't padlocked – and on the lane. 'I'll lead him – he's too unsettled to ride – but you can get there quicker on Plum. You know the way? Straight along, then turn left – about half a mile. Let's hope there's someone in. Are you OK?' he added, and looked at her as if seeing her properly for the first time.

'Yes, fine. Will do.'

Grace turned Plum and set off at a fast trot, knowing better than to canter on the hard road.

Afterwards, reliving the day's drama, she realized that during that wild ride she'd hardly thought about her leg for a moment. She'd simply been riding – hurrying, *galloping*, even! – intent on her mission.

Perhaps the oddest thing in a very strange morning was to find herself acting as a team with Marcus. Thankfully, she found Ian and Gail both at home; her news sent them speeding off in their van to find Charlie. Grace led Plum into the stable and took off her saddle and bridle, and soon Marcus arrived with Sirius. He knew what to do next – rub down the sweaty horses, fill their water buckets and bring them hay from the barn. When both were settled and dry, there seemed little point waiting.

'They'll probably be ages at A & E,' Marcus said. 'We might as well go back to Flambards.'

Only now did it occur to Grace that she'd have to walk across the fields, unless she felt like waiting for Mum to return from a meeting in Chelmsford; the arrangement had been that Ian would drive her back to Flambards after her ride. Marcus whistled to Flash, and was about to set off to collect his bike from the gateway where he'd left it when the same thought must have struck him.

'What about you? You can have my bike if you like – I don't mind running. Can you ride a bike?' He looked at her doubtfully.

'I haven't tried.' Not since It, she meant. 'But I don't see why not. Thanks.'

When they reached the gateway, Marcus held the bike while she mounted, self-conscious, not wanting to look awkward in front of him. Bend her right knee, place her foot carefully on the pedal – she had to look. Then a push forward and away, and she was wheeling sweetly along the lane.

Cycling! Another thing she could do!

Her spirits rose. It was like cantering on Plum – freedom, speed, the joy of movement – and no one would know. She could hear Marcus's trainers pounding the road as he jogged behind, and Flash's eager huffing.

'Oh, it's easy!' she called out, glancing over her shoulder. Next moment her right leg was flying out in front, the front wheel wavered, and before she could correct it the bike rammed into the verge and crashed to the ground. She lay there on her side, shocked and dizzied, her face shoved into rough grass, the bike collapsed on top of her. In an instant Flash was there, panting into her ear, licking.

'Ow!' Carefully she moved an arm, then the other.

'Are you OK?' Marcus was lifting the bike off her; she saw his face taut with anxiety.

'I – think so.' She'd landed mainly on her shoulder, and had wrenched her hip, but was otherwise unhurt. 'It's all right. My leg doesn't fall off. At least it never has done, yet.' She got up, smiling shakily. She knew what had happened. Her right foot, with no feeling, had slipped off the pedal; it was like the problem with stirrups when riding. 'Can I have another go? I'll be more careful this time.'

'Well! If you're sure.'

She took the bike by the handlebars and he stood back, watching her with a hint of amusement – or even admiration?

'Don't say anything to my mum, will you, or yours, about this?' she asked. 'I don't want Mum to stop me doing things.'

He nodded. 'Not if you don't want me to.'

She rode as far as the T-junction, concentrating hard. When Marcus caught up he said, as if he'd just thought of it, 'You know that thing people say about feeling the toes on your missing leg, even though they're not there? Is it true?'

'It's sort of true. I used to get a pain shooting up my leg – still do, sometimes. And you know what the worst thing is? Having an itch, a really tickly itch, and you can't do anything about it because there's nothing to scratch.'

She felt oddly pleased by his question, the way he'd come straight out with it. As if it was a perfectly normal thing to ask, and answer.

At Flambards all was quiet; it was the hour before lunch time. This week's group, ecologists – six of them, so small a group that Roger had been on the point of cancelling the course – had gone out on a field trip for the day.

'I don't know where Jamie is,' Marcus said. 'I was on my way to find him.'

'Perhaps he's down at the lake, with the otters.'

'Yeah. He's crazy about those otters.'

His smile transformed his face. So far she'd only ever seen him smile at Flash; this time it was for Jamie.

Later that afternoon, after a long time at the hospital, Ian came round to Flambards. Charlie had broken one of the bones in her forearm, and was furious – it meant she'd be out of action for the autumn competitions she was training for. She was at home now, with her mother trying to console her.

'Poor Charlie!'

To Grace, it had brought back thoughts of how quickly things could change, how an ordinary day could turn to disaster. She felt for Charlie, even though the fractured ulna would soon mend.

'She sends her thanks,' Ian told her. 'She'd have been frantic if Sirius had got loose with no one to help. To say nothing of having to stagger home with an arm broken.'

'It was Marcus too. I wouldn't have managed if he hadn't been there.'

'Yes, that was a stroke of luck. Oh, and do come over and ride Plum whenever you want,' Ian added. 'Charlie's fine with that.'

To Grace's embarrassment, she was being treated as a heroine – 'Galloping to the rescue like that! When you've only been riding such a short time!' – and required to give her account several times over, for Gail and Ian, for Mum and again for Roger.

'My goodness!' He was last to hear, as he'd been busy trying to find a replacement tutor for one who was ill. 'You really have proved you're a Russell, haven't you?'

Later, getting ready for bed, Grace was thinking how different Marcus had seemed today – purposeful, capable, concerned. She didn't feel wary of him any more.

Marcus is much nicer than I thought, she texted Marie-Louise.

Oh? Tell me more, came the quick reply.

But immediately Grace took off her leg and got into bed, she was too tired to think, let alone explain what had happened. She was aching all over in a way that was oddly enjoyable, the result of her strenuous ride; her shoulder and hip were sore from the bike crash that was her secret. Hers and Marcus's.

CHAPTER ELEVEN

Ghost Soldiers

After that, Grace didn't mind quite so much when Mum invited Sally and Adrian for supper on Thursday. She had only glimpsed Adrian through a window or across the yard since their startling face-to-face meeting, but it wouldn't be too bad if Marcus was there, and Roger was coming as well.

'Couldn't you ask Jamie too?'

'I can't really invite Jamie without Ian and Gail and Charlie. There just isn't the space up here.'

'Marcus would like it better if Jamie came.'

'Marcus doesn't have to come if he doesn't want to,' Mum said.

But Grace found herself hoping he would.

*

Two days after the accident Charlie came down the garden at Marsh House while Grace was brushing out Plum's tail, getting ready to ride.

'Here, these are for you.' Charlie's left arm was strapped up; she handed Grace a carrier bag with her right hand. 'A thank you for the other day.'

In the bag was a riding helmet – 'My old one, but you can keep it' – and a new hardback book called *The Manual of Horsemanship*.

'Thanks! But you didn't have to give me anything.'

Charlie shrugged. 'I'd have been in bad trouble if you hadn't been there.'

'And now? How are you doing?'

'Fed up. Grounded. I'll be riding again as soon as I can, but in the meantime I'll ask Jamie or Marc to keep Sirius exercised. Just quiet walking and trotting, nothing exciting. You can ride out together if you like.'

'Is that a good idea?' Mum objected, when Grace told her this. 'Isn't it another accident waiting to happen? If Charlie, who's so experienced, can be thrown like that – I really worry about you having a fall yourself.'

'It'll be fine, Mum,' Grace said. She was adamant that she was going to ride every day, while she had the chance. 'Plum will look after me.'

Grace's mother finished work early on Thursday and threw herself into a flurry of kitchen activity. She invited people for meals only rarely, and tended to attempt too much and then panic, so Grace was relieved when everything reached the table unspoiled. A lot of it was salad, anyway. Grace had helped with the shopping and preparation and setting the table.

The three Greggs arrived: Sally first – a bit over-talkative, in a way that told Grace she was nervous because Mum could be like that sometimes, saying too much rather than leave space for silence – followed in by her husband and Marcus.

'I don't think you've met Grace, have you?' Mum said to Adrian, and he didn't put her right and say that he had. He did actually look at Grace to say hello – briefly – and there was even a hint of a tight smile. She saw Sally's anxious glance and knew that the edginess was because she couldn't be sure how her husband would behave.

When Roger had come in and everyone was seated, Grace's eyes kept flicking from Marcus to his father and back. Compared to Roger, who took up a lot of space with his height and his long limbs and expansive gestures, Adrian seemed to contain himself in stillness, leaving most of the conversation to the others. But he accepted a second helping of stuffed peppers, listened, and smiled mildly and spoke when directly addressed. Grace got the impression that Sally and Marcus and Roger knew better than to try too hard to involve him in the talk. She was relieved that Mum seemed to have picked this up too, and didn't ask a lot of nosy questions the way she sometimes did with Grace's friends.

Marcus was quiet too – it was as if his father's presence

had a dampening effect – while Sally seemed intent on making Grace the centre of attention. 'I think it's quite amazing, Grace – oh, sorry, *amazing Grace*! I bet you get that all the time – the way you've taken to riding so quickly. You must be a natural.'

'It's her Russell blood,' said Roger.

'Blood is what I'm worried about, after what happened,' Mum said. 'You ride too, Marcus, don't you? Grace said you took charge of Charlie's horse, and knew what to do.'

'Only now and then. I mean, I *can* ride a bit. Jamie taught me when we were just kids. I like horses, but I couldn't care less about all that poncey stuff, dressage and doing everything according to the rules.'

'Same here,' Grace said, thinking of the book Charlie had given her, which was full of strict instructions about everything from clothes to worming powders. 'Not keen on the proper equitation stuff, I mean. I just like being out with Plum, on my own.'

'Polly told me you're going over to Marsh House most days now,' Sally said, 'and needing lifts there and back. I was wondering if you could make use of my bike? It's an old one, not at all smart, but I hardly ever use it. I'm happy to lend it to you for the rest of the time you're here.'

'Oh, how kind of you!' Mum exclaimed. 'Do you think you could ride a bike, Grace?'

'I don't see why not.' Grace caught Marcus's eye across the table, and they shared a quick, furtive smile. She thanked Sally, while Mum made a fuss about not doing too much at first, and practising in the yard, and always wearing a helmet. How lovely to be free to come and go as she wished! Her own bike and her own pony to ride! Of course neither was *really* hers, but almost as good as.

'That's fine, then,' Sally said. 'I'll get it out of the shed tomorrow. Poor Charlie must be fed up. She's so serious about her riding.'

'Lives for it.' Roger held out his wine glass for Mum to top up. 'I don't know what she'll do after A levels. Find a place in a training yard and take the horse with her, maybe. She can't expect her parents to support her indefinitely. It's all horribly expensive. Ian and Gail spend a fortune on that horse, and they're lucky – they've got the stable and paddock at home. I hate to think what livery would cost. But there's still vet's bills and shoeing, and now competition entries, and Ian's bought a trailer. It's more than they can really afford.'

'I hope Charlie's grateful,' Sally said.

Grace rather imagined that Charlie took it all as her right. She couldn't help but be saddened by the talk of expense, bringing her own dreams of independence down with a bump. She knew it would be impossible to continue riding when she went back to Hackney. There were riding schools close to London, even *in* London, but she couldn't expect Mum to pay for lessons. And she wasn't even sure she wanted them. Going to a riding school wouldn't be a bit the same as having Plum to herself.

Mum served the dessert – she'd bought a big apricot tart to serve with cream rather than making something, so that was safe – and the conversation turned to the special event Roger was planning for the Armistice weekend, the hundredth anniversary of the end of the war. Mum was helping with the plans, making a brochure and getting ready for the publicity launch. Local drama groups would be involved, and there would be readings and artwork and displays.

'But events like this will be going on everywhere,' Roger said. 'We want ours to be different, about the local people, so I'm asking around for stories and photos and suchlike. Maybe, Adrian, your family's got something? Old letters, photographs?'

Adrian looked blank, as if Roger was talking about ancient history. Roger went on, undeterred, 'I've got a whole boxful of stuff of Fergus's that was in the attic at Marsh House. I'll go through it this weekend.'

'Fergus?' Sally asked.

'My great-grandfather. The one who was in the Royal Flying Corps.'

'That should be interesting. Adrian, your great-grandfather was in the Army, wasn't he? Invalided out?' Sally looked at him for a response. 'Your Wright great-grandfather, I mean.'

Roger jumped at this. 'Yes! That's Richard Wright, isn't it?'

'Christina's second husband?' said Grace's mother. 'The farming one?'

'Yes, whose grave we saw the other evening. If you could find out anything, Adrian, that'd be great.'

Adrian shrugged. 'I'll ask, if you want.'

Grace reviewed her mental family tree as she helped her mother clear the plates. Marcus and his father were part of it, in their own direct line, even if they weren't blood relations. Everything seemed to lead back to Christina. Decisions made by Christina nearly a hundred years ago had led to them all sitting here now. As in the churchyard, it made her feel a little dizzy.

While her mother put the kettle on, Grace became aware of a change in the atmosphere, centred on Adrian. Roger and Sally were talking to each other but Adrian had withdrawn, his attention no longer in the room; he wore the same mild smile, but his eyes were staring at nothing, as if focused inside his head. He seemed there and not there. Grace could see that Marcus had noticed; so had Sally, who continued chatting brightly to Roger to cover it up, with frequent darting looks at her husband. Marcus was silent, as if his father's mood had a magnetic pull he couldn't resist. His features were set in the closed, troubled expression she'd seen at first. His face – like his father's – seemed made for brooding, his eyes dark under the thick brows, his mouth stern; it was hard now to recall how it was transformed by his rare smiles. Grace tried to catch his eye, but he didn't look up.

'Coffee?' Mum asked everyone.

Adrian stirred himself enough to shake his head. Marcus also said no thanks, and asked Grace's mother if she'd mind if he left now, to give Flash a run before dark.

'No, that's fine. You go.'

'Want to come, Grace?'

She returned his glance and nodded, glad to escape from the tension around the table. Somehow Adrian's silence made everything else seem like empty chatter, background noise to his immersion in whatever absorbed him. Marcus thanked Grace's mother for the meal and Grace followed him downstairs and outside.

In the stable yard, the air was still warm, the sky pearly-pale, streaked with low cloud. Grace heard the shrill overhead cries of swifts; looking up she saw them, dark arrows soaring through the dusk. Before knowing Jamie, she'd have taken them for swallows.

Marcus said nothing as they headed round to the yard behind the Hayloft. Then, as they reached the cottage, he turned to Grace and said flatly, 'This was a *good* day.'

She took a moment to grasp what he meant. 'For your dad?'

He nodded. A scrabbling was heard behind the front door; Marcus turned the key, and Flash burst out as if uncorked. At once Marcus's expression softened as he crouched to fondle the wildly wriggling dog. 'Come on, you! You've had a long wait. Let's go.'

The cottage door opened straight into a sitting room, giving Grace her first glimpse of Marcus's home; she saw a saggy sofa with bright cushions, an overloaded bookshelf, a posy of garden flowers on the sideboard: more homely and cluttered than the tidy Hayloft. Marcus locked up and they headed out past the barn.

'Couldn't your dad have counselling or something?' Grace tried, feeling that what he'd said was too personal to be ignored, almost an admission. 'Therapy?'

Marcus shrugged. 'Yes, he could. Ought to. But he won't. We've tried, Mum and me. He won't admit there's anything wrong. It's like he goes somewhere we can't reach him, he doesn't even see or hear us. And he drags us with him, that's the worst thing. I think of things to tell him, from school – funny things, daft things – but before I even open my mouth it all turns pointless.'

He was staring at the ground as he walked. Grace felt out of her depth, not knowing what to say. She thought briefly of telling Marcus how his father had stared at her in the yard with that odd recognition, but said nothing.

Marcus shot her a glance. 'Like I said, this was one of his better days. I'm surprised he came, to be honest. Mum must have made him.'

'What about work? Does he like that?'

'Yes, it seems to help. Only Mum thinks he shouldn't be on his own so much. That's why I help out when he wants me to. *Try* to help. It's not every day. He pays me, in the holidays. But some days I just can't get anything right.'

Grace thought of her own freedom to spend her time here as she liked. It couldn't be much fun for Marcus, cooped up in a workshop with a moody, fault-finding father.

They were heading that way now, towards the farmyard where Adrian had his workshop. Sheep grazed on either side of the track, and Marcus called Flash sharply to heel.

'I have to watch him. Ought to have him on the lead, really.'

'He wouldn't hurt a sheep, would he?'

'No, but it's his instinct to chase and herd them. They can panic and run into fences, that sort of thing. Or pregnant ewes can abort if they're badly frightened. *Heel*, Flash, that's it. Good boy.'

'Who does the farm belong to?'

'It belongs to a consortium now. There's a tenant in the house and all the ploughing and fencing and stuff's done by contractors. It used to be part of Flambards, years and years ago. My grandad remembers that. *His* grandad used to work here.'

Grace remembered the dinner-table conversation – of course Marcus's family had history here, as well as the Russells. She remembered Granny Izz saying that when she'd lived here it had been a thriving arable farm, employing several men and boys and with its own stables for the heavy horses used for ploughing and harvesting. Her long-ago family and Marcus's might have known each other.

The farmyard felt deserted. A security light flashed on as they approached, but the sprawling brick farmhouse was in darkness, and Marcus said that the tenants were away.

'That's Dad's workshop over there.'

He nodded at an outbuilding with double doors chained and padlocked. There was no sign that anyone ever came here – no animals in sheds, no farm machinery on view. Beyond the farmhouse was a gate leading to another track that looped round through a stubble field towards the woods. They were heading in that direction when Flash stopped, pricked his ears sharply and gave a low *whuff* before racing ahead.

'Jamie,' Marcus said, and Grace heard gladness in his voice. She saw Jamie coming along the track that led round the edge of the wood from the direction of Marsh House.

Had they arranged to meet? Marcus didn't seem surprised, but then Jamie often walked around the woods and meadows on his own. With Flash bounding around him, Jamie waited by the gate at the corner of the field, where three tracks converged.

'Hi,' he called. 'You've been let out, then? I'm looking for bats.'

'*Bats?*'

'Pipistrelles. I often see them between the wood and the farm. There's a roost somewhere near.'

They all stood still, gazing into the fading sky. The first stars were beginning to prick through – Grace saw more and more as she looked, and the thinnest sliver of a new moon in the east, like an edge of fingernail. It was odd how your eyes adjusted as the light faded, seeing more than you'd think possible. She scanned the sky, expecting black bat silhouettes like Hallowe'en decorations.

'Perhaps not tonight.' Jamie crouched to make a fuss of Flash, who had settled in resignation by their feet. 'But did you hear the little owl just now? That *wheuw – wheuw*?'

'Don't owls go *tu-whit-tu-woo*?' Grace asked.

'That'd be a tawny. You might hear those as well. They're around.'

Marcus said suddenly, 'Remember those ghost soldiers, Jame?'

'Yeah.' Jamie looked up at him with a quick smile. 'Course.'

'Your uncle Roger was talking about his First World War stuff. It made me think about them.'

'What ghost soldiers?' Grace asked, her thoughts still on Hallowe'en.

'We saw them in London,' Jamie told her. 'Did you see any of it on TV? It was a sort of stunt. Part of all the First World War things going on, like those poppies at the Tower of London and all that. Me and Marc were on a school trip that day, to the Science Museum. And when we got to Liverpool Street, there were these soldiers. About fifteen of them, in uniform, just standing about, waiting. At first we thought they were real soldiers, but they were in old-fashioned uniforms – you know, khaki and kitbags and stuff. And our teacher realized and we all stopped to look, and so did loads of other people.'

'And then they started singing,' Marcus said. '*We're here because we're here . . .*'

'*Because we're here because we're here.*' Jamie joined in, singing to the tune of 'Auld Lang Syne'. 'It's a song the soldiers used to sing. Like, they didn't even see the point of it, the war.'

'Where were they going?'

'It was like they were heading off to war,' Jamie said. 'It was the first of July. A hundred years since the Battle of the Somme. You know? This massive attack where thousands of people got killed in the first few hours. These guys were there as a kind of living memorial. Mr Hobbs – he's our science teacher – went up to one of the soldiers and asked him about it, but the guy didn't answer, just gave him a card. Then some of us did the same, and got cards too. I've still got mine. Have you, Marc?'

Marcus nodded, and Grace asked, 'What were the cards for?'

'Just little printed cards.' Jamie indicated the size. 'With the name of a soldier, and his regiment, and the date he died. And the date was always the same. First of July, 1916. That's how they were like walking ghosts. All those guys – I don't know if they were actors, or what – each one was pretending to be a soldier who'd died that day and it's like we were there, seeing them go.'

'It was – cool. Really special,' Marcus said.

Jamie nodded. 'We'd done the Battle of the Somme in history. But this made it feel real, like it was happening *now*.'

Marcus looked up at the sky. 'Those young guys, they could have been us two. We both said. We'd have been them, if we'd lived back in those days, a hundred years ago. Just boys doing what they thought was right. They had no idea what was waiting.'

There was a silence. Grace thought of Marcus's father

sitting at the table – a ghost soldier too, a man who'd lost himself somewhere in the past.

'Would *you* fight?'

She was asking both of them, but looking at Marcus. Jamie was about to speak when Marcus said, 'Back then, I would have. Like all the others. Because no one knew.'

Jamie nodded, and Marcus went on, 'D'you remember in English, Jame? We read about one of those war poets – I forget his name, but I do remember he got killed. Someone asked what he was fighting for, and he bent down and picked up a handful of soil and said something like *for this*. For the earth itself.'

'Makes sense to me,' Jamie said. 'I'd fight for this land here. For the fields and woods.'

Grace couldn't stop herself from saying, 'You might have to.'

'Yeah, I will. Not fight exactly. Protest. Lie down in front of the bulldozers, if they get that far, only I hope they won't. Refuse to move.'

'Me too, then,' Marcus said quietly. 'I'll be right there.'

'And me.' Grace wasn't going to be left out, liking the idea of the three of them united in protest. 'We couldn't just stand by and watch.' She imagined them being dragged away shouting, outnumbered. Only if it got to that stage they'd already have lost, wouldn't they?

'Bat!' Jamie grabbed her arm and pointed. 'See?'

Seeing nothing at first Grace scanned the sky, then saw the flickering, wavering flight of something as light and airy as a piece of torn paper. Another, and another. They all three watched in silence for a few moments; then Grace whispered, 'How fantastic! I've never seen real bats before.'

'At least you're not daft about them like some girls,' Jamie said, and she saw the gleam of his teeth in the dim light as he smiled.

'Like some *people.*' She wasn't having that. 'It's all that Hallowe'en stuff, I suppose. Dracula and witches.'

'Some girls – OK, OK, some *people* – think they'll get tangled up in their hair. That's just stupid. Why would they? Bats use echolocation. Fact. They're incredibly accurate fliers. They don't go blundering about like people seem to think.'

Grace stood with head tilted back, gazing. The bats danced in flickering flight, sometimes high, sometimes skimming the grass – now flying fast and direct, now seeming to twist and tumble in the air. She was caught, held in the moment: the air turning cool, the distant stars, the silent presence of the two boys, all of them watching. Even the ghost soldiers they'd been talking about were part of it. She had the sense that she would remember this for ever, as if her own future self was looking back.

When she went back indoors Sally and Adrian had left, and Mum and Roger were drinking wine together: Mum in an armchair, sandals discarded, legs curled up; Roger on the sofa, with Cat Siggy on his lap. The room was softly shadowed, lit by a single lamp.

'Mum! I thought you said Siggy wasn't allowed up here?'

Mum smiled, caught out. 'Well, Roger's here, so I can make an exception. You were out late!'

Grace told them about meeting Jamie, and watching the bats.

'I'd better go.' Roger placed the protesting cat on the floor, stood up and stretched.

Mum got up slowly too. Grace sensed that they could happily have sat talking for a while longer.

'Thanks for a lovely evening, Polly.' At the door Roger paused to kiss Grace's mother on one cheek and then the other. 'Bye, Grace. See you tomorrow.' For a moment it seemed he was going to turn back and kiss her too; then he thought better of it, instead raising a hand in farewell.

Hmm.

Adults did that all the time, didn't they? *Kissy kissy. Mwah mwah. Lovely to see you.* It didn't mean anything. Sally had kissed Mum when she arrived, but Grace couldn't imagine Marcus's dad doing any social kissing. Mum would have been lucky to get a *thank you* from him.

The cat had jumped back to the warm place on the sofa where Roger had sat.

'*Out*, Siggy,' Mum said, and gave him a shove towards the door.

On the point of asking about Adrian, Grace decided not to risk spoiling her mother's mood, or her own. They finished clearing up, Mum humming to herself, Grace thinking about the two boys, and how they'd included her this time, not like the night of the barbecue. Things were different, now that she'd got to know Marcus a little. While Jamie – she thought – hid nothing, she had the sense that Marcus was more complicated, more intriguing. She remembered their secret smile across the table, hugging it to herself.

'What are you grinning about?' Mum asked.

'Oh . . . it was a really good evening, that's all.'

No, Grace told herself, as if talking to Marie-Louise. *It's not what you think. Not like that. I'm not going to be stupid about Marcus. It'd ruin everything.*

But could she stop? Had she noticed, before, this particular feeling of warmth that rushed through her whenever she thought about him? She wanted to be on her own, in bed, to lie there thinking, remembering every detail: how he'd asked if she wanted to go with him and Flash when he could easily have gone on his own; how he'd talked so seriously.

When she woke, in the earliest light of dawn when the birds had just begun singing, a new thought crept into her mind and lodged itself there.

Marcus. Jamie.

Marcus and Jamie.

Marie-Louise had lent her the latest Patrick Ness book, and she'd been reading it in bed and at odd times during the day – keeping it out of her mother's view, because Mum liked to take an interest in what Grace was reading, and Grace felt that she might need protecting from this one. 'It's really . . .' Marie-Louise had said, with a giggle, and when Grace asked 'Really what?' she would only say, 'You'll have to wait and see.' And yes, it was.

You were right, Grace had texted. **It's REALLY really.**

Really touching, she meant. Really startling. Really . . . open. Although she'd reached the end, Grace couldn't let it go, though she had other books waiting; she had to keep flicking back, re-reading. She was in love with Adam, and with Linus too, with both of them. She wanted them to be together, and happy.

Jamie and Marcus. How had she not realized?

She recalled the evening of the barbecue, the boys walking away together, Jamie's head turned towards Marcus, listening, always attuned to his mood. She thought of Marcus's gladness this evening when Jamie walked towards them in the dusk; and how, when she'd come indoors after the bat-watching, Marcus had said he'd walk part of the way back with Jamie, to give Flash a longer run.

They're great friends, Roger had said.

Yes, she could see. And when they were together, no one else mattered.

Perhaps not like Adam and Linus in the novel – her imagination wouldn't stretch *that* far – but then they weren't as old or experienced as those two.

So . . . that made things easier, in a way. Marcus wouldn't notice whether she was soppy about him or not. And that meant she didn't have to give way to the thoughts that had begun to niggle: *Don't be stupid. He's older than you and much better looking. And he's got two legs and two feet. Face it, he'd never fancy you in a million years.*

CHAPTER TWELVE

Marie-Louise

'Why does it always rain on art class days? I wanted to paint outside.'

In the echoey space of the barn, Sushila had set up her easel next to Grace's, as before. Everyone worked quietly during the session, but in the break Sushila asked to look at Grace's sketchbook. Today Grace was trying to draw the otters; their fluid, graceful shapes were so enticing. But how to draw water? Her otters might have been floating in air. When Ian came by, he suggested drawing them *under*water – that would avoid the tricky problem of showing a broken surface. That seemed to work better.

'You've seen otters? Here?' Sushila asked, and Grace told her about the lake and the bats, and Jamie. 'I'd never seen bats or otters before. It's fantastic here. There's so much to see, when you know, like Jamie does. When you look. Some of the course people go down to the lake, but not many.'

'We ought to make more of it,' Sushila said. 'By *we*, I mean Flambards. Did you know I'm going to be a Trustee? My first meeting's next week.'

'Oh! Mum told me about those meetings,' Grace said, not adding that her mother dreaded this next one. 'You're going to be one of the people who decide things? How to keep going?'

'Yes. It's a struggle, I know,' Sushila said. 'That's why I wanted to help, if I can. Is your mum one of the Trustees, then?'

'No – she works here on marketing and publicity.'

'Oh, you're Polly's daughter! Roger introduced us the other day. I should have realized – you're so alike.'

'Are we?' Grace could never see that herself.

Although she knew little about Sushila, she was heartened to know that she'd be involved. The other Trustees – apart from Roger – were just faceless business people, and there was the Mr Naylor her mother had talked about, looming ominously with his calculator and accounts sheets and his housing developments. Grace felt an ache of loss when she thought of the meadow and woods in the stillness of dusk, and the silent, thrilling flight of the bats. She felt it badly enough, but Jamie would be heartbroken if the land was churned up, the habitat destroyed.

The class over, Grace went up to the office to help Mum with printing and folding leaflets. Roger was there at the computer, with a table of figures on the screen. Grace was learning to be wary of tables of figures. Usually, it seemed, they meant bad news. But Roger, instead of looking at them, was telling her mother about a box he'd brought down from the attic, a box that had belonged to his great-grandfather.

'Oh!' Mum was only half-listening, checking her emails while she waited for the photocopier to warm up. 'A reply from BBC Essex. They want to do an interview with you on the Stewart Green show. Let's get a date booked, then I'll put it on Twitter and Facebook.'

'Good work! Thanks. I'll use it to publicize the Armistice weekend.'

'No – it's too soon for that. Better to keep it focused on Flambards generally, and the courses we offer. Then we'll get you invited back in October or November to talk about the First World War stuff.'

Roger threw up both hands in surrender. 'Whatever you say. Anyway, I was telling you about Fergus's box. There's an intriguing thing – an old tape, you know, for a reel-to-reel tape recorder? It's in an envelope that says *Interview with Grandad* in my dad's handwriting, and a date: 11th November, 1970.'

'Armistice Day!' said Mum. 'So *Grandad* – that would be Fergus?'

'Yes. Dad's grandad. And because of the date I think it must be about his wartime experiences. You know how people say we should interview our parents and grandparents before it's too late? Looks like my dad thought of that. He'd have been in his early twenties – Dad, I mean

– and it was five years later that Fergus died. To think of actually hearing Fergus's voice! Problem is, I've got no way of playing the tape.'

'Someone must have an old-fashioned reel-to-reel recorder,' Mum said. 'There are people who collect things like that.'

'Mm. I've got a friend who likes poking around junk-yards and recycling places. He might know where to get hold of one. I'll see what I can do on my day off.'

Sometimes Grace wondered how much work they actually did; they spent so much time chatting.

'Aren't we going to do those leaflets?'

'Sorry, Gracey, yes. Nearly ready.'

When the photocopier had hummed into life and Grace was folding the printed pages and stacking them in boxes, Mum said to Roger, 'I've been looking at wedding venues around the county. I think we could easily compete, with a bit of investment.'

'Weddings?' Roger's attention was now on the spread-sheet on his screen. 'Hmm. We're nowhere near smart enough. We'd have to spend a fortune on the dining room, for a start.'

'We needn't use the dining room. We'd hire a marquee and have it out on the lawn for the whole summer. Look, here's a local company.' Mum passed over her phone. 'See? Swags, chandeliers, pillars of flowers. And we'd use specialist caterers.'

Roger frowned. 'Toilets?'

'We'd hire posh loos too. Seriously, Roger, this place is exactly what people want for their weddings, don't you think? Just imagine the photo opportunities.'

'Don't ask me.' He handed the phone back. 'I'm the last person to know what people want for weddings.'

'Out of paper,' Grace said as the humming stopped. She wondered at Roger's tone; he sounded dismissive, even annoyed. Her mother opened a new packet and fanned out the sheets before stacking them in the tray.

'You could get some costings, I suppose,' Roger said reluctantly, eyes on his screen again. 'Put it to the Trustees if you like. But I know what they'll say. It's not what the Flambards Trust was set up for, to be just another wedding venue.'

'But if it helps keep the place alive?'

Roger only shrugged; the discussion was over.

'We'll do one more box, Grace,' Mum said.

Sally brought the bike round for Grace, who had to demonstrate two circuits of the yard before her mother was convinced that she could ride safely to Marsh House and back. But there was no disputing that the new routine would be easier – Grace coming and going as she pleased, with no need to ask for lifts.

On Monday afternoon she cycled over to ride, and found Plum already in the stable. Jamie came down to the yard and leaned on the half-door to chat while she saddled and bridled the pony.

'Why don't you come too?' she asked, nodding at Sirius, who was pacing up and down the orchard fence. He didn't like being left on his own.

'You must be joking! I'm not riding that man-eater. You can see the mood he's in.'

'But Charlie said you'd exercise him.'

'I know she did. But I'm not going to. I'd rather keep my arms and legs intact.' He stopped, horrified, hearing what he'd said.

Grace looked away. She could have said *Oh, forget it*. People said things like that all the time, without thinking: *Put your best foot forward, stand on your own two feet*. And wouldn't it be worse if Jamie *hadn't* stopped to think?

'You're saying you'd lie down in front of a bulldozer but you won't get up on your sister's horse?' she said, just to fill the awkward gap while Jamie stood red-faced. 'I'd ride him. I wouldn't be scared.'

She wasn't sure that was true, and didn't know why she was saying it.

'That's only cos you don't know enough. You'd be on the ground in no time. He can stay out in the field, or if Charlie wants him exercised she can get one of her horsey friends to do it. I'll walk with you if you want, but not today. I'm going to Chelmsford.'

'What for?'

He hesitated, then, 'Meeting someone from school.'

'Is Marcus going too?'

It was her turn to feel her face glow with heat as she

thought of the text she had sent Marie-Louise this morning: **Guess what? I think Marcus and Jamie might be gay.** To her surprise, Marie-Louise hadn't responded, saying only: **Let's Skype later. Something to tell you.**

'No,' Jamie said. 'He's helping his dad today.'

Only when Jamie had left on his bike, and she was riding Plum across the fields, did she realize that it must have been him who brought the pony in to the stable and brushed her over, ready for riding. She hadn't even said thank you, and felt bad now for being prickly.

Having worked at the weekend, her mother had taken today off and driven to Hackney to do more packing up and to look for possible flats to rent. 'You can come too, if you like,' she had said, but Grace had chosen not to. That was before she knew both boys would be busy elsewhere, and Roger and Irina were occupied with a newly arrived photography group and a replacement tutor who'd been found at short notice and had to be shown around.

Returning to Flambards she took the bike – *her* bike, as she was already thinking of it after just a few days – round to the store beside the barn where it was kept. While she was closing the door, Adrian's white van pulled into the yard and Marcus jumped down from the passenger side and went into the cottage with Flash, not seeing her. A moment later Sally came round the corner from the drive. Preferring to avoid Adrian, Grace was about to walk on past when Sally called out to ask how she was getting on with the bike.

'Fine, thanks! It's great to have it.'

'That was such a lovely evening with you and your mum.' Sally seemed to want to talk; Grace's eyes flicked warily to Adrian, who had been fiddling with something on the dashboard and now got slowly out.

Sally went to him and kissed him on the cheek. 'Hello, my love! Grace is here, look.'

This must be one of Adrian's better days; there had been nothing in Marcus's manner to suggest that he and his dad were at odds with each other. Adrian's eyes came slowly round to meet Grace's, and she saw again that startled flare of recognition before he recovered himself and gave her a quick nod. 'All right there?'

Like the first time, she was puzzled; even a little scared. What did Adrian see when he looked at her – or think he saw?

Sally stood close to him, her hand resting on his arm; she didn't seem to have noticed. 'Your mum's still out, is she?' she said to Grace. 'D'you want to come in with us till she gets back? Marcus is here.'

'Um, no, I'm all right, thanks.'

The words were out before she'd really decided. Going up to the Hayloft, curiosity made her wish she'd agreed. But she knew it would have been awkward. There was something so careful, so deliberate, about the way Sally behaved with Adrian – like the way she'd been at the dinner table, as if he might explode, or crumble into bits. Anyway, Marcus probably wouldn't want her there, and she didn't blame him.

*

Her mother didn't return until nearly seven, bringing a ready meal to heat up for dinner and looking pleased with herself.

'Success! I've found us a flat!'

Oh.

Only now did Grace realize that she'd been hoping the search would be in vain, which was stupid – they'd have to live *some*where.

'Only the third one I looked at. I think it'll suit us just fine,' her mother said. 'It's within walking distance of school, in a quiet side street. No parking, that's a drawback – but it's good for buses, so maybe I won't keep the car once we've moved all our stuff in.'

'But, Mum!' It seemed to Grace that her mother had overlooked something screamingly obvious. 'If we haven't got a car, how will we get *here*? We'll come back sometimes, won't we?'

'Mm, yes.' Mum sounded as if she'd only just thought of that. 'Fair point. But let me show you the flat. Here it is, on Rightmove.' She held out her phone. 'See, it's the upstairs floor of a house. Main room, kitchen, bathroom. And two bedrooms. This one can be yours, at the back.'

Grace looked. 'It's a bit pink!'

'It's *completely* pink. It's a ten-year-old girl's room at the moment. Pink sparkly things wherever you look. Even the books on the shelf are pink and sparkly.'

'What can you see from the windows?'

'Well, nothing much. The street, at the front. Behind,

from your bedroom, you look down on a tiny garden. But that belongs to the ground-floor flat.'

'So we won't have a garden?'

'No, but it's not as if we've got time for gardening, is it? We never did much before – the garden was full of weeds. And the park's not much farther than from our old house. The kitchen and bathroom are really good – look. Newly fitted. And we can paint your bedroom. It doesn't have to stay pink.'

Grace looked away. 'When do we move in?'

'I haven't done the paperwork yet, or paid a deposit. But I hope to get that done this week. Then we can move in at the beginning of September, just before term starts. I've booked another day off next week to finish packing up the house.'

Already August was almost half over. Grace remembered how long the summer holidays had seemed when viewed from the end of July, when she'd felt reluctant to be here; now the time was being eaten up more quickly than she could keep track. She didn't want to think about term starting, but it had been creeping nearer while she wasn't looking. She imagined herself in the pink bedroom, looking out at a small square of garden that wasn't even theirs, with maybe someone's dustbin and a washing line, and nothing but houses and streets.

No riding, no Plum, no otters or bats . . . just a London street, and a walk to the park if she wanted to see trees and grass, maybe the odd duck or pigeon. Flambards, and Christina with it, would fade from her life.

Just as important: there'd be no Marcus or Jamie. Would they come and visit her? Come to London by train, or get Roger or Ian to drive them? She couldn't imagine that. Even if they did, it wouldn't be the *same*.

Could she get used to all that?

Perhaps Mum was right. It *had* been a mistake to come here.

When they'd cleared up after their meal, Mum went over to the house to see if Roger was still there, wanting to tell him the news. Grace turned on Mum's laptop for her Skype talk with Marie-Louise. She would describe the pink sparkly bedroom, making it funny. Marie-Louise would commiserate, and would love coming up with ideas to transform it. She'd soon be back from Paris, and they could fix a date for her visit to Flambards. And Marie-Louise had something to tell her too, she remembered.

From the moment Marie-Louise's face came up on the screen, Grace knew that the *something* wasn't going to be good news. But Marie-Louise didn't come out with it straight away. Instead she talked without much enthusiasm about a visit to her cousins in Étretat and a picnic on the cliffs. She wasn't quite looking at Grace, and she kept twiddling a long strand of hair she'd pulled over her shoulder, corkscrewing it round her finger, the way she did in lessons at school when she was concentrating hard. Or unhappy.

'What's up, M-L? What did you want to tell me?'

Marie-Louise looked directly at Grace for the first time, her eyes shiny with tears. 'Grace, it's awful! I don't even know how to say.' Her mouth twisted, then the words burst out of her: 'We're not coming back. We're staying here in Paris.'

'You mean till the end of the holidays?' Grace's voice was flat with disappointment. 'There won't be time to come here for a visit?'

A pause, then: 'It's worse than that . . . much worse. We're not coming back to London at all. We're going to live here in Paris.'

There was a beat of silence while Grace struggled to understand.

'Not – *no*! You can't mean that!'

'I wish I didn't.' There was a sob in Marie-Louise's voice.

'But *why*?'

'Papa's company is closing the Canary Wharf office, moving everything back to Paris. It's because of that stupid Brexit.' *Breg-zeet*, she said: Marie-Louise always sounded more French when she was in France.

'But – your parents – they can't *do* that!'

'I'm sorry, Grace, so sorry! It's all settled. They've already enrolled me in a school here. But I don't want to go there! I'll hate it. I'll miss you so much . . .'

'Oh, M-L, how awful.' Grace couldn't take it in. 'How will you . . .'

'Maman and Papa say now is better, before I start in Year Ten. It means I shall take the International Baccalaureate, instead of GCSEs. But Grace, we must always be friends. Always I will be your friend. Will you promise to be mine?'

'Yes, yes, of course. Always. I promise, no matter what!'

But making promises made it seem final, settled, unchangeable. Well, it *was* unchangeable. Adult stuff about jobs and flats had made sure of that.

So much had changed in a few minutes. They talked for a bit longer, but nothing seemed worth mentioning. They agreed to talk again soon, and ended the call.

She sat staring at nothing, her head whirling.

No, *no*! No Marie-Louise? School without her? Weekends without her? It was unimaginable. She didn't *want* to imagine.

Marie-Louise had been part of her life since Year Five. She had sounded very French then, newly arrived from Paris with her family. Gradually Grace had drifted away from the other two girls she was friendly with, Anisha and Scarlett, and towards Marie-Louise, who in spite of being new had an easy confidence and self-possession.

Marie-Louise was special; Grace saw that from the start. It was as if they were destined to be best friends, and she felt lucky that Marie-Louise wanted that too.

She could still clearly recall the first afternoon, when they'd shared a table for art. They were making cut-paper collages, following the examples by Matisse their teacher had displayed around the classroom. It was too easy; an infant could do it. All they had to do was cut out shapes in bright colours and stick them down randomly. But Marie-Louise had applied herself to the task with the fierce concentration that Grace soon learned was typical of her. She cut and arranged, stood back to look, huffed at herself, started again, and ended up with a collage that looked very like one of Matisse's, but was also her own.

'You must come and visit me in Paris,' Marie-Louise had said just now. 'I made Maman and Papa promise me that. I want to show you all my favourite places.'

But a short visit would be no substitute for seeing her every day – for sitting next to her in class, eating lunch together, going to each other's homes, helping each other with homework, talking about the books they were reading, making plans, often just being silly together.

Grace's eyes filled with tears. She closed the laptop with a slam, and went downstairs and out.

The beauty of the evening only made things worse. The sky was streaked pink and gold, the sun going down in a blaze over the farm buildings and trees. She heard the crooning of woodpigeons somewhere nearby, and the scream of swifts as they whizzed overhead, impossibly high. Jamie had told her that the swifts would be leaving any day now, for warmer climates: they were late to arrive, he said, and early to leave. In the house the evening meal would be over; people were coming down through the stable yard in twos and threes, heading for the meadow or the lake. It was a photography course this week, and most of them had big cameras slung round their necks. 'Mind, for really sharp results you need a macro lens,' one of them was saying.

Grace's head was thrumming. She stood at the gate, leaning her arms on the top bar.

No. No. I can't do it.

The thought of returning to school without Marie-Louise made her shrink up inside. It felt like the worst thing that could happen – the *worst thing*.

When they first moved up to Westfields she had dreaded being put in different tutor groups, but luckily they were together, and had been inseparable for the last three years. With no Marie-Louise she wouldn't be friendless – there was Carrie, and Jenna, and Luke – but Marie-Louise was her greatest confidante and support. Always, and especially since It. Teachers were always going on about minorities and how important it was to show consideration, understanding, awareness. They usually meant race and religion and colour, and all the LGBT stuff; disability too, and mental health. There were other students with disabilities, but Grace was the only amputee in the whole school. She was in a minority of one.

And without Marie-Louise to be with her, stand up for her, make it seem normal . . . how could she face it?

Lately, Marie-Louise had been sending photos of trendy-looking women with prosthetic limbs or running blades that seemed like fashion accessories. 'See? You don't have to hide your leg, or be ashamed, or feel you're less of a person. You say, *This is me. Here I am.* These girls look amazing, don't they?'

Sharing things with Marie-Louise was a habit. Since being here, whenever she saw or did something new she looked forward to texting Marie-Louise, or telling her on Skype, or taking a photo to send her. Often she found herself hearing what Marie-Louise would say, as if her voice was always there, ready to speak into her ear.

'What now?' she asked miserably, aloud, and Marie-Louise's voice said, *We'll still be friends. We promised, didn't we?*

But what if Marie-Louise went silent? What if she asked a question and there was no reply? Marie-Louise would soon make new friends – she was witty and clever and resourceful, quick to fit in anywhere. Not that Grace wanted her to be unhappy at her new school . . .

She just wanted things to stay the same. To be back as they were. That was a familiar feeling, because of It, and just as hopeless.

You'll forget me.

I won't.

You say that now. Things will change. They always do.

Grace hadn't so much as texted Carrie or Jenna or Luke since coming to Flambards. They'd be hanging out together, maybe talking about her. Or more likely not giving her a thought. If so, she couldn't complain, as she'd hardly thought about them, either.

Aimlessly she wandered up to the house, round the back way to the garden, where she stopped abruptly at the sight of Roger sitting on a bench by himself, smoking a cigarette. She'd never seen him do that before. He didn't notice her and she was struck by his expression: serious, downcast, gazing at nothing. He took a drag and slowly, as if sighing, exhaled smoke that hung in the air. When he did look up and see her, he made as if to hide the cigarette, and gave an embarrassed laugh.

'Caught red-handed! I don't smoke very often these days. Disgusting habit. Tell me off if you like – your mum would, for sure.' He looked at her more closely. 'Hey! What's up?'

She hadn't quite been crying, but now tears welled in her eyes and a big one rolled down her cheek before she could blink it away.

'Did Mum come and see you?' she asked, and her voice wavered.

'Mm. About the flat she's found. She's gone over to tell Sally now.' He paused. 'Is that what's upsetting you?'

'No . . . not exactly.'

'Come and sit down for a minute.' He shifted along the bench, making room. 'You can tell me if you like. Or not, if it's none of my business.'

She told him. He listened, and stared at the ground, frowning; at first he said nothing, then, 'That's really tough, Grace. I'm so sorry.'

He didn't say, *It'll be fine*, or, *Don't worry, you'll soon make new friends*. She was thankful for that. Some grown-ups always thought they had to have an answer, a way out of a problem. Instead he said, 'Tell me about Marie-Louise. What's she like?'

'Well . . . She makes me laugh.'

'Tell me one time when she did,' Roger said.

Grace thought. There was that day in hospital when Luke asked if she'd hold a funeral for her leg. When Grace told

Marie-Louise later – expecting her to say, 'Oh, that's *sick*,' which had been her own reaction – she considered it in all seriousness for a moment before saying, 'In the Catholic church, sometimes people do that. You can, if you want,' and Grace said, 'What, an actual funeral? With a tombstone that says *Here lies the leg of Grace Russell*?' Marie-Louise said yes, and this struck Grace as absurd: 'So I could go and visit my own leg, and take it flowers every week?' Marie-Louise gave a spluttering laugh, and next moment they were giggling together, and leaning against each other. Nurse Liz came in to see whatever was the matter, and they had managed to get the words out to explain, and it sounded like a weird thing to find so irresistibly funny.

It was the first time Grace had properly laughed, since It, even though there had been tears too.

She found herself telling Roger all this. He didn't laugh, didn't say anything at all. He just nodded slowly, and smiled in a rather sad way.

'Wait. I can show you her photo.' She took out her phone and scrolled through her pictures to find the one she'd taken at the Natural History Museum last half term. Marie-Louise was in front of a carved archway that had stone monkeys scrambling up it, and her face, close to one of the monkeys, wore the special twisty smile that Grace's mother said made her look like the Mona Lisa as a cheeky fourteen-year-old.

Roger studied the picture, then handed the phone back. 'She does look nice. And she sounds like a lovely friend.

162

Funny. Kind. She'll still be in your life, Grace, even though you'll miss her badly. I know you will.'

She bit her bottom lip and fumbled in her jeans pocket for a tissue. He sounded as if he knew how she felt; she recalled his look of desolation when she first saw him sitting alone.

'But you haven't told Polly yet?' he said. 'Shall we go and find her?'

'Oh, *no*,' Mum said. 'That's all you need. It's awful for you, Gracey, I know.'

Grace waited for the 'but'. There wasn't one.

'Friends are so important,' Mum said, after a long pause.

Yes, Mum. I know that.

'You can still see Marie-Louise. We'll go to Paris, like she said. Maybe at half term.' Mum gave Grace a cuddle. 'Perhaps it won't seem quite as bad in the morning.'

Yes, Mum, it will. How can it not?

CHAPTER THIRTEEN

Half a Face

As soon as Grace woke up, all the disappointments of yesterday crowded back.

They piled in like a heavy duvet smothering her under its weight. She could only think of all that was lost. Her leg. Her home. Now her best friend. All things that other people took for granted – as she had, before.

She let herself wallow until she was bored with being in bed, having only added to her bad mood by being lazy. She got up and dressed, not bothering with breakfast.

You haven't lost yourself, Grace, Marie-Louise's voice said, slightly reproachful. *Your self. Come on. No one can take that from you.*

Grace didn't feel so sure.

Without thinking she took her pen and sketchbook to the table. Working on one or more of her sketches had become a daily habit, usually alone in the flat while Mum was in the office, sometimes outside. Since she'd started using a fine black pen rather than pencil, her drawing had become bolder and more confident.

But today all pleasure had gone out of it. She opened the pad and looked through the pages, not even getting as far as picking up the pen. She could see only flaws and clumsiness where before she'd been pleased with her efforts.

In secret she'd been working on a detailed picture of the house to give Mum for her birthday in September; then she'd thought of drawing a portrait of Flash to give Marcus – if only she could do it well enough. She'd taken several photos of Flash to work from in private. But she'd never tried drawing a dog before, and she aimed to show Flash's personality, which made it especially hard.

She'd been trying to draw Christina too, from the scanned photograph she now had on her phone. She liked to feel that Christina was always with her, in her pocket or rucksack, for company. But Christina – like Flash – proved hard to catch in a drawing. Although Grace could copy her figure, her pose, her clothes, with reasonable success, she couldn't capture Christina's face or expression. Any face that emerged from her pen seemed to push the real Christina out of sight.

It was when she wasn't trying – when she just sat and thought, or when she was in the house or the stable yard – that she saw Christina most clearly. But today Christina was elusive. Too many gloomy thoughts were getting in the way.

What was the point? Grace shoved back her chair, ripped

out the drawn pages, screwed them up hard and put them in the recycling box.

She went outside and stood by the gate looking down to the woods. The day was grey and overcast, suiting her mood; looking at the doomed meadow added to her sense of everything going wrong. She couldn't even find the energy to go over and ride Plum. She thought about going down to the lake to see if Jamie was there, then remembered that she'd been snotty with him yesterday.

Too much was shifting and changing. The meadow was hazed with pollen and thistledown, and she saw hints of summer edging towards autumn: green blackberries were showing in the hedgerow, and walking along the drive between house and stable yard she'd been surprised to see spiky green conker cases among leaves that were already crisping. A change in the light – lower, slanting – deepened the colours, firing the greens of summer into autumn richness. But she was in no mood to be grateful for such abundant beauty.

Everything said that her time here was running out. And possibly Flambards' time was running out too. Hopelessness tugged at her. She pictured bulldozers moving in to churn up the field in front of her, and new houses springing up like Lego. The woods and lake would be made tame and suburban, with concrete paths and lights, and bins for dog poo. She'd hate to be here to see that.

Why did we come, if it's all going to be spoiled?

But in spite of the imminent wrench of leaving, she

wouldn't have chosen not to be here, to spend the summer holidays in London instead. Anyway, Marie-Louise wasn't there, and London would be no fun without her.

The ping of a text message arriving made her think for a second that Marie-Louise really was telepathic. But it was Mum: **Come to the office, quick! Something for you to hear.**

As Grace entered, Roger gave her a quick sympathetic smile that acknowledged their conversation of yesterday evening. Her mother was fidgety with excitement. 'Come in and sit down, Gracey!'

As so often, she and Roger seemed not to be working, though Mum was wearing her glasses as if trying to look businesslike. On Roger's desk was a bulky tape recorder, the old-fashioned reel-to-reel kind he'd said he needed.

'Where did you get that?'

Roger explained that Ian had phoned someone in the music department at school, who had this ancient machine in a store cupboard, and had gone in specially to fetch it.

'We've been listening to Fergus,' Mum told Grace. 'Roger's great-grandfather, the one who was a pilot. He's talking about William – *our* William!'

'And they *did* know each other,' Roger said. 'Let me find the place.'

The tape recorder was an unwieldy piece of equipment. The controls made loud clicks and clunks as Roger wound the thin tape forward and back, stopping now and then to listen. He was afraid of breaking it, he said, and would make a new digital recording later. 'This is too precious to lose.'

After several false starts, he said, 'This is it,' and they all settled to concentrate. The sound quality was poor. There were two voices: a young-sounding man asking questions, and an older one answering.

'This is Fergus,' Roger said.

'. . . Yes, I went into the Royal Flying Corps soon after the war broke out,' said the cracked old voice. 'There was no RAF back then, not till 1918. I'd always been keen on aviation, so I joined a flying club when I went up to Cambridge. That was where most of us came from at the beginning – from amateur flying clubs. When I was stationed at Saint Omer I was in the same squadron as William Russell. Will, everyone called him.'

Grace looked at her mother; they both leaned closer to the machine.

'He was born and brought up at Flambards – not that I'd heard of it, back then. I didn't come to live in Essex till after the war. He was a quiet, serious sort of chap, not easy to get to know, but I liked him at once. He'd been designing aircraft, as an amateur, and that was what he loved. He was immensely clever, though he made light of it – knew more than most of the ground crew about engines and mainte-nance, having worked through it all himself.'

'And he was shot down?' said the younger voice.

'Yes, barely a month after I met him.' There was a sigh. 'Crash-landed in a hayfield and died of his wounds later that same day. I was so sorry. I often wondered what he'd have gone on to do, with all his talent and ambition. And his poor young wife, Christina, widowed at twenty-one – he'd spoken of her and everything he'd put her through. I had no idea then that I'd end up being her neighbour, or that we'd become such great friends.'

His voice in the room was almost ghostly – the voice of someone long dead, but someone who had known Christina and Will as friends, and was speaking of these things as if they'd only just happened. Tingles ran down Grace's spine as she listened intently, not wanting to miss a single thing.

'But all that was later,' Fergus went on, 'when the war was over. *Mark* Russell, Will's brother, I met in hospital a couple of weeks later. It was only two days after we lost Will that I was shot down in flames myself. We didn't have parachutes, not that I could have got out even if I'd had one. Never expected to make it – in fact I wasn't even sure I *wanted* to, the state I was in –'

Grace looked down, hearing her own thoughts from the hospital bed: *I might as well die. What's the point of living like this?* Across the years, Fergus spoke of something she understood too well.

'– and Mark was terribly injured too. He was Army, but in the general chaos we were thrown into a ward together. Somehow we both survived, and one thing led to another and I ended up working with Mark on the cars, and making a life for myself here. It's strange how that worked out – Mark told me that this was the very place where Will learned to fly, with an interesting old chap called Dermot, a bit of an eccentric. He saw Will's ability when he was just a lad, and encouraged him.'

'This Mr Dermot actually lived *here*?' the younger voice said. 'At Marsh House?'

'Yes – Will was living at Flambards then, of course. Born and brought up there. Will never got on with his father, who was fanatical about horses and hunting, by all accounts. Will never took to that, unlike Mark, who was such a bold rider. They were such different characters. Will had a wonky leg, he told me, after a hunting accident when he was fourteen. When he began serious flying he had to have his leg broken and re-set – it was difficult for him to manage the controls otherwise. He really was a remarkable young man. Such determination. He saved up and flew himself to Switzerland and back in his flimsy little aircraft to get treatment from some leading surgeon there. I remember him telling me that as if it's what anybody would have done.'

'That's amazing, Grandad!' said the younger man. 'But let's go back to you and your injuries. It was a while before you had facial reconstruction, you said?'

There was a sigh that was partly a wheezing laugh. 'Oh, I was a sight, I can tell you, with my half a face. Enough to terrify myself, let alone anyone else. Used to give myself a jolt if I looked in a mirror, though I avoided that as much as I could. Children used to scream and run away in the street – they thought I was a monster. That's why it suited me to bury myself here in the country, where local people got used to me and were kind. Especially your gran, and Christina.

170

They persuaded me to go to the Sidcup hospital for the re-construction job. That certainly made a difference. I still look peculiar, but people don't mistake me for something from a *Hammer Horror* film any more.'

'You look like Grandad,' the other voice said, and there was a pause that seemed to be filled with a hug and a laugh.

'I've been lucky, I know, the way things have turned out,' Fergus went on. 'You've seen the photos, haven't you? Before and after? I used to be quite a nice-looking chap. I can say that without being vain – it was so long ago. Then the flamer, and that turned me into a horrifying gargoyle. I was a hero as well, for being in the RFC and fighting for my country, but that was soon forgotten once the war was over. No one wanted to look me in the face.'

'Oh, Grandad, that must have been heartbreaking!'

'Mm, mm. But in the hospital I saw people worse off than me. Faces half blown off, mangled beyond recognition. It was astonishing the poor chaps could still be alive. But they were, and they had to get by, somehow. Some of them wore masks – tin masks, we called them. I tried it for a while, but it was hot and stifling behind one of those. And they were just as frightening to strangers. Just imagine. So people were going to feel ill at the sight of me, whichever way.'

'How did you cope with that?'

Another sigh. 'I learned to live inside myself, I suppose. I had my piano – I could lose myself in music. I made some friends in hospital and we got together to play jazz. And I still had my mind. I hadn't lost any of that.'

'You still haven't,' said the younger voice.

'Not like some poor chaps. The things they'd seen, been through. I remember one lad—'

Roger pressed a button to stop the tape. They all looked at each other in the pause that followed.

'There's a lot more,' he said. 'Too much to listen to the whole thing now. But when I've made the recording I'll give you a copy on a memory stick.'

Grace stared out of the window, her eyes focusing on an earlier century. Her mind was full of Will and Christina and poor Fergus. She was looking at the drive as it curved round towards the lane, thinking that Will and Christina must have walked or ridden along it, countless times, leaving Flambards or coming home. They would have been in this room, in the dining room and the kitchen. In the stable yard. In the meadow and woods. This had been their home; they were everywhere. Still with that sense of her gaze travelling back a hundred years and more, she looked at Mum and saw that she too had a slightly dazed, unfocused look. Roger was winding back the tape; it whirred and whirred and then stopped with a loud click.

'Have you got those photos Fergus mentioned?' Mum asked.

'Yes, they're at Ian's. They were in the box. I'll show you if you like – but I warn you, they're pretty shocking.'

'Maybe not just now, then.'

'I'll bring the other one over though. From before the war, when he was at university.'

'Can we look at the photos Mum gave you?' Grace's voice came out husky. 'The ones of Will and Christina, I mean.'

'Yes, of course.' Roger sorted through a box file, brought out the three photographs and handed them over.

Before, Grace had concentrated on Christina, pretty in a light-coloured blouse, strands of hair escaping under the brim of a shady hat, unaware of the tragedies that would soon afflict her. Now her eyes were drawn to Will. He and Christina were in a field, grass mown short and dotted with daisies, standing proudly beside a small aircraft with struts and slender wings and a passenger seat open to the sky.

Grace showed Roger and her mother. 'Was this the plane he flew to Switzerland?'

'I don't know. I imagine so.'

There he stood: Will, who would so soon die in a hayfield in France, who would never be any older than twenty-two. Who was clever and determined enough to know how to make a plane fly, and brave enough to pilot it – alone! – all the distant miles over sea and land and mountains to Switzerland. How did he even know the way?

'Hello, Great-great-grandfather,' she whispered.

'He'd be astonished to hear you say that,' Roger said, and she gave him a quick smile.

Will in the photo looked barely old enough to be a father – just a boy, not a great deal older than Jamie or Marcus. The face smiling at her from the photograph was thin, even gaunt. He wore a peaked cap back to front, which gave him a jokey and even quite modern look. He and Christina were holding hands, and she was laughing too, a little giddily, making Grace wonder what they'd just been doing or saying, and what they were going to do next. Maybe they'd just made a safe landing in the plane, or maybe they were going to climb into it and take off. They were so *alive*.

In the last few minutes, Fergus had sprung to life too – no longer just a name on the family tree, on a gravestone, someone Roger talked about, but a voice that had spoken to her. Here, now, he had introduced her to the young Will and to his own younger self, as if the time between had suddenly shrunk to nothing.

When she left the office and went back to the stable yard it felt like waking up from a vivid dream. She saw Will, walking back to the house, lurching heavily on his wonky leg; she imagined he smiled at her, friendly but puzzled. She saw Christina mounted on a big horse, sidesaddle in a dark blue riding habit, a groom helping her adjust the stirrups. Mark would be here too, but she couldn't see Mark as clearly.

'Ooh, I bet the place is haunted!' Marie-Louise had said, with a spooky shiver, when Grace had first shown her a photograph of Flambards. She hadn't been serious, but maybe she was right. It was haunted by Will and Christina's young selves.

'I'm here,' she said aloud. 'Christina. Will. This is me, Grace. I'm only here because of you two.'

What would they think of that?

It was Cat Siggy who answered, trotting up to her in a

pleased, purring rush, butting up against her to be stroked. Grace bent to scoop him up in her arms, burying her face in his fur.

Sometimes Grace saw everyone other than herself as whole and perfect, but of course that wasn't true. Will with his wonky leg and Fergus with his burned face had told her that. And back then, after the war – she'd seen photos of men on crutches with one trouser leg rolled up, men in wheelchairs with no legs at all. It would have been a common sight. Some former soldiers had been reduced to begging, parading their disabilities, asking for pity.

But imagine being Fergus! Imagine being exposed to the sky in an aircraft that might as well be made of cardboard, taking to the air over the scarred front line and beyond, knowing how heavily the odds weighed against you – then the horror of being trapped and burned, the agonizing recovery, and trying to find some kind of normal life, when people reacted with revulsion at the sight of you, shielding their eyes, turning away in disgust – who could live with that? Wouldn't you want to hide yourself away, never willingly showing your face to another human being? Wouldn't you want to end your life?

If Fergus had done that, there'd be no Roger, no Ian, no Jamie or Charlie.

But he hadn't ended it. Hadn't given up. He'd settled here, worked, made new friends, played jazz piano. He'd had his terrible face patched up; he'd married, and had a son and a grandson. He had apparently been happy, and – as Grace

175

had just heard on the tape – loved. He even said he'd been lucky. *Lucky!*

Grace thought of telling all this to Marie-Louise; later she would Skype. Her head had gone swimmy, as if she'd been whirled round fast on a fairground ride and was waiting for the world to stop spinning.

CHAPTER FOURTEEN

Bruised

Grace rode Plum every afternoon, usually alone. Often Charlie was down by the stables, grooming Sirius one-handed, or, once, exercising him on a long rein in the paddock, which she called lungeing. To do this she stood in the middle of the marked-out schooling area while the horse circled her at a trot or canter, obeying (or not obeying) her voice commands.

'I'll start riding soon,' she told Grace. 'I don't care what the doctor says. Being grounded is doing my head in.'

One afternoon she insisted on giving Grace another lesson in the paddock. She made her trot without stirrups, which Grace didn't enjoy at all, being jolted and unbalanced until she learned to stop resisting and let her back soften, instead of sitting rigidly upright. There were endless transitions and turns, circles and halts. 'Don't let her slop along! She's behind the bit. Keep up the impulsion.'

It was too much like bossing, Grace thought: Charlie bossing her while she in turn bossed Plum. She much preferred the times when she rode out alone into the fields – the lovely freedom, Plum more willing beneath her than when she was made to trot pointlessly from H to F in the schooling ring. Together they seemed part of the landscape, the pony's hooves brushing through grass and stubble or treading the leafiness of woodland tracks. Sometimes, on the rise of a field, Grace would stop to look and listen, and it seemed that Plum listened too, her black-tipped ears sharply pricked, alert to the screech of a pheasant or the quick scurry of rabbits.

'Plum, I love you!' Grace leaned forward, face in the pony's thick mane, arms dropping around her neck. They were so used to each other that Plum had become an extension of herself, hardly needing a squeeze of leg or a touch on the rein to go forward into a canter when a grass track stretched invitingly ahead, or to stand quietly when Grace wanted to just sit and look. Once, in the woods, a fallow deer moved slowly across the path in front of them, dappled coat in dappled shade under the trees. Catching her breath, Grace remembered Jamie telling her that he got closer to wild animals when mounted on Plum than when he was on foot.

Cycling back to Flambards, late on Wednesday afternoon, her spirits rose at the sight of Marcus cycling down the main drive, Flash running ahead. Head down, he was pedalling hard; he hadn't seen her. As Flash bounded towards Grace and leaped around her Marcus glanced up, unsmiling. For a moment it seemed he'd carry straight on without stopping; then, as if diverted from some more pressing purpose, he came to a halt and gave her a reluctant sidelong glance.

She saw a bruise on his cheek, dark blue tinged with red, close to his eye.

'Ouch,' she exclaimed. 'What happened? That must have hurt!'

'It's nothing,' he said, but touched the place tenderly. 'Had an argument with a plank, in the workshop.'

'Does anyone know? Shouldn't you get First Aid or something?'

'Nah. Looks worse than it is.' He gave a wincing smile, making light of it.

'Are you going to see Jamie? He's not there. He's gone to Chelmsford, his dad said.'

Marcus shook his head. 'No. Just going out for a bit.' He seemed anxious to move on, fidgeting the bike forward and back.

'Why does he keep going to Chelmsford, anyway?'

'Hasn't he told you?'

'No?'

'There's this girl he likes.'

'*Girl?*'

'Yes. An actual girl.' He gave her a quick, amused look. 'Why so surprised?'

She had his attention now. He let go of the handlebars and sat upright, arms folded, waiting for an answer. Flash flopped down on the grass to wait.

'Well, I didn't think . . .' She faltered.

'Didn't think what? That he likes girls?'

On the point of saying, *That's not what I meant*, Grace fell silent. That *was* what she'd meant.

'You thought Jamie was gay,' Marcus stated.

She was mortified that he'd read her thoughts so accurately. 'I – did sort of wonder.'

'Would it matter?'

'Course not! Why would it?'

She thought for a moment he might be angry, but he only laughed.

'So, let me guess. You thought I was too. Stands to reason. Two boys go around together, they've got to be gay. Does that mean you and your friend Marie-wotsit are lesbians?'

'Marie-Louise? Don't be stupid.'

'What's stupid about that?'

'Because we're just not. And there's a boy she likes in Paris.' Marie-Louise had been talking about a Swiss boy who lived in a neighbouring flat, making Grace realize that she was already finding some compensation for not coming back. 'OK, so I got that wrong. And I didn't even think it out loud. So – Jamie's got a girlfriend. What's her name? Is she nice?'

'Skye. With an *e*, like the island. She's in the year below us at school. Yeah, she's cool.'

'So why didn't Jamie just say he's seeing her?'

Marcus shrugged. 'Probably knows you think he's gay. Doesn't want to disappoint you.' He whistled to Flash, and gave her a grin that looked painful, with the bruising on his cheek.

'Why would I be . . .'

But Marcus was already leaning into his pedals and riding on. He called, 'See you' over his shoulder, and left her feeling in the wrong, disturbed by his spiky mood. As she cycled slowly towards the house, the conversation replayed itself in her head, and what she heard this time was: *Jamie let you think he's gay, because if you knew he fancied girls, you might wonder why not you. And – come on – who's ever going to fancy you?*

He hadn't said that. He hadn't. She shook her head vigorously as if to fling the horrible thought out of her head. And Jamie couldn't even have known what she'd supposed. Marcus's expression really hadn't been mocking, sneering, like the version her mind was inventing. But she couldn't dislodge the feeling that everything had turned hollow and pointless.

A cramping pain reminded her that her period was due, and made her feel both worse and better – worse, because it was a drag, and better, because she could blame it for her dreary mood. But it seemed too much to cope with, right now.

'I know. A design fault,' her mother had once said. 'We just have to put up with it.'

Lucky boys, not having the fuss and bother of periods. Not having to mark dates on the calendar. *Another* thing that wasn't fair.

She stopped at the house, to head for the loo along the corridor behind the stairs. Afterwards she'd look in to see if her mother was still at her desk. As she propped the bike against the wall of the porch she noticed a pair of well-worn walking boots beside the steps, with laces trailing. She crossed the hallway and stopped dead by the noticeboard as she heard muffled sobs coming from the office. Someone was crying in there! Not Mum, surely? But no, next moment Mum's voice could be heard, soothing.

The door was open. Inside she saw Sally sitting at Mum's desk, bent forward, head in her hands; Mum had pulled up another chair and sat turned towards her, a hand on her arm. She looked up, saw Grace, and said, 'Give us a moment, please, Gracey?'

As Grace backed off, Sally glanced up too, blinked rapidly and stood.

'I'd better go. Sorry.'

'No, wait . . .' Grace's mother protested.

Gulping back sobs, Sally edged past Grace and into the hall. Two guests were coming in at the front door; she swerved round them, turning her face away, then sat on the porch steps to pull on her boots. Grace saw her hands shaking as she fumbled with the laces. Mum followed, gestured to Grace to go back into the office, and went to sit on the step beside Sally.

'I'll help, you know I will,' Grace heard her saying, in a low voice.

What was that all about? Grace thought of how odd

Marcus had been just now: his bruised face, his quick cover-up. There must be a connection.

Marcus had had a blazing row with his mum? She couldn't imagine that.

No. His dad. A row with his dad was much more likely. And – argument with a plank? Wasn't that the sort of thing people said to gloss over something worse?

His dad had hit him.

How hadn't she realized? He was anxious to get away – where? – and she'd held him up with embarrassing chatter. She hadn't been thinking straight. So pleased to see him at first, then slapped down by his offhandedness – she should have realized something was wrong.

Something serious.

In the office she gazed around aimlessly, too restless to sit down. She wondered where Roger was. His computer was on, open at a document headed, 'Flambards Trust, Agenda for Trustees' Meeting 16th August, 2018', followed by a numbered list. Her eyes scanned down, stopping with a jolt at item four, 'Proposed Sale of Long Meadow to Naylor Homes: Flambards Fields development'.

Outrage rose in her – *Flambards Fields*? So it was an actual agenda item, then, to be seriously discussed? Not just a distant possibility? *Flambards Fields*, where there would no longer *be* a field?

But there wasn't time to dwell on that. A gurning ache reminded her that she needed the loo, and she headed there, her mind galloping. Today had turned unpredictable, things going wrong, spiralling off in unexpected directions. When she returned to the office she saw, through the window, Sally hurrying away, dabbing at her eyes with a tissue. A moment later Mum came back in, her expression stern.

'What's up?' Grace asked. 'I met Marcus just now, saw his face. Did his dad hit him? Is that why Sally's upset?'

Her mother gave the slightest nod. 'She wants to move herself and Marcus to her parents' house in the village. For a few days at least. She's gone to pack a few things, then I'll drive her there.'

'But what about . . .'

'Could you help me out, Gracey? Stay here and look after the office till Roger gets back? Just in case of phone calls. He shouldn't be long. I'll be as quick as I can.' She barely waited for an answer before she was out of the door again.

Grace sat down at her mother's desk, feeling jittered but important, as if she was running the whole place. All was quiet, though she'd heard sounds from the kitchen as she came in, and knew that Irina would be there if any complicated questions needed answering.

Her thoughts flipped back to Marcus: his bruised face, his evasiveness. What could have happened to make Adrian hit out? Deliberately? Surely it must have been – if it was only an accident, Sally wouldn't be planning to move out. Had Marcus done something wrong in the workshop, messed something up? She felt a surge of indignation for Marcus, mixed – she realized – with concern for Adrian, and a strange sense of being complicit, because of the way he'd stared at her with that strange, fearful recognition. A fear of what he might do?

But nothing could excuse hitting out at Marcus – and *hard*, to judge from the darkening, bloodied bruise. The blow must have been dangerously close to his eye.

Living with a father who could do that – no wonder Marcus was often unhappy, and Sally on edge. Things had been difficult with her own parents, but she could never, ever imagine Dad hitting or hurting her. No matter what.

Oh, why hadn't Marcus *said*? Then she wouldn't have blathered on so idiotically. She wished he'd come back. Her eyes strained through the window to the farthest turn of the drive, yearning for a glimpse of Flash running ahead of Marcus's bike.

The phone rang only once: someone asking whether the guest bedrooms were wheelchair friendly, to which Grace was able to answer yes, two of the stable yard rooms had easy access. Then a car came up the drive, a big four-by-four, and she heard the door slam; it had stopped outside the house instead of going round to the car park. A man in red trousers and a quilted waistcoat came towards the entrance, and moments later his heavy tread arrived at the office door. He stopped and stared.

'Oh. No one here?' Apparently she didn't count as a person. 'Is Roger around?'

'Yes, somewhere,' she told him, though Mum hadn't actually specified. 'He'll be back soon.'

'And Polly? Polly Russell? Isn't she working today?'

'She was, but she had to leave.'

'Hmm. Left you in charge, have they?'

'Only for a little while. Shall I take a message?' She reached for a pen and a Post-it Note.

'If you would. Though I'll hang on a few minutes.'

She had smiled pleasantly as she spoke, but he didn't smile back.

'Tell them I called in, will you? The name's Rex Naylor,' he told her. 'I didn't expect to find the place deserted.'

Oh. Grace looked at him with wary interest. So this was the Mr Naylor who had the future of Flambards in his pocket, who was poised to put up a new signboard and bring in the diggers. She'd pictured him as big, smug and round-bellied like the fat cat businessmen of political cartoons. This real Mr Naylor was not very tall, oldish, about the age of Grandad Neil, with an air of expecting people to do what he said, and double quick.

'It's N-A-Y,' he prompted as she wrote. 'Not as in hard as nails.'

She guessed from his tone that this was a well-worn joke. Ha ha.

'And you are?' he asked.

'I'm Grace. Grace Russell.'

'Ah! So you're Polly's daughter.' He looked at her curiously. 'Why not say so?'

Thankfully, at that moment Roger came in, doing a double take as he saw Mr Naylor standing there.

'Rex! Hello – but I wasn't expecting you today?'

They shook hands, Mr Naylor still looking stern. He said, 'Evidently not. What's going on? I hope you don't make a habit of this – leaving a child in charge. The office needs to be properly staffed at all times.'

'No, we don't,' Roger said smoothly, and gestured to the visitor to sit down. 'There's been an emergency. I had to go over to the farm, and Grace kindly helped out. Thank you for that, Grace.'

'Hmm. I'll take up ten minutes of your time if you're not too busy elsewhere. A few points about tomorrow's meeting.'

Roger agreed, and asked Grace if she'd mind going to the kitchen to ask Pam to bring tea. Thankfully, she escaped. She didn't like the look of Mr Naylor one little bit, but at least she'd seen him. Seen the enemy.

With an hour to go before the evening meal, Grace hung about outside the house, unsure what to do. She texted Jamie: **Is Marcus there?** But his quick reply said: **Not seen him 2day.** She hadn't swapped numbers with Marcus, and resolved to ask him next time they met. Restlessly waiting for her mother to come back, she thought of messaging Marie-Louise, but decided it wouldn't feel right, not yet – too much like relishing someone else's drama.

Mr Naylor stayed for half an hour, and Grace saw Roger looking unhappy at the end of it. He locked up the office and told Grace he was going over to the farm to see if Adrian was in his workshop.

She and her mother had taken to having their evening meal in the dining room, with Roger too, quite often. Tonight, as they took their seats, a place was set for him although he hadn't yet returned from the farm. The long main table was occupied by the photography group who by now seemed to know each other well, their laughter and chatter at odds with the anxious mood at the corner table where Grace sat with her mother. Mum was preoccupied with her phone, sending and receiving messages, and reading some of them to Grace.

'Oh, dear. I drove Sally round to her parents, but she doesn't know where Marcus is, and his phone's turned off. He didn't say where he was going, did he, when you saw him earlier?'

'No.'

'She thought he'd want to be with Jamie.'

Grace coloured up, thinking of her stupid assumption. 'No. I texted Jamie but he hasn't seen him. I expect he's gone somewhere on his own, with Flash.'

Her mother sighed. 'That's another problem. Sally wants Marcus to stay with her parents too, only he can't take the dog – they've got two ancient cats. And he won't leave Flash with Adrian, that's for sure.'

'Couldn't *we* look after Flash? Have him to stay with us?'

'I did think of that. I suggested it to Sally. But she says he'd never settle without Marcus.'

Grace told her about Mr Naylor turning up unexpectedly in the office, and how he'd seemed to be telling Roger off. 'But he's not Roger's boss, is he?'

'Not exactly. Roger works for the Flambards Trust. But Rex Naylor pulls the strings, being the main sponsor. We could have done without him turning up today, on top of everything. Just when I was skiving off. I'm sure that's how he saw it.'

'He seemed to think *everyone* was skiving,' Grace said. 'I thought he was horrible.'

'Can't say I like him, either. He's good at putting people's backs up. But he does get things done.'

'Things that make money for him!'

Her mother pulled a face. 'It's not that simple. Without his money, the Flambards Trust wouldn't exist, and we wouldn't be here. He's not a person to get on the wrong side of.'

Irina brought their food and Grace poked at it, not feeling much like eating. Everything seemed so gloomy today. At last, when they'd nearly finished, Roger came in. Both Grace and her mother looked up alertly.

'Did you find him?' Mum asked.

'Yes, he was still in the workshop, just sitting there. He was gutted. Said he didn't mean it, what happened. But, well . . .'

He shook his head; Grace knew he'd have said more if she hadn't been there.

'This can't be ignored. Or excused,' Mum said. 'To my mind it should be reported, but Sally just won't. I asked if he's ever done that before, but she said no. He's got angry, thrown things and smashed things, but never actually hit anyone.'

'Perhaps some cooling-off time is a good idea. Might make him realize how serious things are,' Roger said. 'At least we're on hand, and Sally's got her parents. They're not on their own, either of them.' He picked up his phone in response to a buzz. 'Oh. Text from Ian. Marcus is over there now, and Ian says he can stay the night.'

'That's good. What about Adrian? Will he be OK on his own?'

'I wanted him to come back with me, but he wouldn't. Said he'd clear up and go on home. I'll go and see him in the cottage when we're finished here.'

Roger ate his meal quickly, refused dessert and coffee and left.

'Why doesn't Sally leave Marcus's dad for good, if he's so awful?' Grace asked her mother.

Mum gave a wistful smile. 'Because – it may seem unlikely, but she loves him.'

Grace thought of the way Sally had looked at Adrian in the yard that time, how she'd spoken to him so tenderly. Yes.

But how could you love a man like that?

CHAPTER FIFTEEN

Dearest Christina

Next morning Grace and Mum were in the office early to listen to Roger on BBC Essex.

'So – tell us about the exciting things going on at Flambards,' said the presenter, and Roger did: talking about courses for everyone, photography, dance, cookery, crafts, writing, and more. 'The courses so far have been residential, but we're holding open days with taster classes. I hope people will come and see for themselves – try a class, listen to live music, stay for lunch. For next year we're planning a series on gardening, with guest speakers and demonstrations, and one-day yoga workshops.'

Mum smiled approvingly; these were her ideas.

'And we hear there'll be a special First World War weekend?' the presenter said. 'You'll be back to tell us more at the start of November – but just to give listeners an idea. You'll be drawing on the history of Flambards itself, I gather, and some of the people who lived there?'

When the interview ended and the presenter introduced his next music track, Mum sat back, looking pleased.

'Great! Roger did well there. I'll invite Stewart Green to the launch evening, along with local journalists, and that might get us some more coverage. Let's hope the Trustees were listening. Especially Rex Naylor.'

The meeting was due to start in an hour, giving time for Roger to drive back. Grace helped her mother to sort out the papers and spreadsheets and get the classroom ready. The radio thing had been good, but still – so much could change in the next couple of hours, and all she could do was wait.

People began to drift in, and Pam trundled a trolley round from the kitchen with coffee and biscuits. She pulled a face as she passed, and Grace guessed that she knew her job here was under threat.

Grace had pictured the Trustees as smart people in suits, sitting round a table like a Cabinet meeting, but those arriving looked so ordinary – mainly oldish, chatting to each other as they came into the hallway, some in jeans and shirts as if they'd just been gardening or walking their dogs. Could they really make such crucial decisions?

Among them was Sushila, giving Grace a little wave and a smile as she entered. She stood out from the others, dressed in a kingfisher-blue salwar kameez and scarf in bright red making a gorgeous clash, and hair swept up elegantly.

She carried a document folder, obviously wanting to look smart and organized at her first meeting. Mr Naylor parked his four-by-four at the front of the house, as he'd done yesterday, instead of using the car park like everyone else, and gave Grace a curt nod as he passed her in the entrance hall.

Mum ushered them all into the meeting room; Roger arrived, a little out of breath, and joined them, closing the door behind him.

Back in the office, Grace's phone pinged: Jamie.

Otters. Now. Come and see? Hide.

Coming! she returned.

She was glad of a distraction, to make things a bit more normal.

In the woods she crept along the far side of the lake, already seeing the splash and ripple as the otters played. As silently as she could she opened the door of the hide and sidled in, sitting on the bench beside Jamie, who had his camera ready as well as his binoculars. The otter and cub were swimming, dark flat-headed shapes in shining water.

'They've been here a while. I've got lots of good shots.'

They sat and watched as the otters put on a display: dashing in and out of the shallows, shaking themselves, sliding in again to roll and twist with easy, sinuous grace. Their energy seemed boundless. When at last they had slithered away into the deep undergrowth at the far end, Jamie took a notebook and pen out of his rucksack and made a quick entry.

'I saw a common hawker, earlier. Dragonfly,' he added, in response to Grace's blank expression. 'And the otters. Dad told me my notes might be useful.'

'Useful for what?'

'If there's a planning application to cover the field in houses and demolish half the wood.'

His voice was bitter. Abruptly Grace felt all the joy of the wild encounter draining away. Down here it was easy to ignore the rest of the world, with its pressing need for houses, shops, children's playgrounds, but today it was intruding.

'Where's Marcus?'

'Gone out for a run, with Flash. You'll see him later if you come over to ride. He's staying with us for a few days.'

'Is he OK?'

'His face has gone technicolour, but otherwise yes. You know what happened?'

'Sort of.'

'His dad – he just loses it, sometimes.' Jamie puffed out his cheeks. 'Can't imagine my dad ever hitting me.'

'Me neither.'

He looked at her. 'Where *is* your dad?'

'Lives with his girlfriend in Stoke Newington. They're having a baby soon,' she added, remembering. Dad and Chloe hadn't been much in her thoughts.

Jamie scanned the lake with his binoculars again. 'Marc thinks his mum and dad'll get divorced.'

'Does he want that?'

'Dunno. It's bad if they do. Bad if they don't.'

Grace was silent, thinking of the time when she'd thought her parents divorcing was the worst thing that could happen. Now – it was just the way things were.

'His dad's never been the same since he came back from Afghanistan,' Jamie said, still scanning the water. 'I've known him years – me and Marc have been friends since junior school. Adrian used to take us on camping trips and do football coaching and stuff like that. But then – out there he saw people on fire and bits of bodies on the ground and awful stuff like that. And his best friend got hit in a mortar attack and Adrian tried to save him but he died right there in front of him.'

How could anyone forget such horrors? Grace was silent for a few moments before asking, 'Shouldn't he get help, then? I had therapy after my accident, more than I even wanted. There must be something for him.'

'Oh, there is,' Jamie said. 'But he takes a tough-guy line. Nothing the matter. Nothing he can't cope with. Only he's getting worse, not better. You never know what sort of mood he'll be in. And there was that time when he got confused about—'

He stopped abruptly, holding himself tense.

'About what?'

'When he got confused about something.'

Grace looked at him expectantly, but he was looking closely into the reeds, adjusting the focus of his binoculars.

'How do you know all that about Afghanistan?' she asked. 'Did Marcus tell you?'

'No. Uncle Rodge did. Marcus hardly ever talks about him. Except once when he told me he'd never be good enough for his dad—' He grabbed Grace's arm. 'Kingfisher! Quick! On the post behind the reed mace . . .'

Grace gazed in panicky haste and saw, just in time, the vibrant turquoise of head and back, rusty orange belly, long sharp beak: impossibly exotic, it looked. Then the bird took off from its post and flew low above the water in a flash of jewelled colour, vanishing in to the density of reeds.

'My first one!' she said, and Jamie wrote the date and *Kingfisher* in his book. Watching, she asked, 'Have you only just started that list?'

'No – I've got records going back months.' He turned the pages to show her – dates in a column, and notes in his small, meticulous handwriting. 'Birds, insects, badgers – all my sightings are in here. The otters might count for something, and the bats. What we need is a real rarity, something to show this is a significant site for wildlife. A great-crested newt would be good. I keep looking.'

'Would anyone listen?'

Jamie shrugged. 'Who knows? It's hard to imagine a newt or a dragonfly stopping the bulldozers, but there you go. It'd be worth a try. They're having their meeting right now, aren't they? Uncle Rodge was a bit wound up about it.'

'You ought to be there! Showing them your photos and telling them what's here.'

Jamie hesitated for a moment, then said, 'Bit late now. They're probably deciding to sell off the whole place. It's all about money. That's all anyone cares about. Fact.'

'*Some* people do. But Roger and my mum are thinking of whatever they can to make a go of Flambards. Isn't there a way of – I don't know – putting on courses for people who'd come specially to see birds and bats and otters? Turning it into a proper nature reserve?'

Jamie seemed in no mood to consider anything other than loss and disappointment. Grace recognized the feeling. It made a change to see someone else mired in gloom, herself the one trying to stay buoyant.

'It's not going to make much difference to you, is it?' Jamie said. 'You're only here for a couple more weeks.'

'Jamie!' She was stung. 'You know it matters! Yes, we're going back to London – it's not a hundred miles away, is it? Besides, I don't want to go. Mum and I, we . . .'

Belong here, she had nearly said.

'What?'

'We, I, we love it here. But it's not about us, is it? It's about the place and the people. *Our* people, the Russells. Did Roger play you the tape? Your . . . what is he . . . great-great-grandfather, Fergus?'

'Yes.' Jamie picked up his binoculars. 'But I don't see what that's got to do with it. It's the future that's important, not the past. Everyone's got ancestors. We can't expect them to be kept alive for ever. Flambards isn't a museum.'

'I know it's not a museum! No one wants it to be.'

Grace had talked herself into a muddle. They seemed to be disagreeing, but she wasn't sure what about. They both

197

wanted Flambards to be kept as it was, and especially the woods and the lake. But if Jamie wanted it all to himself, he surely couldn't have it.

'There's got to be a way,' she said. 'There's just got to be. And I hope they're coming up with it right now.'

All Mum would say, when Grace asked, was that the feeling of the Trustees was split, and that they'd scheduled another meeting for next week. 'But I wasn't there for all of it, not being one of them.'

'All these meetings! Do they actually do any good?'

'Let's hope so. Your art class friend, Sushila, had some good ideas, Roger said. She's a school governor, and she talked about running courses for schools – day courses and residential – and working with the local education authorities, London ones too. Bringing children and teenagers here for outdoor and environmental education.'

'That doesn't sound very exciting.' Grace didn't think much of the idea of gangs of kids trooping about – she had come to think of it as her own special place, and didn't want to share. Even though, as she'd just pointed out to Jamie, that might be the only way Flambards could be saved.

'Think about it,' her mother said. 'You'd never been anywhere like this, had you? And now you love it. I talked to Sushila after the meeting – she's nice, isn't she? She was saying that lots of children who live in towns don't get out into the countryside at all, or see wild animals and birds, or learn about trees and ecosystems. And that makes it hard for them to understand how important it is to look after the environment. She says most of the people who come to Flambards at the moment are well-off middle-aged people who can afford to do whatever they want, and that's fine, but we could offer it to others who might not otherwise get the chance. She's a breath of fresh air. Very persuasive.'

Grace didn't see Sushila at Friday's art class. Her father – on his own, this time, as Chloe was at work – took her out to the cinema and to Frankie and Benny's afterwards. He liked the American diner ambience, with the old film photos and music, and Grace had learned to like it too. He and Chloe were leaving next day for their Lake District holiday, and he repeated his invitation for Grace to go with them.

'It's not too late to change your mind! You could quickly pack a few things and come back with me tonight. We're leaving early.'

'Oh, but I can't,' she said quickly. 'I want to be at Flambards.'

'You'll be leaving soon, though, won't you? It's only a couple of weeks before you move into this flat your mum's found.'

'I know. That's why I don't want to miss any of the time that's left. Thanks, though.'

Even while sitting in the cinema she'd felt her thoughts edging back to Flambards. She enjoyed the film, one that Marie-Louise had already seen and told her about, but it seemed a waste of a sunny afternoon to be sitting in stuffy darkness. Leaving for a whole week would be unthinkable, with her Flambards time dwindling fast.

Dad drove her back, saying that he'd have a quick word with Grace's mother to remind her about the holiday. They found the office empty; Mum and Roger were sitting together on the terrace bench outside the dining room in the quiet hour before the evening meal.

It was the first time Roger and Grace's father had met. Her mother introduced them. They shook hands and smiled and exchanged friendly remarks, but Grace had a sense that they were sizing each other up, like rivals. Mum was wearing her flowered dress, rather than her usual working clothes of jeans and top. Noticing earrings and make-up, Grace wondered why she'd made a special effort.

'Are you going out somewhere?' she asked, when Dad had left.

'No – no.' Her mother took out two pages of writing from a document folder she'd been looking through with Roger. 'Can I show this to Grace?'

'Course. Go ahead.'

'Roger found this in the box of papers,' Mum said. 'It's a letter Fergus wrote to Christina. And there's a card from Christina to Fergus too.'

The letter was written on two sheets of fine notepaper, headed *Marsh House, New Year's Day, 1921*, in a flowing hand: tiny, but neat and easy to read.

'My dearest Christina,' Grace read aloud.

'No, sit down and read it to yourself.' Mum stood up,

making room. 'Back in a minute. I'm going inside to phone Sally.'

Roger got up too, and wandered over to the rose arch, where he stood looking out over the fields. Grace settled on the bench to concentrate, holding the small script close to her face.

My dear Christina,

Only by telling myself that I need never send it am I finding the courage to sit down and address this letter to you.

As I think you must be aware, I have come to regard you as a dear and treasured friend. You have done as much as anyone could to help me pick myself up from the wreckage of my life, and to begin building something worth having. You have been more than kind, and as the weeks have passed I have delighted in your company. Your laughter, your generosity and especially your willingness to acknowledge me publicly as your friend, though others flinch in disgust and turn away, have given me a hope and optimism I never expected to find again. Your example has encouraged others to follow, and to endeavour to see the man beneath the grotesque exterior.

I know that you have had grievous troubles of your own. That you have confided in me gives me hope that I have at least earned your trust.

Perceptive as you are, however, I don't think you will guess what I'm about to have the effrontery to ask, so I must be frank.

Christina – would you consider letting our friendship evolve into a closer kind of loving companionship? To avoid possible misunderstanding, I had better put it even more plainly – will you marry me? Would you do me the very great honour of being my wife?

There. Now I have shocked even myself by putting my request so bluntly. Besides, I am well aware that there are two excellent reasons why not, without even considering my less than pleasing appearance.

Firstly, you are already married.

Secondly, I know that you are in love with Mark.

I would never have imagined myself proposing to a married woman – what a thing to do! – but I am well aware that your marriage to Dick is over in all but name, and that you will soon embark on divorce proceedings. The second point is more compelling. Mark is my good friend, and I am betraying his trust by so much as thinking of you in this way. However, the law does not permit you to marry Will's brother, and you have told me that for the sake of the children you will not compromise respectability by living with him unmarried.

So you are in love with Mark, and I, dearest Christina, am deeply in love with you. You see how I cannot prevent myself from repeating your name, whispering it aloud as I write. Christina. Such a lovely word to say, to write, and for me it encapsulates all that is you, your lightness and beauty, your seriousness and grace. Christina.

What, then, can I offer you that you might

possibly value? You are not in need of a home, or of financial security. Loving companionship, however, after your losses – that, maybe, is something you do need, and would value. Devotion, loyalty and love would be abundantly yours; I would be the best stepfather I possibly could to Tom and Isobel, and would regard it as an honour and a privilege to take that role in their lives. If, however, your affections remain strongly with Mark, marriage to me would give you respectability in the eyes of the world, and protect the children from scandal. In return – all I ask, Christina, is for you to share your time with me.

If your answer to this preposterous suggestion is a definite No, I will quite understand, and will never mention this again. On the other hand, if you are willing at least to consider

The letter ended there, in mid-sentence.

Unfinished.

Unsigned.

Grace turned over the page in case there was more: but nothing.

Fergus couldn't have sent it. If he had, why would it be stored in his box of papers?

Had Christina ever known that he loved her?

Grace re-read Fergus's words, not sure she had fully understood. Aware of Roger quietly watching her, she stood and went over to him, holding out the letter with the feeling that the lost words were still waiting to be said.

'He didn't finish it? Never sent it?'

'No. He must have lost his nerve, or something happened to stop him. Or maybe he was writing it mainly for himself. It's possible, I suppose, that this was only a first draft, and he did copy out and send it, but I don't think so.'

'Dick – that must be short for Richard? And – she *did* marry Mark! We know that.'

'Yes. The law was changed later that year – 1921 – so that a woman could marry her dead husband's brother. So many women lost their husbands in the war that it can't have been unusual. And that must have put an end to his hopes.'

Grace hesitated. 'But – have I got this wrong, or is he actually saying here' – she glanced down at the neat, controlled handwriting – 'that Christina could have *both* of them? Marry him, but still be with Mark?'

'I think that *is* what he's saying, yes. What an offer! Generous, selfless, desperate – depends how you look at it.' Roger's mouth twisted and for a moment he seemed to be blinking back tears. 'It's possible, I suppose, that instead of sending the letter he told her how he felt, in person. But I don't think so, to judge from this other message.' He went to the folder on the bench and took out a greetings card with a faded flower design on the front. 'Read this. It's from Christina to him, later that year, just after she married Mark.'

The writing inside was larger and more feminine than Fergus's, with loops and flourishes, and Grace felt a little faint at the thought that she was looking at Christina's handwriting, at a message Christina must have considered and paused over and finally signed, with flamboyant strokes of her pen.

My dearest Fergus,

Just a quick note to thank you for being best man at our wedding. You know Mark never thinks of thanking anyone, but he told me you were the very BEST best man he could have had. Wasn't it fun? I so enjoyed our elegant day, and hope you did too. I know all the local farmers and hunt people are being sniffy, and talking behind our backs about the scandal of me getting married for a third time, and to my brother-in-law. It was lucky the church wouldn't have us, so we could do the deed in Chelmsford, out of their sight. I certainly don't plan to do it again – three weddings is more than enough for anyone! Now all I want to do is live happily with Mark and the children – and you, our dear friend, close by.

With my fondest wishes,
Christina

PS Here's a pressed flower from the bunch I carried. It's the nearest thing to throwing the whole bouquet at you – to give you a little push, dearest Fergus, to propose to your nice Miss Portman. I am looking forward to another special day, and to seeing you comfortably settled. It can be Mark's turn to be best man for you. We will see you both here for dinner next Thursday evening.

Grace read this twice, stroked her fingertips over Christina's signature, then looked at Roger.

'No, she can't have known, can she?'

He shook his head. 'I don't think so.'

'Miss Portman? Was she . . .'

'Yes. She and Fergus did get married. Helen Portman was my great-grandmother.'

'So he was best man at Christina's wedding, when he'd wanted to marry her himself.' Grace imagined Fergus standing next to Mark, smartly dressed and correct. Was he able to conceal his feelings behind his half-a-face, trying to be happy for his friends, but unable to stop thinking how things might have been? As before, thinking of Fergus and Christina and the tuggings of love and friendship and chance that had led to this present, she felt dizzy. And Christina's note! Grace liked the way she sounded: bright, happy, sparky. As might be expected from someone who'd just got married. Almost she *heard* her, as if she'd sprung out of the photographs to speak quite loudly in Grace's ear.

'Was the flower still there?' she asked, and Roger nodded.

'Yes, but in faded bits that fell out when I opened the card. I couldn't tell what sort of flower it was.'

Mum came back, saying that Sally was on her way to join them, and they all looked at the letter and card again, exclaiming and wondering.

'What's puzzling me,' Roger said, indicating the card Grace was still holding, 'is that Christina says *children*. And Fergus offers to be a stepfather to *Tom*. Tom and Isobel. I can't make sense of that. Who's Tom? I didn't think Christina had another child until the birth of her and Mark's son, in 1922. That was a year after their wedding.'

'I wondered about that too,' Grace's mother said. 'I'm sure Granny Izz didn't have another brother. She never talked about a brother called Tom – only the younger one, Robert, her half-brother, who died in the Battle of Britain.'

'So where did this Tom come from? And what happened to him?'

'Maybe he was just staying here for some reason?' Mum suggested. 'A relative we don't know about?'

'Maybe. I'm almost certain he wasn't born at Flambards, but I'll have another look at the parish records and the census returns. A mystery!' Roger rubbed his hands together. 'Something to keep me busy in my spare moments.'

It was the last night for this week's guests, who began to assemble in the garden to take group pictures with their tutor. Roger was called on to take photographs, and while he was obligingly clicking away a succession of cameras people handed him, Sally arrived. She held a bottle of wine and looked a little self-conscious, wearing dressier clothes than usual – light trousers, a floaty top and jewellery. It seemed that the three of them – Mum, Roger and Sally – were making an occasion of the evening meal, to cheer Sally up. But when they'd done the ritual grown-up kissing, Roger said, 'Have fun. See you tomorrow,' and left.

'He's taking Adrian to eat at the pub,' Mum told Grace. 'It's just us and Sally tonight.'

So, not a party, then – more like a two-pronged manoeuvre at sorting things out. Still full of her late lunch at Frankie and Benny's, Grace excused herself. She'd only be in the way.

Having missed her ride today she cycled over to Marsh House to see if Jamie and Marcus were there, and to take Plum some apple pieces. Arriving, she was surprised to find Marcus and Charlie walking in from the paddock with Sirius between them. Marcus wore a helmet, and Sirius was saddled and bridled.

'Have you been *riding*?'

Marcus grinned. 'Yes. Charlie persuaded me.'

Grace felt a little put out, seeing him and Charlie together, and at ease in each other's company.

'He did well! A bit rough round the edges, but potentially very good,' Charlie said. 'Honestly, Marcus, you could really be a rider, if you wanted.'

'It's fun, now and then.' Marcus gave a small shrug. 'I don't want to spend my whole life trotting round and round in circles, the way you horsey people do. It's not for me.'

Plum, watching from the orchard gate, made the little nickering sound through her nostrils that was her greeting to Grace, who found it both touching and heartbreaking, knowing that she wouldn't be around much longer. When she left, Plum's future would be as uncertain as that of Flambards. Jamie had told her that his parents thought the pony should be sold to a good home where she'd be regularly ridden. He and Charlie both opposed that, and Grace's daily riding had given Plum a reprieve, but when Grace was gone, what then?

As the pony crunched apple, wrinkling her nose into Grace's palm, Grace felt ungenerously put out by Marcus's success. She'd been the one receiving praise for taking to riding like a natural; now it seemed that Marcus could easily outclass her if he chose. Though she didn't imagine he could enjoy being given orders by Charlie in instructor mode.

While Charlie fussed over Sirius, Marcus came over to lean on the fence next to Grace. At closer range she saw that the bruise on his cheek had turned multicoloured, blues and purples shading to yellow. She hadn't spoken to him since their conversation in the drive.

'Are you OK?' It was the nearest she could manage to a direct question.

'Yeah,' he said, as if it didn't much matter.

'How long are you staying here?' she asked, immediately realizing it was a question too far. Marcus didn't answer, giving only a small shake of his head.

'Are you coming in?' Jamie was coming down through the garden, with Flash bounding ahead to hurl himself at Marcus. 'Dad's making pizza. Oh, hi, Grace. D'you want to come too?'

Grace said that she ought to start back. Dusk was beginning to settle hazily over the fields; darkness was coming earlier now, in the second half of August. She called goodbye to the boys and Charlie, turned on the front light of her bike, and rode away.

After only a few yards Flash overtook her, leaping ahead, turning to look at her smiley-faced, eager for a run. She stopped, for a moment thinking that Marcus must be coming too – perhaps he wanted to tell her something. Then she heard a shout and a whistle from behind, and saw him standing by the gate. It was only Flash being exuberant, running off. Marcus had been saying that Flash was less obedient than he used to be, needing more regular training. The dog ignored his calls at first, leaping around Grace; then, in response to a more emphatic shout, gave in and ran to him. Marcus waved and turned back towards the house, and Grace continued alone.

She'd had the feeling, back there by the paddock before Jamie came out, that he'd wanted to say something, but if he had, he could have come after Flash now. Conflicting feelings tugged at her, filling her with a confused yearning. Marcus often made her feel like this. It was his way of some-times talking to her quite seriously, more often closing up, unreachable, but obviously troubled.

Her thoughts returned to Fergus, writing his long-ago letter in the house behind her. She imagined him gazing out of the window, perhaps into the first dusk of the new year, while he composed his words so carefully. The flower Christina had saved had crumbled into dust, but the lane between Flambards and Marsh House, running smoothly between high hedges, felt charged with new meaning. Something hummed and crackled between the two places, connecting the lives lived there, both now and in the past.

She liked to find patterns; they seemed to give her a place, making sense of things that might otherwise feel random. This lane, with its gateways and hedges and heavy-leaved trees, and the signposted T-junction half a mile on, must have been as familiar to Fergus as it was becoming now to her. She pictured him in an early open-topped motor car (she was vague about the details, but imagined it huge, with great shining flanks, and Fergus behind the wheel in goggles and a cap) setting out for Flambards to see Christina; his heart full of the things he would never dare say.

CHAPTER SIXTEEN

Kicks

'I want to see the manager. Roger Clark. Is he here?'

'No, it's his day off. There's someone in the office, though.' Grace pointed the way.

The newcomer frowned. She was an oldish woman, slim, silver-haired, with eyes that looked swimmy behind the lenses of her glasses; she wore red jeans and a red cardigan over a red-and-white striped shirt. Trotting behind her was a miniature dachshund, with legs that looked too short to make much progress.

'No, it's Roger Clark I want to see. The one that was talking on the wireless.'

'Shall I ask him to phone you when he's back?'

'Oh, all right then.' The woman sounded mildly put out. She scooped up the little dog and put it into her handbag, where it seemed quite happy, gazing around with big, soulful eyes. It wore a shiny collar with a bow, the same bright red as its owner's clothes. Grace wondered if it had a selection of collars to coordinate with various outfits, or if both dog and woman always wore red.

She led the way to the office, where Irina was tidying up. The decorators were in the house, finishing off the painting of the flat that would soon be Roger's, but otherwise not much was happening. The weekend's course had been cancelled through lack of numbers (a downward dip of the teetering balance that was Flambards' future) and no new guests were arriving till Monday.

'Tell your dad my mother used to work here,' the woman said, as they paused at the front steps.

Grace stared at her, not immediately understanding. 'No, Roger's not my dad! My mum works in the office, but she's not here either.'

'Righty ho. Can you tell him, my name's Duncan, Mrs Marion Duncan, and my mother's Mrs Wright, Jenny Wright. I thought he might like to know about my mum's time here, as he's interested in the goings-on back in the old days.'

'He definitely would,' Grace agreed.

Wright? That was the name of Christina's second husband, Richard, and Grace remembered that there were lots of them in the churchyard. Roger had said that Adrian was descended from the Wrights, and that meant so was Marcus. Maybe this woman was a relation of theirs?

They went into the office, where Irina greeted the visitor

most charmingly, exclaimed over the pretty dachshund and wrote down the name and phone number on a note for Roger.

Mrs Duncan left, her little dog trotting briskly by her side, and Grace followed her outside. She was at a loose end today, and thought she might as well head down to the lake to see if Jamie was there.

Her mother had gone out, saying she'd be back late afternoon. Grace assumed that she was going somewhere with Sally, though she hadn't said. They seemed to be good friends now; Mum would surely keep in touch with Sally after the move back to London.

'It's great that you get on so well with the boys,' Mum had said, more than once. Yes, Grace did: with both of them together and more particularly with each of them separately. Well, most of the time. But everything was beginning to feel fragile and temporary. The links to Marcus and Jamie, so important now, would surely fade without daily contact – another loss, to add to the absence of Marie-Louise. She couldn't imagine the boys bothering to keep in touch when she'd gone. Already she felt wistful at the thought of leaving them: wistful and lonely.

Hesitating on the porch steps, she realized that the house was empty today apart from the decorators. No guests were staying, Pam had the weekend off and only Irina was around. Inside, sunlight slanted into the hall; the carpeted sweep of staircase beckoned her.

She couldn't resist. Surely no one would mind if she

explored a bit? Quietly she went back inside, and up.

From the upstairs landing, a corridor stretched left and right, with doors to the bedrooms all open. At the farthest end a second, smaller staircase led up to the flat that would soon be Roger's. Grace rather envied him that, fond though she was of the Hayloft. But one of these bedrooms must have been Christina's.

She peeped into one room, then the next. In both, large windows faced the tree-lined drive that led to the stableyard. The rooms were simply furnished, made up ready for next week's guests: each had a white bedspread, a cane chair with a red cushion, a wardrobe and a desk with a reading lamp. Christina must have looked out of these windows, wondering if it would be a fine day for riding.

Standing there, Grace had the odd feeling, just for a second, that she was Christina, and that if she let herself believe it she might see herself – Grace, years into the future – walking round from the yard. What would Christina think of her?

She went back to the landing. The space of the house stretched around her: high ceilings, the generous width of the staircase, and the stillness of air that felt timeless, but vibrant with echoes of the lives lived here. She walked slowly down, running her hand along the curve of the banister rail. Christina must have done this, countless times.

With a jolt she saw that Irina was standing by the notice-board, looking up at her and smiling.

'Exploring?'

'I couldn't resist. While no one's here.'

Irina nodded. 'I do that sometimes. Pretend I live here. It's so different from home.'

Irina lodged with someone in the village, but Grace guessed that *home* meant Germany.

'What's it like, at home?'

'In Leipzig? We live in a flat in the city centre. I like that better – it's too quiet for me here.' Irina turned towards the kitchen. 'Time for a break. Pam made chocolate brownies yesterday – want to try them?'

Half an hour later, walking past the cottages and greenhouse, Grace noticed to her surprise that the yellow Fiat was parked there. Strange – she thought Mum had gone out in it, with Sally.

She was heading for the lake, intending to take the path that looped back to the woods. Beyond the cattle grid, the sheep were out in the field beside the track, and she saw that they were alert, all looking in the same direction, towards the farm buildings. When a black-and-white collie shot out from behind the barn they huddled together, bleating, shifting anxiously.

Flash.

On his own? She couldn't see Marcus, or anyone else, but the dog seemed intent, circling behind the sheep, panicking them by running from side to side. This wasn't like the shepherding she'd seen on *Countryfile*, with the dog obeying orders, calm and watchful. Flash was excitable, skittish, doing this only for himself.

'Flash!' Grace yelled, and hurried over, her leg and foot awkward on the uneven ground. Would he come to her? He often did, but only if he felt like it.

The sheep crowded towards the corner of the field nearest the barns, jostling, front runners jammed against the fence while some of those behind reared on to the backs of others in an effort to get away from the threatening dog. The flock divided as she approached, a small group peeling away from the rest in their fear of her.

She heard a shout of anger. A dark-haired man – Adrian – darted through the gap between the buildings and vaulted the fence by the water trough.

'Come here, you!' he yelled, more roar than shout.

Flash, enjoying his game, bucked and leaped. For the sheep it was not a game; Grace saw ears flicking, eyes rolling back, mouths bleating in fear. Next moment she was rolling on the ground, barged off-balance in the surge of what she realized now were quite hefty animals. Hauling herself up she heard Adrian shout again. As he reached the dog, his face contorted in fury, he kicked out hard, shouting something incomprehensible. Flash cringed and whined as Adrian kicked him a second and third time. He shouted something incomprehensible, kicking again and again.

'Stop! *Stop* it!' Grace cried, appalled. She heard another yell: 'Get off him! Get back!' and saw Marcus sprinting to the fence.

But she was nearer.

Though frightened of Adrian, aware that he was a fit,

217

strong man gripped by anger, she lurched over and tried to grab his sleeve, to give Flash a moment to run free. Adrian shook her off and for a moment their eyes met before he turned back to Flash, ready for another blow. In the same instant, in desperation, she swung her right leg forward with all the strength she could summon.

He gave a yelp as her artificial foot slammed into his shin, the shock enough to stop him. The impact of her prosthetic, solid and metallic, shuddered through her, wrenching her knee and hip. Losing balance she flumped down hard on ground, trampled into clods and tufts by the cloven hooves of sheep. She lay there for a moment too winded and shaken to move. Adrian looked at her in astonishment, clutching his leg, his face screwed up in pain.

Marcus flung himself over the fence. Ignoring his father he ran to the dog, who lay whimpering on his side. As Marcus crouched, touching him with gentle fingers, Flash raised his head and stirred his tail feebly. Only now did Marcus turn towards Adrian, in a fury to match his father's.

'Don't touch him!' His words were forced between clenched teeth. 'I hate you! Don't you dare touch him ever again!'

As father and son faced each other Grace saw how alike they were: thick black hair, dark eyebrows drawn low over flashing eyes. For a second she thought Marcus was going to hurl himself at his father. Then, all at once, Adrian seemed to come to himself, gazing horrified from Flash to Marcus to Grace and back to the cowering dog. He dropped to his knees, slowly raising both hands to cover his eyes.

Grace was trembling, stunned by the savagery of Adrian's attack on Flash, and almost as much by the violence of her own retaliation. She watched Adrian uncertainly. He looked likely to collapse in tears, while Marcus turned away, giving all his attention to Flash. The sheep had run back and now stood in a wary, shifting semi-circle, waiting. Someone needed to take charge, but there was no one around: just the stricken man, the furious boy and herself.

Before she could think what to say or do, Adrian let out a wail, jumped to his feet and ran, colliding with the fence as if not seeing it. He heaved himself over and stumbled on, passing between the buildings. Marcus was crouched over Flash, talking softly. An engine started up, and Adrian's white van sped off down the farm track towards the lane.

'Marcus!' Grace wasn't sure he'd even noticed. 'Marcus! Where will he go? He shouldn't be driving, not in that state. Can you call your mum?'

He showed no sign of having heard; he was all concern for the dog, hatred for the man who'd hurt him. Flash seemed too shocked to do more than lift his head, showing the whites of his eyes and flattening his ears.

'Flash, Flash! Good boy.' Marcus's voice was soft, crooning. 'You're all right, all right now.'

'Does he need a vet?'

'Not sure. But if I take him, and say he's been kicked . . .'

Grace thought she understood. If a vet examined Flash she would surely ask how he'd been injured, and Marcus would either have to lie, or say that it had been a vicious attack from his father. Maybe the vet would report that to the RSPCA or the police. Marcus, it seemed, still had some loyalty left for his father, even if it was fiercely divided.

Flash lurched to his feet and stood trembling. Marcus ran careful hands over his sides, his back, his jaw, while the brown mournful eyes looked up at him for reassurance.

'I think he's OK,' Marcus said. 'He's not flinching when I touch his ribs and back. Thank God.'

'But your dad. Where will he go?'

Marcus's mouth twisted. 'Don't know. Don't care.'

'Has he done that before?'

'To Flash? No, or I'd kill him.' Marcus glanced up wildly for a moment; then the anger left him and he drooped over the dog, shaking his head. 'It's my fault! I should have seen it coming, kept him away from the sheep, or on his lead. He's been getting too full of himself. He could be shot for that – if a farmer saw him worrying sheep. It happens. I should have been more careful—' He broke off, looking at her properly. 'Are *you* OK? He knocked you over, didn't he?'

'I think I knocked myself over. Lost my balance. Your dad didn't shove me or anything.'

'But you went for him. You kicked him. Made him stop.' He met her eyes for a moment then looked down, shaking his head. 'That was—'

'A bit mad.'

'No, awesome, is what I meant.'

Grace was still shocked, even a little impressed, at the

strength of the impulse that had overtaken her. 'I've never kicked anyone before. With – with my leg, I mean. Well, why would I? It hurt, but it must have hurt him more.'

'Your bionic leg! It's a secret weapon! Don't ever kick me, will you?'

The tension of the incident had dissolved into shaky laughter, but only momentarily.

'I promise not to,' she said. 'But shouldn't we tell your mum or something? About what happened, and your dad driving off like that?'

'Yes.' Marcus was serious again. 'She's over at Flambards. I'd better go and find her. I think Flash is OK now. We'll see how well he can walk.'

They began to make their way, slowly, for the dog's sake. What to do next, Grace wasn't sure, with her mother not around.

'Wait a minute,' she said, remembering. 'Hasn't your mum gone out with *my* mum?'

'No – she's working today, doing the lawn edges. I helped her move some sacks of compost this morning.'

Puzzling over this, and the Fiat still in the yard, Grace concluded that her mother must be spending her day off with Roger, not with Sally. And without having mentioned it. But there was no time to examine that thought, in the urgency of finding Sally and telling her what had happened.

And there Sally was, just as Marcus had said: in her sun hat, jeans and checked shirt, working along the edge of the lawn outside the dining room with long-handled clippers.

Grace waited on the terrace while Marcus went to his mother and spoke to her. She heard Sally's cry of alarm; the shears fell to the ground as she clapped both hands to her mouth. She took Marcus's arm and gazed into his face in concern; she bent to examine Flash, who was by now looking quite pleased with the attention. Then she put her arm round Marcus and they moved off together in the direction of the cottage, while Grace dropped back out of sight, not wanting to intrude into this new family crisis.

What now? Should she tell someone? Get help?

After several minutes' dithering she sent a text message to her mother, receiving a quick reply: OK. Sally phoned Roger just now. We're on our way. Mx

This latest episode couldn't be contained or smoothed over, Grace knew.

She was battered and sore from falling over twice, and especially the impact on her leg from having kicked Adrian so hard, but more than that she felt dazed by the speed at which an ordinary quiet Saturday had overheated. How could this awful situation ever be put right? It was frightening, out of control. If Adrian wasn't helped in some way, he'd do serious harm to someone. Possibly to himself.

But she remembered the moment back there when he'd stopped, appalled, as if he were two separate people: the one who lashed out in anger and the one who watched, pushed to the sidelines, helpless.

Which of them was in control now? And could he actually

be blamed, if he was mentally ill, as surely he must be? Now, even Adrian couldn't pretend that nothing was wrong. No one could.

At last Mum and Roger arrived, shortly joined by Ian and Jamie, who had been searching the lanes in response to a call from Roger, but without result. They all spent some time discussing what should be done now, and whether the police should be called: Grace and her mother both thought yes, Ian thought no, and Roger said they should wait longer to see if Adrian returned either to the cottage or to the farm. While they were still debating, Sally came in to tell them that she'd had a phone call: Adrian had driven to the house of an ex-Army friend, Phil, in Maldon.

'It was Phil who rang. He says Adrian's in quite a state. He'll stay the night there and Phil says he'll bring him back tomorrow. I offered to go over, but Phil thought best not.' She collapsed on a chair, exhausted. 'I can't think straight, what to do for the best. I can't face telling my parents all this – it'd upset them terribly. But how can I not?'

It was a strange evening. Mum took Sally up to the Hayloft, and at Ian's suggestion Grace went over to Marsh House, with Jamie, Marcus and Flash.

No one said much when they got there. Charlie was out with friends; Marcus sat quietly in a corner of the kitchen with Flash, while Jamie hung around nearby. Grace went down to the field to see the horses. When she came back, Ian and Gail were putting together a meal for everyone, trying to be bracing and ordinary.

223

A car pulled up outside, and Grace saw Marcus's startled look. Jamie went to see, and came back a few moments later, followed by a tall blonde girl.

'I forgot about Skye coming over,' he told his parents. 'It's all right, isn't it? Her dad's waiting outside in case it isn't.'

'No, it's fine,' Ian said. 'Come on in, Skye!'

Grace looked with wary interest at Skye, who was long-legged and slim in Lycra shorts, trainers and an outsize sweatshirt with pushed-up sleeves.

'Sorry.' Skye gave a quick smile. 'Bad timing, Jamie says.'

Ian went out to speak to her dad and invite him in for a drink, while Jamie gestured awkwardly by way of intro-duction. 'Er, Skye, you don't know Grace, do you?'

'Hi, Grace! Jamie's told me about you.'

Unsure as ever what that meant, Grace smiled back. She suppressed a twinge of envy of Skye's smooth tanned legs, that looked as if they did a lot of running; she remembered for a moment how that felt, the surge forward, legs pumping strongly, full of go. Skye's face was open and friendly, with greenish eyes that looked at Grace with genuine interest. Her straight pale blonde hair was pulled back in a ponytail. She was a good-looking girl, Grace saw, who seemed not to place much importance on her appearance.

Skye's arrival had broken the tension. Soon she was asking Grace about riding, and how she managed with her leg, and whether she'd get a running blade. 'That'd be cool!' Her frankness was infectious, and soon they were chatting quite easily, Grace telling Skye that in a few months she was hoping to get a general purpose athletic limb, rather than a running blade. 'Because those are *only* for running. Have you seen how the blade runners can't stand still on them while they're waiting for a race? How they have to keep moving about? The limb I'm getting will have a springy ankle and a foot, so I can move in all directions, and stand still. And wear trainers.'

Jamie and Marcus talked quietly together, Flash lying at Marcus's feet. Grace saw Jamie ask a question and Marcus lower his eyes, with a quick shake of his head. She longed to talk to him, but perhaps it was best to leave that to Jamie.

Skye's dad ended up staying for the whole evening. Late-ish, he dropped Grace off at Flambards; Skye waved goodbye and called out, 'See you again soon!' and Grace went indoors, surprised that something good had come out of this strange day.

Sally had gone. Grace found her mother alone in the flat, tidying the kitchen.

'What's happened?' Grace asked.

'Nothing. Sally and I talked, and looked at some websites, then Roger came over and I got us some food. That was about it.'

'What about when he – when Adrian comes back?'

Her mother shook her head, lips pressed together. 'I don't know. Sally doesn't know. It's complicated.'

'But if he *doesn't* come back, where will he go?' Grace thought of the horrified expression on Adrian's face when he saw what he'd done.

'There's no easy answer to that,' Mum said. 'But Sally told me she'd given him an ultimatum, after he hit Marcus. Either he gets help, or . . .' She shrugged.

'Or it's all over?'

'I can't really tell you any more, Gracey. Sally told me lots of things in confidence.'

'OK,' Grace said; then, remembering, 'Why didn't you say you were going out with Roger today? Where did you go?'

'To Hyde Hall, a place with lovely gardens the other side of Chelmsford.' Her mother seemed glad to change the subject. 'We wanted to get ideas – look at their programme of events and special days.'

'To copy?'

'Well, not copy exactly. Get some ideas and adapt them to what we can do here. A craft fair, for instance. We could think about holding a craft fair.'

'So it was *work*, then? On your day off?'

'I suppose we could call it that. But it was a nice kind of work.' She smiled; a rather smug, secretive smile, Grace thought. 'We'd have stayed longer if all this with Adrian hadn't happened.'

A pause; then Grace said, 'Mum? You like Roger, don't you?'

'Yes, of course. Don't you?'

'Yes! But I mean *like* like. And he likes you, doesn't he?'

'Possibly.' Her mother coloured up, pretending to busy herself at the sink.

'More than possibly! He does! And he's not married or anything, is he? He went a bit funny that time you were talking about weddings.'

'No, he's never been married. He was going to, but his girlfriend pulled out at the last minute and went off with someone else. It's taken him a long time to get over that.'

'You mean he hasn't had another girlfriend since?'

'He has, but no one special.'

So he'd told Mum all about that. They were close enough for confidences. And she'd probably talked to him about Dad. Grace knew well enough that Roger was a good person to talk to, a listener and careful considerer.

'Maybe you two could . . . ?'

Mum laughed. 'No, Grace – no. I've no intention of marrying again. Once was enough. I may be a Russell, but I'm not planning to follow Christina.'

Grace hadn't meant *marrying,* exactly. 'Will you still see Roger when we go back to London, though?'

'Perhaps. If he wants.'

Later, in her room, she messaged Marie-Louise: Guess what? My mum and Roger are a Thing. And pretending they're not.

Today's more dramatic events would have to wait for a proper conversation on Skype.

CHAPTER SEVENTEEN

Perfectionist

Roger moved into the Flambards flat on Sunday, helped by Ian and the boys. Mum and Grace went up to see. It was spacious and clean, still smelling of fresh paint. Roger had opened all the windows, most of which looked out over the garden and the meadow and woods beyond. They all admired the view, Grace hoping that it would always be there for Roger to look at, not obscured by the brand-new houses and garages of Mr Naylor's Flambards Fields.

'It'll be great to live here on site,' Roger said. 'And it makes more room at Ian and Gail's, with Marcus staying for I don't know how long.'

Grace and her mother spent most of the afternoon unpacking boxes of books and arranging them on shelves, which took a long time as Mum kept exclaiming over books she'd either read or wanted to read, and ended up with a pile to take back to the flat and a promise to lend Roger some of hers. Borrowing books, Grace thought; sharing books, talking about them. What clearer sign could there be that they liked each other? Surreptitiously she sent a text to Marie-Louise, who replied: **Aha! Proof.**

Only later, back in the Hayloft, did Grace remember the dachshund lady whose message Roger wouldn't have seen yet, as the office had been locked up all day. Although it could easily wait till the morning she thought she'd tell him now, and went back over to the house while her mother was in the shower.

Unusually, the front door was locked. There would be no guests until tomorrow, and she had no key.

She stood outside, looking through the library windows, feeling that the house had closed itself against her. She had no right of entry. Perversely, that made her yearn to be inside, while no one was there – to breathe the air, walk through the rooms, have the place to herself.

Dusk was falling, the sky streaked pink, the last wood-pigeons cooing in the chestnut trees. The air was cool and still. Turning, Grace imagined Christina walking round from the stables, tired from a day outdoors; she'd be looking forward to a hot bath and a hot dinner, her muscles aching the way Grace's sometimes did after riding. And Christina would have ridden with far more skill and dash, and for longer. The door would be open for her, perhaps with an old dog waiting, getting up slowly from the mat as she approached, thumping its tail in greeting. This was Christina's home. She belonged here.

The crunch of feet on gravel made the back of her neck prickle. For a tingling instant she believed it really was Christina approaching round the bend in the drive. Her eyes went swimmy, then focused on Roger, who was walking as if lost in thought, abruptly becoming alert when he saw Grace by the porch.

He seemed taken aback, then recovered. 'Oh – hello! I was just having a walk round, now that I properly live here. It's nice having the place to ourselves for a change. I was imagining I was one of the old Russells.' He gave an embarrassed laugh. 'You made me jump. I was thinking about Christina. For a minute I thought you were her, standing there.'

'That's weird! I was just thinking about her too.' Grace was touched, even flattered. 'Sometimes it seems as if she really *is* here.'

'It does,' Roger agreed. 'Were you trying to go in? Sorry, I locked up, as there's no one in.'

In those few moments Grace had forgotten why she'd been looking for him. Remembering, she explained about yesterday's visitor. 'And there's a note in the study from Irina, with the phone number.'

'Marion Duncan, you said? And her mother was a Wright?'

'Yes. Jenny Wright.'

'Jenny Wright. Now, how does she fit in? I'll go and look at the family trees.' He looked at his watch. 'It's a bit late to phone now. I'll do it tomorrow. Thanks, Grace.'

When Roger did make the call, next morning, Grace was in the office helping her mother with lists for the Bank Holiday weekend.

'Well!' He rang off, greatly animated. 'I assumed Mrs Duncan's mother must be dead – but it turns out she's still around, ninety-eight, a bit deaf, but with all her marbles. She worked here till the house was sold, and knew Christina right up till she died!' He and Grace's mother looked at each other; then he remembered Grace was there too, and smiled at her.

'That's brilliant!' Mum exclaimed. 'Could we meet her? Would she talk to us?'

We. Us. The family history was a joint project now, not only Roger's.

'Yes, she's in a care home on the edge of Chelmsford.' Roger waved a piece of paper with a handwritten address. 'I looked her up in the family tree. She was married to the Thomas Wright who's always puzzled me because he suddenly appears on the census with Richard and Amy but with no record of his birth – adopted, I assume. She'll know about that.'

'When can we go and see her?'

'Soon as possible, I hope. It's a busy week, from tomorrow . . . but I'll phone and find out.'

Adrian did not return. Grace knew from her mother that Sally had visited him in Maldon, but she was still going back

231

to her parents' cottage each evening, while Marcus stayed on at Marsh House. How would things be resolved? Grace had the sense that something was simmering, and that everyone was watching carefully. Her mother was anxious to support Sally however she could; but surely Marcus would never forgive his father for the attack on Flash, let alone trust him not to do it again.

Marcus said nothing at all about his family situation, and was as withdrawn and unhappy as when Grace first saw him. He spent time with Jamie, more often alone with Flash. She wished she knew how to help. In secret she worked on her Flash drawings, beginning at last to feel pleased with her efforts.

One morning she met Marcus heading over towards the farm, with Flash by his side. She noticed that he kept the dog on a lead now whenever they were anywhere near sheep, and was stricter with him than before.

'Is he back, your dad?'

'No.' He shook his head vigorously. 'No. Mum wants me to go to the workshop to check an order from one of his customers, see if it's ready to collect. Come with me?'

'Yeah, course.' As always when she had his attention, Grace felt a flush of pleasure; besides, she was curious to see where his father worked. As they approached the cattle grid Marcus spoke sharply to Flash and made him walk to heel, but still the sheep eyed him warily all the way through to the farmyard.

Marcus unlocked the workshop and slid back the double

doors. The spacious interior smelled of wood and sawdust and varnish; there was a workbench, open shelving and storage units tall enough for long pieces of wood. Everything was orderly, meticulously so: tools in crates and drawers, larger ones hanging on hooks. Several doors were finished, leaning against a wall.

'This is what he was working on last week,' Marcus said. 'I was doing the varnishing.' He showed Grace a pair of finished doors, panelled and stained a dark walnut brown. 'It just needs the handles fitted, but I can do that. I know which ones.' He ran a hand over the wood as if it were the shining coat of a horse or a dog, asking to be stroked.

Grace had never given doors or handles the slightest attention, but looking around she saw evidence of skill and craftsmanship: the beauty of the wood, the richness of the dark stain, and even the handles, dark and heavy and traditional, curved to fit the hand, so that something as simple as opening a door would give pleasure. It surprised her; she had been half-expecting chaos and shoddiness, not this almost loving attention to detail and finish.

'He's a perfectionist,' Marcus said when she remarked on it. 'About his work, at any rate. He can't bear anything that's not quite right.' There was a pause before he added what Grace was already thinking: 'Especially himself.'

Grace remembered something Jamie had started to tell her once: that Marcus thought he could never be good enough for his dad. She didn't understand that. Wouldn't most fathers be proud of a son like Marcus?

'Do you want him to come back?'

'Yes. No. I don't know.' He looked away. 'I want things back like they used to be, before.'

She knew that feeling, all too well. It was as if there was a deep sorrow within him that answered something in her. Not knowing what to say, she could only express silent sympathy.

Now that Marcus was staying at Marsh House, he had been persuaded by Charlie to take Sirius out for light exercise. Grace rode with him, preferring his company to Charlie's constant demands and criticisms. Marcus said little, but seemed quite at ease on Sirius, more relaxed on horseback than at any other time. On their second ride, reaching a broad uphill track at the side of a field, he let Sirius surge forward into a fast controlled canter. Plum did her best to keep up, Grace leaning forward, easily in balance now as she thrilled to the speed and the thrum of hooves. When Marcus pulled up by the hedgerow at the top he turned to her, smiling broadly. Flash caught up, panting and excited, and they walked on, the horses side by side. Sirius was meant to be having only slow exercise, but the burst of speed and energy had been a release of tension that Grace sensed Marcus had needed.

They returned to Marsh House to find Skye there with Jamie, brought out to see them by the clatter of hooves. 'Ooh, don't you two look cool! Wait – can you make them stand still?' She produced her phone to take photographs. 'One more. And another. Sit, Flash – I want you in it too. Are you on Instagram, Grace?'

In spite of Skye's friendliness and the lovely ride, Grace felt newly sad as she unsaddled Plum and brushed her down. She led the pony out to the orchard with an end-of-holiday feeling; these leisurely afternoons were running out so fast.

'Oh, Plum. I'll miss you.' Grace offered a Polo mint, which she had discovered the pony loved. Plum's whiskery nose tickled the palm of her hand as she took it, and crunched noisily. 'Will you miss me?'

In little more than a week she and Mum would be in London, and school would start, and all this would be pushed into the past: a summer holiday, soon obliterated by timetables and bells and homework, all the clamour of school life. Without Marie-Louise. She didn't want to think about any of that.

She cycled back, overtaken by Roger's car as she rode up the Flambards drive. After working hard to get ready for tomorrow's meeting, he and Mum had finished early and driven to Chelmsford to visit Mrs Duncan's mother at the care home. Roger stopped, and Grace's mother lowered the window on the passenger side.

'Grace, come up to the Hayloft! Mrs Wright told us some amazing things.'

'Oh, what?'

'You can listen for yourself. We've made a recording.'

Upstairs, Grace sensed their suppressed excitement. They all sat at the table, Mum with a notebook and pen ready.

'I started to make notes while she was talking, but then

235

it got too exciting – there was more than I could get, all at once.'

'Here she is.' Roger showed Grace a photo on his phone: a very old lady, white-haired in a pink cardigan, with eyes that seemed glazed over with a pearly sheen. 'She's frail, in a wheelchair, can't do much for herself – but pin-sharp.'

'And with a fantastic memory, which is brilliant for us,' Mum said. 'Listen to this.'

CHAPTER EIGHTEEN

No Accident

Roger touched the screen, and his own voice said, 'So, Mrs Wright, you worked at Flambards for a good many years?'

'Yes, I did. Same as my grandad before me,' said a husky old-lady voice – slow, enunciating carefully, as if conscious of being recorded. 'He was head groom at Flambards for years – Fowler, his name. I was a Fowler before I got married. I started just after my Thomas was killed – in the D-Day Landings, that was – and stayed on there till I retired. Mrs Christina was always good to me.'

'And that's Christina *Russell* you're talking about?'

'Yes, that's what I always called her – Mrs Christina. She'd been Wright for a couple of years, mind, when she was married to Dick, my father-in-law.'

'Dick? So that was Richard Wright?' asked Mum's voice.

'Yes, but everyone called him Dick. Anyhow, that didn't last long, like lots of people said it wouldn't from the start. Everyone round here thought Christina was a flighty piece, but she'd gone through a lot. And it was shocking the way Mr Mark died. So after three husbands she ended up living alone when she was still quite young.'

'Shocking? What do you mean by—' said Roger's voice, but Mrs Wright talked on without pausing. Grace glanced up at the actual Roger, who put a finger to his lips and said, 'Hang on! She comes to that, in a bit.'

'Course, I lived out, in the village. Me and my Tom, we had the cottage next to the old forge. Then when he was killed I was left with the two kids. Just five and three they were, when they lost their dad. Like I said, Mrs Christina was always kind to me and the kids, used to give them Christmas presents, and a nice tip for me, and a bit more now and then. I think she felt a bit guilty – there was bad feeling between the Russells and the Wrights. Not her fault, at least not all of it, but there you are.'

'She felt guilty? For what?'

'Oh . . . we never talked about it so it was easy to forget. Now you most probably don't know this – but my Tom was a Russell too, as well as a Wright.'

Two voices in unison – Roger's and Grace's mother's – said, 'What?'

'Oh yes. Dick took him in and brought him up as his son, but he wasn't really. Anyone could see he was the spitting image of Mr Mark, more and more as he grew up.' A

238

throaty chuckle. 'No surprise there. He was Mark's son.'

'Mark? Christina's husband, Mark?' said Mum's voice, and Roger's: 'But how could—'

'Well now. Dick's sister, Violet, was my Tom's mother, so Dick was actually his uncle. Violet was a maid up at Flambards, oh, before the first war, that was. Same time as Dick worked in the stables and my old grandad was head groom. Young Mark – a bit of a tearaway, he was, by all accounts, and handsome enough to turn any girl's head – got Violet into trouble. She left and went to London, had the baby – my Tom, that was – and married someone else. But when Tom was still a small boy, he was brought back to Flambards to be near his Uncle Dick and the horses – always loved horses, he did. For a while he lived with Mrs Christina and Dick, while they were married, but then that came to an end and Christina married Mr Mark soon after. Well, even though Tom knew by then that Mark was his real father, he was much closer to his Uncle Dick, who he'd known all his life. And – to tell you the truth – he was a bit scared of Mark, with his temper, and I don't blame him, from all I heard. So when Mark married Mrs Christina, Tom left Flambards and went back to his Uncle Dick.'

'So – Dick brought up Mark's son as his own?' said Roger's voice.

'That's right. So Tom went from living at Flambards to being a farm boy, not that he minded. Changed his name to Wright. Dick did get married again but he never had kids of his own, so Tom was as good as his son. I told you Dick was

239

my father-in-law, but strictly speaking he was my *uncle*-in-law. Mr Mark was really my father-in-law, only I never saw him that way and I'm quite sure he never gave it a thought.'

'My goodness!' said Mum's voice. 'I think I need a diagram. Christina and all her husbands – it's hard to keep up.'

Roger paused the recording to tell Grace, 'We'll make one. But this solves the mystery of the Tom in Fergus's letter we were wondering about. It was this *same* Tom who went to live with Richard Wright – I'd thought they were two different people. Wait for this next bit, though.'

They all listened intently.

'Oh, but you must know my great-grandson, mustn't you?' the voice said. 'Adrian. Adrian Gregg. Served in the Army for a good few years. I don't see him at all these days, but I heard he's living in one of the Flambards cottages with his wife. You can see the Russell in him, and he's got a temper to match, so they say. I don't think he even knows. Some things are best forgotten.' Again, the husky laugh. 'Probably shouldn't be telling you now, but if you're doing a family tree you might as well get everything right.'

'Adrian's your son's grandson?'

'That's right. Got a son of his own too. A teenager, by now.'

'Marcus!' said Mum's voice. 'Yes, we know him too.'

Roger pressed *pause* and looked at Grace for a reaction; she stared back.

'Adrian? And Marcus?' she exclaimed. 'So they're Russells, like us? They're *relations*?'

240

'Yes,' her mother said. 'Descended from Mark. That makes them third or fourth cousins to you and me, or something like that. We all go back to the first William Russell, the hunting-mad one, the father of Mark and our Will.'

'But – don't they *know* that?'

'No, it seems not,' Roger said. 'And wait – there's more. I'll go on right to the end now without stopping.'

His recorded voice took over. 'You said something about Mark – that it was shocking, the way he died. What did you mean by that?'

There was a ruminative sigh, then: 'I was only a baby at the time, course, but everyone in the village knew about his terrible accident. Only it wasn't.'

'Wasn't an accident?' said Mum's voice.

'No, no.'

Grace caught her breath, for a moment imagining that Christina had *murdered* Mark; but surely not. I *know* Christina, she found herself thinking. She'd never do that.

'Mrs Christina told me the truth of it later,' the old lady went on. 'Mr Mark, he'd been in the fighting over in France, and he was injured so bad he nearly died. They brought him back in a terrible state and he had to be nursed at home for months, the hospitals were so stretched. Internal injuries it was. And he was never the same, after. Had to rest, couldn't eat proper food. It was a wonder he fathered another son, if you get my meaning. And for a strong, vigorous chap like he'd always been, it was a torment. He loved his riding and hunting and his horses – Mrs Christina did too, all her life

241

– but he'd go out for a day's hunting and it'd nearly finish him. He'd have to spend the next couple of days resting to get over it, and he couldn't stand that, hated any kind of weakness. But he'd keep doing it, all the same, and paying the price. He'd always had a temper on him, like his father before him, old Russell. Mrs Christina told me she knew that when she married him.'

'So what did she tell you about the, erm, accident?'

'They'd had one of their quarrels, she told me, a real shouting match. She never did say what about. Mr Mark, he goes storming out of the house and down to the stables, and he gets up on one of his horses and goes haring off. Ragtime, its name. I remember that – it was a name I liked. From what she said, he'd have gone off on a mad gallop, the mood he was in – he always rode hard, I knew that much from my grandad. There was a big gravel pit at the edge of the woods, back then – years later it was filled with water for the lake that's there now. Mr Mark jumped the horse over a fence and right into the quarry. Broke his neck, and the poor horse's as well.'

A pause, and an intake of breath, then Roger's voice said, 'He did it deliberately, you mean? Are you sure about that?'

'That's what Mrs Christina told me. She was the one who found him. When he didn't come back she went out on her own horse, looking.'

'How awful!' Mum's voice was barely audible.

'Accidental death was the coroner's verdict. But Mrs Christina knew it couldn't have been an accident. Mr Mark knew his way around those fields and woods like the back of his hand – he'd been riding there all his life. He knew the quarry was there, the other side of the fence. It could only have been on purpose. But she kept all that to herself at the time. Didn't want it known.'

There was a pause in which both Roger and Grace's mother started to speak, then the old lady gave a slow sigh. 'Broke my grandad's heart, it did. I remember he cried – for the horse, not for Mr Mark, begging your pardon. Grandad loved horses, spent his whole life looking after them, and at Flambards they always had the best. He said ever since Mr Mark was a boy, he was a tough one, a real thruster – always thought of himself, never his horse. If one went lame or broke down he'd just sell it and buy himself another. And to kill a lovely horse like that Ragtime . . . Grandad couldn't bear to think about it. It was unforgivable, he said.'

'Poor Christina. After all she'd gone through,' said Roger's voice. 'And the son she had with Mark was killed too, in the Battle of Britain.'

'I know. Robert, that was – a lovely young man. A pilot, like her first husband. Proper knocked her for six, that did, when he was shot down. Must have been like losing her William all over again. But she was tough too, in her own way – she was a Russell, remember. Picked herself up and carried on. After Mark died she lived on at Flambards with her daughter Isobel—'

'My grandmother!' Mum said.

'Oh yes, you told me that. I never saw much of Isobel,

Izzy they called her. By the time I went to work there she'd left to do war work and never came back. Never really a country girl, she wasn't. So Mrs Christina was on her own again when she gave me the job. I started off as her servant, but ended up as more of a companion. She was always sprightly, right up to the end. Went out riding nearly every day, and hunting, well into her seventies. She had shares in a racehorse as well. Used to love a day at the races.'

'I remember that,' said Grace's mother. 'Granny Izz said she was never going to settle down to an old age of knitting in front of the television.'

There was a pause, then Roger spoke again. 'Christina was young when Mark died – still only in her late twenties. Was there ever any question of her marrying again?'

'Not that I knew about. But late in life she had a gentleman friend she saw a lot of. And he *was* a gentleman – Mr Ashley-Clark, from over at Marsh House, who used to fix and sell cars.'

'He was my great-grandfather!' Roger's voice had a smile in it.

'What? Oh – yes, your name's Clark, isn't it? You told me. Oh, that poor lovely gentleman – he'd been a flyer, you know, as a young man, one of the first. He flew in the first war, like Mrs Christina's first husband that got killed before his daughter – young Izzy – was even born. Very brave they must have been, them pilots. Poor Mr Ashley-Clark – half his face was burned away. Terrible. I remember when I was a little girl, us children in the village used to scream when we saw him and run off – it was mean of us, treating him like a monster, but we were just kids who didn't know any better. Then later he had work done and didn't look quite as bad, at least not like before. And in spite of everything, he got married and had a son. But you don't need me to tell you that' – another laugh – 'cos here's you, sat here large as life, to prove it.'

'That's right! His son was my grandfather.'

'Mr Ashley-Clark and his wife Helen were very friendly with Mrs Christina for years and years. And then he was widowed. When would it be now? Let me see . . . in the sixties, it would have been, that year there was a man on the moon . . .'

'1969.'

'That's it. And after, it was natural the two of them liked spending time together. They'd see each other most days.'

'I wonder they didn't marry,' Mum's voice said, and Grace guessed she was thinking of Fergus's unsent letter. 'Still, it's nice to know.'

Other voices came in then, a loud cheerful one asking if they all wanted tea, and someone else wanting the television on.

'One more thing, though.' Mrs Wright's voice became confidential. 'Her first husband, Will. The flyer. She told me once – an anniversary, I think it was – he was the love of her life. She'd never have wanted anyone else if he'd lived.'

The recording ended there with thanks and exclamations from Roger and Mum. Roger sat cradling his phone as if in wonder at what it contained. He, Grace and her mother looked at each other in the sudden silence, absorbing what they'd heard.

'Oh, but there must be more!' Grace said after a few moments. 'I want to know *everything*. Christina must have told her lots of things about Will, and about Flambards. We've got to get it all before she – you know. While she's still around. While she still remembers.'

'I know. She was getting tired, but she said afterwards we could go again. But – there's so much there to be going on with!'

There was. Roger went over to the office for his family tree folder, and he and Mum sat at the table making their diagram, listening to the recording again, pausing to make notes. Grace went downstairs and out into the yard.

A few of the guests were coming or going from the stable bedrooms, heading for their evening session over in the house; a three-quarter moon was visible through the trees beyond the cottages, even though it was still daylight.

When she thought herself back into the past, Grace saw the younger Christina on a horse, or with Will. But now it was Mark she was thinking of – Mark with his terrible temper, Mark who looked just like Adrian, Mark who had stormed down here in a rage and had a horse saddled and galloped off, hunting himself to his own death. Killing a beautiful horse along with him.

What had he been thinking?

Trying to picture Mark, it was Adrian's face she saw,

clenched in anger; Adrian's destructive energy, that could lash out or just as quickly turn inwards.

Mark had come down here hot and blazing from a row with Christina. What had they quarrelled about? Did Christina blame herself when he didn't come back, or was she in a fury too, leaving him to burn out his rage in a wild gallop? But then she'd gone out searching; she was the one who found him. Grace saw Christina riding up to the edge of the quarry, looking down at the smashed bodies of horse and rider, knowing at once what had happened – that Mark had chosen this rather than carry on living with his wrecked body. She pictured the horse, catching its rider's urgency – leaping out into space, realizing too late that there was no safe landing, crashing . . .

Christina would have known that, would have understood how it happened.

Now there was Adrian, in a direct line. And Marcus. They were *family*, sort of. It gave her and Marcus an extra bond.

Grace thought of Sally, loving Adrian but hating his violence, and Marcus, drawn into himself: the family split three ways, seeing no end to their unhappiness. New generations at Flambards. People hurting each other, as it seemed they always had.

In spite of thinking about the long-ago tragedy she realized that she was hungry; her mother and Roger seemed so absorbed as to have forgotten about food. She went indoors to look for something to eat.

CHAPTER NINETEEN

Missing

'Roger's been thinking about the readings for the Armistice weekend,' said Grace's mother. 'Poems, extracts. He wondered if you'd like to do one?'

'Me? Why me?'

They were having breakfast in the flat. The dreaded day had come; this morning the Trustees would decide the fate of Flambards. Mum's folder and laptop were ready on the table, she had put on make-up and earrings and her smart jacket hung over the back of a chair, but she was chatting about anything other than the meeting as if to put off the decision that would be made today.

She passed Grace a slice of toast. 'He thought it would be good to have young voices. And you read well.'

'What would I read?'

'We thought a piece by Vera Brittain. She wrote a

wonderful book about the First World War, *Testament of Youth*. A memoir. You should read it some day. Roger's going to ask Marcus as well. Jamie too, only Roger thinks he'll need more persuading.'

'Well, he's doing his talk today. And that's *really* important. After that, how hard can it be just to read out a poem?'

Grace was pleased with her own small contribution to the meeting. To both Roger and Sushila, separately, she had put the idea of Jamie speaking to the Trustees about the wildlife of the wood and lake, and showing them his photographs. He was now an agenda item, which had daunted him at first. 'But I hate talking in front of people! I never do in lessons, if I can help it.'

'Oh, come on!' Grace had told him. 'Which would you rather – have your say, or wait for them to make up their minds without you, then wish you'd done it when you had the chance? Besides, if you want to be a wildlife presenter like Chris Packham, you'll have to get used to it, won't you?'

Now she felt anxious for him, butterflies in her own stomach as if she was the one preparing to talk.

Her mother poured coffee. 'Shall I tell Roger that's a yes, then, about the reading?'

'OK then.'

When Mum headed over to the house, Grace was at a loss to know what to do with herself. In just a couple of hours, plans for the special weekend might seem pointless. Would it still happen? And if it did, would she even want to be here?

So much could happen between now and November. She and Mum would have to drive up from London, probably not even staying overnight. It might be a time to mourn their own losses, rather than those of a hundred years ago.

She didn't want to think of being back in London. Soon they'd pack their things; the pink-bedroomed flat awaited them, though Mum hadn't said exactly when. Perhaps she too wanted to put it out of her mind now that she was so involved here – with Sally and with Roger, as well as with her work.

Heavy with gloom, Grace went outside. This was getting to be a habit: another meeting, and a helpless wait while people argued and made decisions. Except that Jamie was involved this time. The sky was grey, the air cool, hinting at autumn; the potted geraniums in the yard scattered their petals to the ground like scarlet tears.

Today her ghosts were absent: she had no sense of Christina or Will being close. Bad sign, she wondered? Had they already fled, sensing change? Instead she heard the slam of car doors and calls of greetings as the Trustees arrived and made their way to the house. It was all down to them. Mr Naylor wasn't among them and she supposed that as usual he'd parked outside the porch, as if he found it too much effort to walk from the car park.

As she passed the meeting room she saw Jamie inside, with Roger. On the screen was the title picture she'd helped him choose: one of his photos of the otter and cub, with the heading *Wildlife at Flambards*.

Good luck, she texted, though he was no doubt too busy to look. **You tell them!**

Knowing that he'd give his presentation and then leave, she waited in the office, helping Irina, while the meeting began. Her ears were tuned for footsteps in the corridor and as soon as she heard them she hurried out, intercepting Jamie on his way to the door.

'How did it go?'

He pulled a wry face. 'OK. Ish. Hard to tell. Some of them asked questions, but old man Naylor didn't say a word. Just wrote down a few notes. Come down to the lake? I can't face hanging around here. Skye said she was coming over too. I'll text her to say we're on our way.'

They walked across the meadow, meeting Skye on the path through the woods; she had run over from Marsh House. They settled themselves in the hide and Jamie took out his notebook. Skye hadn't yet seen the otters and was disappointed that they were nowhere in sight. She was usually so cheerful, a good person – Grace thought – to have around, but with little to see from the hide today she was soon bored.

'I think I'll run some more. See you later.'

Grace watched her jogging along the side of the lake, envious of her strong legs and easy stride, wishing she could go too. It could have been so different, meeting someone fit and athletic like Skye, matching her energy. If only . . . That useless, pointless *if only* – it still teased her with its jibes and reminders. No amount of dreaming could make It unhappen. Would she ever stop wishing?

Jamie looked downcast: whether because of the meeting, or because Skye had so quickly tired of his birdwatching, Grace couldn't tell. The lake was listless, with little to ruffle the grey surface other than a solitary coot that gave its loud *prrruk* and disappeared into the reeds.

He huffed, wrote *Coot 1* and the date in his notebook, then slammed it shut. 'This is pointless. Might as well give up.'

Giving up wasn't a good omen. Nothing was.

'Marc's on a real downer,' he said abruptly. 'Have you seen him?'

'Not since we went riding yesterday. He was quiet, but seemed OK.'

'I've no idea what'll happen about his dad. He's clammed right up.'

'And he's still at yours? He can't stay for ever, can he?'

'Mum and Dad don't mind. There's room, as long as he wants, now Uncle Rodge has moved out. But his mum wants them to be together. He sees her every day at Flambards, but it'll be different when school starts. I s'pose if Adrian's cleared off for good, Sally and Marc can go back to the cottage.'

'Do you think he *has* cleared off, then?'

Jamie shrugged. 'Dunno. Might be best if he did. I can't see how things'll work out otherwise, not since he went for Flash. Marc might get over being hit in the face, but attacking Flash – that's something else. Fact.' He lowered the flap, and the hide was instantly dark, just a crack of light showing through. 'I'm going home. Catch you later if you come over to ride. Uncle Rodge says he'll text me when the meeting's finished.'

Grace looked at her watch; it wouldn't be over yet. They parted at the wood's edge and she walked slowly back to Flambards, where she saw, to her surprise, that Adrian's white van was parked outside the cottage. Had he returned last night?

Her mother might know, from Sally. She went on past the side of the house and the meeting room, trying not to stare in too obviously. The Trustees were seated round a table with papers spread in front of them, and Sushila – in purple and green today – was talking earnestly, with many gestures. And everyone seemed to be listening to her intently, so that at least looked hopeful.

She found her mother in the office; she had made her presentation with Roger, then withdrawn, like last time.

'Mum? How was it?'

Her mother made a *so-so* face. 'OK, as far as I could tell. They'll be a while yet. Jamie's bit was good – he had some great photos, and he knows such a lot. D'you want to help for a bit?'

Grace read names from lists, while her mother double-checked bookings for the next few courses – none of them full, she noticed. The office door was open, and all was quiet. When Irina brought coffee her footsteps were loud on the tiles of the hall floor.

At last they heard voices, and people coming along the corridor. Grace listened alertly. The volume of sound – several people talking at once, even someone laughing – must surely be promising?

Grace's mother stood up, and at that moment Roger strode in.

'We did it, Polly – we did it!'

'Oh!'

He threw his arms around her in a bear hug, lifting her right off her feet; then he noticed Grace was there and swept her into the hug as well.

Almost too squashed to speak, she managed, 'You mean Flambards is safe?'

Letting go, they all stood back and looked at each other a little giddily.

'For at least two years, yes,' Roger said. 'And there'll be no sale, no building. Oh, it's the best we could have hoped for!'

Grace sagged with relief, thinking of Jamie, the otters, the bats. The Trustees were filtering through the hall on their way out, some of them looking in at the office door. 'Well done, Roger!'

'Polly too! So pleased.'

'It's the right thing for Flambards, I know it is.'

'Sushila!' Roger said, seeing her behind the others. 'Come in for a minute. It was Sushila's ideas for involving school groups that swung it,' he told Grace and her mother. 'She was *brilliant*. No one could have resisted.'

Sushila smiled modestly. 'Well, one or two of them did try. But I'm so glad everyone else was in favour. Outdoor and environmental education is so important. And Jamie showed us all what a really good site this is for wildlife. Well done him! And you, Grace, telling me about the otters and the birds – that started me thinking this way, so you can take some of the credit.'

'We'll tell you all about it at lunch,' said Roger. 'Sushila, you'll stay, won't you?'

Sushila agreed, and Grace's mother said she'd go and fetch Sally while Roger went to the kitchen for the champagne he'd put in the fridge just in case. Grace texted Jamie, who replied instantly with a whole row of grinning faces. She had Marcus's number now, and texted him as well. There was no answer, but she knew that he didn't always have his phone turned on.

There was a celebratory mood at lunch, not dimmed by the small number of students on this week's mosaics course and the half-empty dining room. Roger poured champagne, and Grace's mother said, as he hesitated over a glass for Grace, 'Yes, go on, she can have some.'

'Someone's birthday?' the tutor called across.

'Better than that,' Roger said. 'Better than *all* our birthdays.'

They all reached across the table to clink glasses. 'To Flambards! To the future!'

The talk was all of the new plans: a possible new teaching space, bunkhouse-style accommodation for groups of children, adaptations for special needs. Best of all, as Grace saw it, a proposal to manage the lake and meadow as a proper nature reserve. 'With expert help,' Roger said. 'We're going to approach the Essex Wildlife Trust for advice.'

'Oh, won't Jamie be delighted!' Sally said.

'It was his idea,' Sushila said. 'And wasn't that astonishing about Mr Naylor's granddaughter?'

'What's that?' Sally asked.

'We really thought we'd have a fight on our hands, to persuade him about opening up to schools,' Roger explained. 'But it turns out he's got a step-granddaughter with cerebral palsy, so he's well aware of special needs provision, or lack of. When Sushila started explaining her ideas she won him over straight away. We're going to look into extra grants we can apply for, and plan some fundraising of our own, and he'll do match-funding. It worked brilliantly.'

'It's lovely to think of children coming to Flambards. It makes the best use of what we've got here. Sharing it. Opening up all sorts of possibilities.'

How quickly a day could change! Grace sipped her champagne, feeling the fizziness slip down her throat, the bubbles spreading to her head, her whole body. After all the doubt and worry, this had turned into the kind of day where nothing could go wrong, where everyone was full of optimism and hope and pride in a job well done.

After that, as they ate, the conversation split into two halves: Roger talking to Sushila and Grace, while Grace's mother and Sally talked quietly together. Half-listening to all of it, Grace switched her attention when she heard Sally saying, 'He doesn't say much, just pretends everything's fine, but he feels things so deeply,' and realized that she meant Marcus.

Grace's mother made sympathetic mmm-ing noises.

'But this is such good news.' Sally took a sip from her glass. 'At least I'll still have a job, and the cottage. Even if I don't know when Adrian's coming back. Whether, even.'

Grace had forgotten about seeing the white van earlier, but now she said, 'Oh, Sally! I think he *has* come back. His van's parked in the yard.'

'What? Is it?' Sally looked astonished. 'Are you sure it's his?'

'I think so. It's there by the cottage. At least it was when I came by, about an hour ago.'

'Excuse me.' Sally pushed back her chair. 'I'd better go.'

Grace saw glances of concern flash between Mum and Roger.

Sally hadn't returned by the time lunch was finished.

Grace cycled over to Marsh House and found Charlie grooming Sirius outside his stable.

'So, good news!' Charlie said at once. 'Thank God for that. Uncle Roger must be relieved, and your mum. Jamie's gone off somewhere with Skye, but Marc's over there' – she gestured – 'mending the fence.'

Marcus was by the water trough, nailing up a rail, with Flash watching closely. Grace collected Plum's headcollar

257

and went through the gate. Plum's head went up as she saw Grace, and she made her sweet nickering sound of greeting, which alerted Marcus.

'Hi there,' he called. 'If you're riding I'll go with you.'

He sounded reasonably cheerful, in spite of what Jamie had said earlier.

'Great!' She gave Plum a Polo mint and buckled the head-collar; then realized that he probably hadn't heard. 'Your dad's come back – did you know?'

'What?' He swung round to face her.

'His van was there in the yard. Your mum went to find him.'

He stood for a moment uncertainly, then made a few more blows with his hammer, put away his tools and said, 'I'm going over. C'mon, Flash.'

He set off up the field, and Grace heard a brief, 'Got to go,' as he passed Charlie and headed for his bike. She followed more slowly, leading Plum.

'What's that all about?' Charlie asked.

Grace explained about Adrian, and Charlie pulled a face.

'Right. Let's see what happens next. Something's got to change. Poor old Sally's at her wits' end, anyone can see that.' She carried on brushing Sirius's neck with firm strokes; fine dust and hair rose from the chestnut sheen. Grace had never known that a horse's coat could be so glossy; glancing colours in the sunlight like shot silk. Charlie looked round at her, and went on, 'He's been getting more and more weird, Adrian, I mean. All those days when he doesn't speak to anyone or just switches off in mid-conversation. And then there was that thing when he first heard about you.'

'When he what?'

'Didn't you know? When he heard about you and your mum coming, and Uncle Rodge told him about—' Charlie stopped abruptly and bent over the box that contained her grooming kit. 'Oh. Sorry. Me and my big mouth.'

'*What?*' Grace stared at her, baffled.

'I don't suppose anyone's told you. Forget it.' Charlie picked up a cloth that looked like a tea towel and smoothed it over Sirius's neck.

'No! You'll have to tell me now!'

Charlie gave an *oh well* shrug. 'Uncle Roger told him you'd lost your leg in an accident and you've got a prosthetic limb. I mean he wasn't just telling Adrian, we were all here, my parents and Sally and Marcus and Jamie and me, having Sunday lunch. And Adrian sort of froze, and went quiet, like he does. Then – all of a sudden – he asked if you'd stepped on a landmine. Came out with it just like that.'

'A—'

'A landmine, right. Though Uncle Rodge had already told us it was a car that hit you. A landmine! I mean, as if!'

Grace's thoughts were racing; she couldn't speak.

'I mean it was completely daft, wasn't it?' Charlie went on. 'Funny, even. How could he think that? But it just shows what's going on in his head. Proves he needs help. P'raps now, after all this, he'll actually get it. Otherwise he'll end up in a mental home or something.'

259

'So what happened?' Grace managed. 'After he said that?'

'Oh, I can't remember.' Charlie was brushing Sirius's mane now. 'I think Uncle Rodge took him off into the garden and they talked for ages. Then they came back in as if nothing had happened. Nothing *does* happen, that's the problem. Until it does.'

Grace thought of Marcus heading back to Flambards. To what? To a blazing row? To more silence? She couldn't see how it would end well.

'Anyway, you'd better forget I told you,' Charlie said. 'I shouldn't have. Are you riding? I'll come with you, as Marc's cleared off.'

'What about your arm?' Grace would have preferred to ride on her own.

'Sod my arm. I'm sick of everyone fussing about it. It'll be fine.'

The word had lodged in Grace's mind, chanting itself to the rhythm of Plum's hooves on the tarmac road.

Landmine.

Landmine.

He thought I was a victim of war. He thought I'd stepped on a landmine and blown my leg off.

This was obviously the thing Jamie had been about to mention, that time in the hide, but thought better of it sooner than Charlie had done.

But at least I know now. And they all did *know. Marcus. Marcus knew.*

*What if it's me coming here that's made his dad go weird?
He looks at me and sees the war. Afghanistan. Everything
he thought he'd left behind.*

He sees me as a damaged person. Which I am.

Like him. Only in a different way.

*It's not his fault, is it? How he is. How can it be? He's a
victim too. He's seen too much, been through too much. He
can't forget.*

'OK?' Charlie called out as they turned through an open
gateway. 'Ready to go?'

She tried to shake the disturbing thoughts away, giving
herself over to the joy of a fast uphill canter.

Later, cycling back to Flambards, she met Marcus and Flash
coming in the opposite direction. They stopped, and Marcus
spoke first.

'He's not there. No sign. Must have been some other van
you saw.'

'I'm sorry!'

Marcus shrugged. 'No need. Probably best if he stays
away.'

'Do you really think that?'

'I don't know what I think.'

'But he needs help, doesn't he?'

'Yes, he does. But you haven't tried persuading him, like
Mum has and I have.'

'Now, though?'

Grace wanted to tell him what Charlie had said, to ask

what he made of it, but he was impatient to be on his way.

'Who knows? See you tomorrow, I expect. Come on, Flash.'

Grace cycled on, full of frustrated energy, doubting now that she'd actually seen the van. All her fizzy happiness about the Flambards news had gone flat. Instead she was thinking about Marcus's dad: remembering the moment when she'd kicked him, and he'd stared at her wildly, startled and in pain.

And Marcus: unhappy again, when they could have gone out riding together if she'd kept quiet. She didn't know if he even knew yet about being a Russell, descended from Mark. With everyone focused on the meeting and the worry about Adrian there had hardly been time to think about that, let alone talk about it.

She'd only made things worse.

Early, before Grace and her mother were up, there was a loud rapping on the door of the Hayloft. Mum went to answer, and while Grace was donning her leg she heard Sally's voice, raised in concern.

'. . . must have been here, but now I've no idea where he is! It's all my fault!'

'Wait, wait,' said her mother's voice. 'What's happened? Isn't he still in Maldon, with his friend?'

'That's what I thought. I'd decided to go there this evening and try to persuade him to come back. So first thing I came over to the cottage to tidy up, and found a phone message from Phil – from last night! Hours ago! He was checking that Adrian had got back OK.'

'Back here?'

'Yes . . . so I phoned him – Phil I mean – and he said Adrian left there yesterday morning. Packed his bag and left. He was coming here – said he'd got work waiting and was keen to get on with it.'

'But he *didn't* come back?'

'No, I think he did.' Sally looked up as Grace entered the room. 'When you saw the van, Grace – you were quite right. The cupboard door was open in the bedroom and there was dried mud on the rug. It looks as if he went indoors just to get something, and then I noticed his Barbour coat wasn't on the peg by the door – he'd taken that. If only I'd got there in time . . . where can he have gone?'

'Are you sure he didn't spend the night there?'

Sally shook her head vigorously. 'No. The bed hadn't been slept in. And besides, the van had gone when I went to check at lunchtime, and it wasn't there later when Marcus came over. Where is he? Oh, why didn't I make more effort to get him back?'

Her voice broke in a sob. Mum passed a box of tissues; Sally grabbed two and blew her nose, then answered her own question.

'I was scared to. That's why. I just couldn't see how things would work. And he was obviously in no hurry to see me. So I carried on doing nothing, putting it off. Letting Phil decide what was best.'

'Come and sit down. Don't blame yourself,' Grace's mother soothed.

'I *do*! Where can he be? Why was I so stupid? I shouldn't have left him to come back alone. I should have gone and fetched him.' Sally let Grace's mother guide her to a chair, but sat down reluctantly, ready to spring up again. 'Should I call the police?'

'Wait – you've tried his mobile?'

'Turned off. And Phil hasn't heard from him since yesterday morning. He's worried too. He and his wife left for work, and Adrian let himself out later. Phil said Adrian seemed fine when they said goodbye. He was asking about the nearest place to get petrol.'

'So, he drove himself here, called briefly at the cottage yesterday, took his coat and went off again.'

'Why would he need a coat?' Grace asked. 'It's not cold. Unless he was going to stay out all night?'

Sally gazed at her, while Mum asked, 'Are there other friends he might have gone to? Relations?'

'He doesn't get on with his parents. I can't believe he'd go there.'

'Could he be in the workshop? Maybe he slept there for some reason, or even worked through the night?'

'No, no. I went over there after I spoke to Phil. It's all locked up, and the van's not in the yard.'

'OK,' Mum said. 'Let's have some tea – can you do that, Grace? – and I'll phone Roger and Ian and we'll all think what to do.'

264

She made the calls, explaining, but no one had heard anything. By this time Grace saw that she was almost as worried as Sally, though trying to appear calm.

'He could be *any*where.' Sally sounded despairing. 'How can we even start looking?'

'Have you got a key to the workshop?' Mum asked.

He might be in there. He might have barricaded himself in, Grace thought, and knew that the same thing had occurred to her mother.

Her brain swirled with awful possibilities. Adrian might easily harm himself, his anger turning inward. She thought of the confusion and fear she had seen when he looked at her.

Fear of his own mind and what it could do?

'No,' Sally was saying, mopping at her eyes. 'There's only one spare, and Marcus has got that.'

'I'll phone Ian again. Get him and Marcus to go over with the key.'

But a phone call from Roger, twenty minutes later, confirmed that Ian and the boys had joined him at the farm, and there was no trace of Adrian or his van. Marcus had opened up the workshop, and was certain that nothing had been touched or moved since he last went in.

Grace and her mother had dressed quickly, and within half an hour everyone assembled in the office. Grace saw Marcus's expression, set and unmoving, and knew better than to try to catch his eye.

'So it wasn't true, what he said!' Sally was still jittery

with panic. 'About being keen to get on with work? He hasn't even *been* there.'

'It's time to call the police, I think,' Roger said.

No one disagreed.

CHAPTER TWENTY

Love, Even

Roger made the call, soon passing the receiver to Sally so that she could give full details. Immediately the situation felt more serious. The laughter of a group of guests passing through the hall on their way to breakfast felt out of place, as if from a different world untouched by crisis.

'What now?'

'We can't just wait.'

'Someone needs to be here, though.'

'I'm going to drive round the lanes,' Ian said, 'just in case. Anyone want to come with me?'

Roger went with Ian while Grace's mother and Sally stayed in the office to make or receive phone calls. Jamie said that he'd look in the fields and woods nearby, and although that seemed pointless, Grace decided to go too, for the sake of doing something practical instead of just standing about.

'Marc?' Jamie stopped in the doorway. 'Come with us?'

Marcus shook his head, looking at the floor. 'I'll stay with Mum.'

The weather was unpromising: the sky grey and featureless, a cool wind from the east carrying moisture that was almost drizzle. At this early hour the grass was night-damp, laced with cobwebs; normally Jamie would stop to look for interesting spiders, but he walked on almost too fast for Grace to keep pace. As they passed through the deserted farmyard they heard footsteps pounding behind and saw Marcus sprinting to join them, Flash lolloping joyfully alongside.

Grace stopped dead, thinking there must be news, but all Marcus said as he slowed was, 'I'll come with you. Got to do *some*thing.'

They walked on, not speaking. Jamie led the way along the track out of the yard, the way the three of them had walked on the night of the bats. This time, instead of turning right towards the meadow and the gate into the woods, he took the left fork, keeping to the broader, beaten-mud track that swept round behind the woods and on up the gentle hill towards Marsh House. There was another gate on this side, the one Grace had ridden through on her first ride with Charlie, and many times since. As the track curved round, separated from the wood by a barbed-wire fence, she saw the gleam of white through foliage: looked again, and grabbed Marcus's arm.

'There – look! Is that the van?'

'Yes – there—'

The boys were off, running, too fast for Grace to keep up. She jog-trotted awkwardly behind, soon seeing that the van had been driven under low branches and into dense shrubs and brambles as far as it could go. It wasn't locked; Marcus had opened the driver's door and was leaning in.

'No. Not here,' Marcus said. 'The keys are in the ignition, though.'

'Looks like he slept in here.' Jamie had swung open the back doors.

Grace and Marcus came round to look, seeing a tangled blanket, a rucksack and some empty beer cans.

'Why would he sleep here? Not in the cottage?'

Briefly Marcus met her eye, not replying.

He's gone into the woods, she thought.

Jamie was trying his phone. 'Ach – useless! No signal. You two keep looking. I'll run back to the farm and phone from there.'

Marcus slammed the doors shut and turned away into the trees, whistling Flash to heel. Following, Grace realized that this was the track where Charlie had had her accident. When Marcus took the left turn where two paths crossed she thought he was heading for the lake.

It seemed inevitable.

The lake. Where the gravel pit used to be.

In her mind she saw Mark on his horse, face set in anger or determination, galloping fast across the fields, not stopping for the gate but riding hard at it and soaring over. Into the twisty paths, ducking low branches, the horse eager to do what its rider wanted until it found itself leaping into empty space and falling to its death on the gravel.

To both their deaths.

What desperation had driven Mark to do that?

Mark then. Adrian now.

Although no one had said so aloud, Grace knew that they all shared the fear of Adrian doing something drastic – that he might hang himself or take an overdose. That had been in Marcus's mind just now, she felt sure, as he looked inside the van, and earlier, at the workshop. He must have dreaded what he'd find.

She scurried after him, pushing back twigs, freeing herself from the clutch of brambles. She knew it was pointless to make conversation and expect him to reply, but she saw the miserable hunch of his shoulders, and wished she could say something to help.

He turned to glare at her. 'This is my fault!'

The way he spoke made it sound like *hers*.

'No, Marcus, it isn't! How can it be your fault?'

He struggled to speak for a moment, then, 'I told him I hated him. You were there! You heard! And I really did, then, because of what he did to Flash. But I didn't mean it, I know it's not . . .' His voice wavered; he rubbed angrily at his eyes, turned and strode on. 'Not his fault, how he is. If only . . .'

Let it be all right, Grace whispered silently, and it felt like praying, though she never did that. *Please let it be all right*.

They reached another meeting of paths, and Marcus

stopped again, so abruptly that she almost walked into him.

'The lake,' she said. 'He's at the lake. In the hide perhaps, or . . .'

A slide show of awful possibilities flashed through her mind. Marcus looked at her, then turned left and plunged on, quickly outpacing her. As the first glimmer of water came into view she heard him give a shout, breaking into a run. Reaching the lake's edge she stood for a moment seeing nothing at first, only the black-and-white of Flash as he ran ahead. She heard Flash give a whine, and saw him stop, uncertain.

There, by the curve of shore farther round, was a huddled figure, completely still, well-camouflaged in a khaki coat with a hood pulled low over his head.

'Dad!' Marcus shouted, and was there in a few bounds, stooping. 'Dad . . .'

For a terrible moment Grace thought Adrian was dead, frozen there in rigor mortis. He looked too small to be a grown man, hunched and clenched as if to make himself insignificant.

She saw his head turn stiffly, and he made a strange jerky movement with one arm. He stared at Marcus, unrecognizing at first, then turned away, put both hands to his face and began to weep. Flash whined again too, and lay down a few yards away.

Never had Grace heard such a sound, a wailing howl of despair, eerie in the quiet of the trees; never had she heard an adult give way so dramatically to utter grief. She stopped, holding herself still. Marcus knelt beside his father and put his arms round him and spoke quietly.

After a few moments Flash came to Grace and pushed his nose into her hand, as if he too needed comforting. Looping her fingers through his collar she drew back, telling him softly to come with her. Adrian seemed unlikely to harm either himself or Marcus, not now, and she thought she'd be most useful by going back to the van to tell the others where to come.

Before she'd gone far along the track, Flash's ears pricked and he gave a *whuff* of recognition. She heard the crack of twigs ahead and saw the tall dark shape of Sirius through sapling trees, ridden one-handed by Charlie. Oh, thank goodness – Charlie on Sirius would be faster than anyone else at getting help.

'Charlie!' she yelled. 'Over here!'

The pockets of Adrian's coat had been weighted with stones.

That was the detail that stood out in Grace's mind, from all the activity, doubt and confusion that followed. He had gone to the lake intending to drown himself; he had made preparations.

She thought of him selecting the stones, weighing them in his hand. Heavy enough? Another? A few bigger ones, to be quite sure? As if drowning himself was a practical task, to be confronted as methodically as fitting a door hinge or sanding down a piece of wood.

Unmaking. Ending. Giving up. Giving in.

But he *hadn't*. When it came to the moment, he hadn't

272

taken those final steps into the water. He had stayed on the bank, contemplating, but not doing it. Whether through fear, or because the will to live had after all proved stronger, who could know? Whether he *would* have done it, if Marcus hadn't found him . . .

Charlie had galloped back to find the others. Within minutes, Ian was driving his own van down to the gate, bringing Sally, Roger and Jamie. Roger and Marcus helped Adrian to walk slowly – numbed into stiffness, walking with difficulty like a frail old man – to the wood's edge, and Ian drove him back to the house. Marcus and Sally went with them while Roger carefully backed Adrian's van out of the clutch of shrubs and brambles and then followed.

At Flambards they found a police car parked in front of the porch, and two sergeants, a young WPC and an older man, in the office with Grace's mother. Students were starting to arrive for Ian's art class, and Grace remembered that it was, after all, a normal Friday. The mosaics guests were leaving, carrying bags down from their rooms and looking on curiously, pretending not to be too keenly interested.

Adrian was silent now, silent and confused. He sat in the office, wrapped in a blanket, seeming not to know where he was. Grace stayed at a respectful distance, hovering, until her mother came out and closed the door behind her.

'Sally thinks he's suffering from hypothermia,' she told Grace, who was surprised at that – she'd thought hypothermia afflicted people stranded on mountainsides in blizzards. But her mother said that both sergeants had agreed, and called for an ambulance. Adrian had been out all night, either in the van or by the lake, probably hadn't eaten for some while, and was suffering from extreme stress: all that could cause hypothermia.

'Besides,' she added in a low voice, 'he may have taken something, for all we know. He needs to be thoroughly checked over.'

It was only just gone ten, but it felt as if hours had passed since Sally's knock on the door. Grace felt the oddness of being dumped back into an ordinary grey Friday morning. Ian had quite forgotten about his art class and had to make hasty preparations; Marcus and Sally went with Roger to the hospital, following the ambulance. Charlie, after causing quite a stir by bringing Sirius into the yard, where he was admired and photographed by several of the departing guests, rode back to Marsh House, and Grace's mother returned to her office desk. A new group would be arriving this afternoon and everything must be ready. The usual routines were taking over.

Grace went to Ian's class, wanting to be with other people without needing to talk. Sushila wasn't there today, and Grace simply sat and drew and thought, going over and over the events of the morning. Without quite intending to she began drawing the two stooped figures, Marcus and his father, under the trees. Although cartoonish in its simple lines, the pose made her think of a religious sculpture, expressing pity and forgiveness. Love, even. But she didn't want Ian or anyone else to see that, and soon turned her page.

274

There was an extra kindness in Ian's manner today, in his comments on the work. Everyone involved in the crisis seemed newly aware of how they treated each other, and the importance of looking after people.

What would happen now in Marcus's family Grace had no idea – only the sense that something had ended. Pretending was surely over, and recovery could begin. Marcus didn't really hate his father. Maybe Adrian's anger had burned itself out, fizzled out in the cold and damp of early morning and the stark realization of what he'd been about to do. How different the future would look if Adrian's drowned body had been pulled out of the lake! Then there could be no return to normality. Especially for Marcus, who'd have blamed himself for ever.

She began sketching a worn old walking boot that was in Ian's crate of oddments. She liked the way it was shaped to the foot of an unknown person, the deep cracks in the leather testifying to miles walked and weather endured.

CHAPTER TWENTY-ONE

The Me of Then, the Me of Now

'What will happen now? Will Adrian be all right?'
Grace and her mother were in the Hayloft,
having a quick sandwich lunch.

'I hope so,' Mum said carefully. 'It's too early to know.
This has certainly been a – a point of no return. After today,
no one can pretend things are normal. Even Adrian can't go
on insisting he doesn't need help. It was awful, frightening
– but maybe for the best.' After a pause, she went on, 'Poor
man. Phil, the Army friend, told Sally something Adrian had
never mentioned to her.'

'What?'

'Something that happened out in Afghanistan. Some
insurgents had been killed in an attack and were lying by
the side of the road where they'd fallen. Adrian's unit went
to check if they were dead or injured – carefully, in case it

was a trap. They *were* dead, five of them. And two were just boys, teenagers – too young even to be fighting. For a moment he thought one of them had a look of Marcus. After that – *years* after, even now – he keeps dreaming, hallucinating even – seeing this boy's face and Marcus's, as if they're the same person.'

Grace was silent, digesting this.

Her mother sighed deeply. 'How would you get over that? Seeing – killing – what you thought was the enemy, and finding they were hardly more than children? And he'd never told Sally about it. Never told anyone. That was hard for her to take – knowing he'd kept it to himself for so long, tormenting himself. And then finally he told someone else, someone who'd been in the Army too, and had some idea what it was like.'

'Will she move back to the cottage now?'

'Yes. She never really wanted them to be apart, only things went too far. It'll be different now.'

Grace thought of how Sally turned to Mum whenever she was worried or upset. For practical help, for understanding. They'd become close, just as Grace wanted to think that Marcus and Jamie were her own special friends. It seemed to her that they all needed each other.

'The other night – no, it was only *last* night, though it seems ages ago – Sally showed me some family photos,' said Mum. 'There was one in particular, taken a few years ago when Marcus was quite young – the three of them piled on a sledge, laughing. You could see what a handsome man Adrian was – well, still is, isn't he? – and them all having fun together in the snow. I don't think I've ever seen Sally look as happy as that, either – not surprisingly. She was saying she'll never get that Adrian back, but perhaps he's not altogether gone, either.'

'Mmm. She'll have Roger around to help, even after we've gone. You'll stay friends with them, won't you?'

'Yes, of course,' her mother said, and seemed about to go on, but fell silent. Grace waited, looking at her expectantly, then raised the subject they'd both been avoiding.

'Mum? About that – you haven't said when we're leaving, but it must be quite soon, mustn't it? How many days have we got left? I need to *know*.'

'Yes, course you do. Sorry.' Her mother gave her a doubtful look. 'There's something we need to talk about. I didn't think today was the right time, though, with all this.'

'No, go on,' Grace said, with a sense of foreboding. 'What?'

Mum seemed to be choosing her words carefully. 'I know how difficult things are for you, with Marie-Louise not coming back, and Dad leaving, and – well, everything.'

'Right. You could say that,' Grace said, still wary.

'How . . . how would you feel about not going back, Gracey? Staying here?'

Grace stared, not understanding. 'What, you mean *live* here? But how can we? What about school?'

'You could change schools. There's Hales Green, where Marcus and Jamie go. Ian and Gail both teach there too. I've looked into it, checked there's a place for you.'

Grace's mind blurred in panic. *I can't! Everything strange. Being different, being looked at and pitied, people saying all the same old things* . . . She saw herself in a packed corridor, being jostled, curious stares directed at her, whispers and overheard remarks. 'That's her. The new girl, the one with . . .'

A minority of one, facing that all over again.

No. No. I can't do it.

'It's a good school,' Mum went on, talking fast as if she had to seize the moment, 'and you'd already know the two boys, even if they're in the year above you. It's a big thing, to start all over again at a new school, especially with, you know, your leg and everything. But if you *did* think you could do it, the start of Year Ten isn't a bad time.' She gave Grace a doubtful look. 'Perhaps it's unreasonable of me to ask, though. If you'd really rather not . . .'

'You mean nothing's decided?' Grace asked, though it was clear enough that Mum wanted her to agree.

Her mother put an arm round her and hugged her close. 'Course not, Gracey! I wouldn't decide without asking you. I want you to be happy. If this is too much . . .'

Yes, Grace thought. *It is too much. More change. A huge change.*

But, but . . .

It'll be awful anyway, going back to Westfields. No Marie-Louise. I'd be on my own.

Here . . . Flambards, and everything . . . Jamie and Plum . . . and Marcus . . . I wouldn't have to leave them.

I could be here. I could stay.

She closed her eyes and swallowed hard.

I can do it.

And suddenly she was full of elation. Determination. Hope.

'Oh, *Mum*!' she burst out. 'I thought you were going to tell me something really awful!'

Her mother looked at her in transparent relief. 'So – could you get used to the idea? Do you want to have a think?'

'I've already thought. Yes, let's go for it. D'you really mean it?'

'Of course I do! I'd hardly joke about something so important, would I?'

Grace sat down, stood up again, clapped her hands over her mouth and gazed around the room and out of the window. 'Oh, Mum – wow! It's brilliant . . . There's Skye too. I'll already have a friend in the same year. But . . .' Her mind was buzzing with questions that rushed in all at once. 'But what about you? Your job – how will that work?'

'The Trustees want to keep me on till Christmas, three days a week, and I can still go back to my freelance stuff. After that – well, it depends how things go here.'

'What about that flat, though? The pink bedroom flat? I thought you'd signed the papers and everything?'

'No,' her mother said, after a moment. 'I didn't sign after all. It's probably gone by now.'

'Mum! Why didn't you tell me?'

'I needed to see how things turned out. You know, at the meeting, and . . . everything.'

280

'Devious or what?'

'Well, I'm lucky it worked out. I'm so glad you're pleased.'

'*Pleased?* Understatement! It's the best thing that could have happened!'

Grace went over and hugged her mother and they rocked together for a few moments, laughing.

'So – this will be home, this flat?'

'For a little bit longer, at least.'

Grace looked at her closely. 'There's more though, isn't there?' she said; then got it. 'Aha! *Roger*. He's part of this, isn't he? You and him?'

'Erm, yes.' Mum had the secretive, pleased look Grace had often noticed when Roger was mentioned.

'So you're together now?'

'Yes . . . we are. Will be. Want to be.'

'So what if I'd said no, I want to go back to London?'

'We'd have worked something out. It wouldn't have been impossible. But this is better, so much better!'

Mum and Roger, Grace thought. Roger and Mum. They already seemed like a sort of team, looking to each other for company and support, spending time together when they didn't need to.

Yes, she could live with that. She nodded approval. 'That's cool.'

'I'm glad you think so!'

'Well, it's not as if I didn't *know*. It's pretty obvious.'

Her mother laughed. 'Is it? And I thought we were being so discreet. So . . . you and I will stay on here in the Hayloft, at first. See how things work out. When we've all had time to get used to things, we can move in with Roger. That would be better, because this flat is really meant for visiting tutors to use. His flat over in the house has got plenty of space, with two bedrooms. You could have your own room, a lovely one, bigger than yours here.'

'We can live in the house? In actual *Flambards*?' For a moment she felt dizzy with the rightness of it. 'And – you and Roger. Will you get *married*?'

Her mother shook her head, laughing. 'I don't know about that. We haven't talked about it, and I don't think either of us sees it as important. Weddings. Stuff. Fuss. We just want to be together.'

'Does Dad know?'

'I haven't told him, no. I think he might have started to guess. I'll talk to him soon about the change of school and everything.'

'He can't complain. He's got Chloe, and they'll soon have their baby. I don't see why you shouldn't have someone nice too. But – what if it doesn't work out, you and Roger?'

'There's no certainty, Grace. All I can say is that we both want it to, very much. And we're both old enough to know what we want.'

'So – do you *love* him?'

'Yes! Yes, I do,' her mother said, in a surprised way, as if it felt strange to say so. 'And I know I can trust him. Completely. I hope you feel that too. You do, don't you?'

'Yes,' Grace said, but was struck by a new doubt. 'The

only thing is . . . he wants to be with you, but it means he gets lumbered with me, as well. Is he OK with that?'

'Oh, Gracey! Of course he is!' Mum gave her another big hug. 'More than OK – he'll be absolutely delighted. We'll talk more about everything. With Roger too. But for now I need to get back to the office.' She carried their plates to the sink. 'It's so good that you're keen! I hoped you would be.'

Grace followed her downstairs and out, but while her mother sped along the drive towards the house she dawdled behind. This was her favourite place for imagining she saw Will or Christina, or sometimes Mark, coming or going to the stables, passing her without seeing, wrapped up in their own concerns.

I'm here, she told them silently, just in case they were around. *And I'm not going anywhere. I'm here to stay.*

'You know Roger mentioned the photographs he'd found, of Fergus?' her mother said later, in the office. 'I've got them here. He showed me earlier. You can see them if you like, but I warn you they're a bit shocking.'

Because of Fergus's burned face, she meant.

Grace hesitated, curiosity fighting reluctance. Curiosity won, and she moved closer to her mother's desk.

'This was him, before, when he was at Cambridge.' Her mother held out a black-and-white portrait. 'Nice looking, wasn't he?'

Yes, he was. Fergus wore a collar and tie that looked uncomfortably tight, and had neat fairish hair brushed back from a high forehead; he smiled diffidently, as if he didn't much like having his photograph taken, but was being polite about it.

'Then this.' Mum handed over a second picture.

Grace took it, looked, and almost dropped it. Her eyes went swimmy with horror. In this photograph Fergus had become a sort of hideous Mona Lisa – the two halves of his face didn't match, but the mismatch was grotesque, not mysterious like the painting. One half was just about recognizable as the same person she'd just been looking at. The other half hardly resembled a face at all. The hair was burned away to a few tufts, and there was no eye at all – just the trace of an eyebrow and a lid that dropped to the scarred and puckered skin that stretched from nose to an ear that had its lobe missing. It was a frightening mockery of a human face, and yet . . . it was the same person, a young man still in his twenties who'd have to find a way to live with the wreckage he showed to the world.

This was Fergus, whose voice she had heard and whose letter she'd read; Fergus who had loved Christina, and never told her. This was him.

She looked away, then made herself look back, concentrating on the undamaged half, with its eye that still somehow had a kindly expression – as if this time his concern was for the person looking at him. For *her*, she could almost have thought. He didn't want to shock or frighten her.

'Oh, poor man, poor Fergus! How could you – how could you even *live*, knowing you looked like that?'

'But he did live. He made a new life. And – look – this is him after the facial reconstruction. It's still alarming, but better. There was all this pioneer work on skin grafts at a special hospital in Sidcup – Roger's found out quite a lot about it. By the time Fergus had his treatment they knew how to avoid infection, and it was generally quite successful.'

The third picture showed an older Fergus, still with a face lopsided and distorted, but the skin on what had been the burnt side now smooth and unblemished. He wore glasses and an eye-patch, and although Grace could see that children might still run away at the sight of him in either real or imagined fear, it was a big improvement.

How brave he must have been! Brave, in the first place, to fly at all. Then, when so terribly disfigured, not to give up on life. And brave to go through surgery, knowing that at best he could be roughly patched up, never given his own complete face back. That could never happen.

But she'd heard the humour and kindness in his voice; his affection for Will and for Christina. His voice alone told her that he was a kind man, a man she'd have liked to know.

'Are you OK?' her mother asked.

'Yes. Fine. I'm just going outside for a bit.'

There was something she had to do, on her own. Something that had been on her mind for a while.

She went into the garden, to the bench by the rose arch, and sat there for a moment gazing across at the flowerbeds.

Young Fergus, a clever student, brave enough to fly an aeroplane – he must have thought he had a bright future.

His Before and After had been more drastic even than her own. He had two legs, yes, but he faced that awful choice – hide himself away, or know that whenever he appeared in public people would turn away in horror. His face would always be the first thing they saw, and most wouldn't get beyond that to the person inside. The thought had crossed Grace's mind more than once: at least it wasn't my face that was damaged. I still look the same. And if it *had* been her face, modern surgery could do more than clumsy patching up.

She took out her phone and flicked back through the photographs stored there till she reached the one she was looking for.

The one of herself. Before. Taken by Marie-Louise.

She had sometimes cried over it, sometimes raged; she had often been on the point of deleting it, but could never quite bring herself to.

There she stood, on the running track at school, squinting into bright sun, holding up a hand to shield her eyes. In Lycra shorts and trainers and a sports vest she was lined up with three others, ready to run. Her eyes went to her right leg: thigh, knee, calf, tapering down to the slenderness of ankle, ankle bone, foot: the lost leg and foot she had mourned. She felt the clench of her missing toes as she looked, felt the flexion of a foot that was no longer there, the springiness of her ankle. How beautiful a foot was, how wonderfully made, how perfectly suited to standing and running and dancing. Nails that could be painted, toes that could wear rings; slim shapely ankles, feet that could be shown off in sandals, toes that could wriggle in the sand of a beach.

Things she had rarely thought about, Before.

That was me. The me with two legs, two feet, like everyone else. Then.

But the Me of Then was a person she no longer quite recognized. That Grace was a child, more than a year younger. She had never been to Flambards, never met Marcus or Jamie or Roger, Sally or Adrian or Skye; had never ridden a pony, watched otters or bats or listened to owls. She had never fallen in love with a place and its ghosts; had never seen a man drive himself to the brink of suicide, pulled back to live again. She felt quite dizzy with the swirl of experience.

The Me of Then wouldn't understand things she now felt she did understand, or at least was beginning to.

Would I go back? Would I change places with her?

To get my leg back? Like a shot.

But the other things? Would I change them?

No.

This is the Me of Now. This is Grace Russell, the Me I live with. And I think she'll be all right.

She hesitated, about to delete the photograph, but decided to keep it.

CHAPTER TWENTY-TWO

Do You Remember?

Late October

On the first weekend of autumn half-term, Marcus and Grace were heading back to Flambards, walking through the farmyard. Flash was on his lead because of the sheep; he stayed obediently at heel, though still eyeing them as if he knew he was meant to be a sheepdog, impatient for a proper job.

Later this afternoon there'd be a practice reading with Roger in the barn; then Grace would start packing for her trip to Paris. She and her mother were going there on Eurostar and spending most of the half-term break with Marie-Louise and her parents. She'd miss Marcus's birthday on Friday and felt wistful about that, but she had something special to give him – later today, if she could find the chance.

It had made for a smooth transition to Hales Green,

having Marcus and Jamie as friends 'looking out for you', as Jamie put it, and Skye in the same tutor group. At school she and Marcus referred to each other as cousins, although really they were only sort-of cousins. Telling people, 'I've got a cousin in Year Eleven' made her feel that she already belonged, especially when one girl said, with instant respect, 'Marcus Gregg? He's your cousin?' And she could count Jamie as an unofficial step-cousin as well, with her mum and Roger together now.

Every morning Grace and Marcus walked down the drive to wait for the school bus, and then back each afternoon. They often did homework together, in the cottage or the library or in Roger's flat in the main house, where Grace now lived; Marcus helped Grace with her maths, while she was better than him at French because of all the time she'd spent with Marie-Louise. The boys had mock GCSEs approaching soon, and Grace knew that Marcus worked hard at his studies while keeping up a front of not being much bothered.

She liked thinking of him as a Russell relation, with Russell blood and Russell looks, even if not – she felt sure – the temperament to lash out and hurt others. Adrian was the one for that. But maybe not any more.

'He won't ever be the Dad I remember, from when I was little,' Marcus had told her. 'He won't ever forget. Shouldn't, probably. But it's like he's got through the awful stuff and he's slowly coming out the other side.'

They'd reached the end of the sheep field. Marcus closed

the gate and put the chain-loop over, then said, prompted by nothing Grace was aware of, 'I think you're incredibly brave.'

'Me?' She was astonished. 'Why?'

'You know. Your accident, and everything since.' He gave her a quick sidelong smile. 'The way you just get on with things.'

'I don't exactly have much choice!'

'I know, but – you're special, Grace. Really special. I hope you know that.'

She felt too overwhelmed to reply. Marcus unclipped Flash's lead and they both watched him run ahead in great ground-devouring leaps.

You're special too, Marcus. I hope you know.

She had no idea what had made him say such a thing, but a moment later it became clear: he was looking for bravery in himself, of a different kind. When she asked if he had plans for his birthday next week, he hesitated, then said, 'Yes. I have got a plan. I'm going to come out to Mum and Dad.'

He looked at her for a response. She gazed back, surprised – but, she realized, not *very* surprised.

'You mean you're gay? But – that time when we talked in the drive – you said you weren't!'

Marcus smiled. 'I didn't say that. I said Jamie wasn't. And obviously he isn't. Does it matter?'

'Of course it doesn't matter! Does anyone know?'

'Jamie does. And Roger, since last week. And, erm, Liam. You know, Liam Solomon, in the sixth form?'

290

'Right. I've seen you talking to him a couple of times,' Grace said, recalling a tall, rather handsome mixed-race boy who was admired by several girls in her year. 'Cool! So you've told Roger but not your mum, though? Why all the secrecy?'

Marcus gave her a *do you really need to ask* look. 'Because of Dad. I don't know how he'll take it. I could never have told him, the way he was before – might as well stick my arm in a piranha tank.' He shook his head vigorously, walking on. 'No way I'd have risked it. Now, though, with Liam on the scene – at least I *hope* he's on the scene – well, it's time. I'm not looking forward to it, but things are different now. Mum'll be fine. Dad . . . who knows?'

'He might be OK with it. After all, he was hiding stuff himself. He knows how awful that was.'

'That's what Roger says. No more secrets.'

Grace saw that the episode at the lake, Adrian's slow recovery since and Sally's devotedness, had made honesty not only possible, but essential.

'Do it,' she said. 'It'll be all right.'

When she examined her own feelings, she found that she was glad. *I love him*, she thought. He had just made it possible to think that, without complication. And he loved her too, in a way. Hadn't he almost said so?

That needn't ever change.

Later, starting on her packing, she thought again of what he'd said about being brave, treasuring his words even though they made little sense. Fergus had been brave, and

Will was undoubtedly brave, and so was Christina, to ride those big horses and fly the Channel. And Marcus's father, to face horrors that had almost driven him to kill himself.

Her, though?

Surely not. You couldn't be called brave just for having an accident. That was nothing more than being in the wrong place at the wrong time. All the same, she glowed at the thought that Marcus thought she was brave, and special. With that to remember, she could face *anything*.

After all, she was a Russell.

She thought affectionately of her kindly ghosts, Christina and Will, who could stay here undisturbed by earth-movers and destruction. Flambards was safe, and so were the lake and the woods and their creatures, and Jamie had a new project, working with an expert from the Essex Wildlife Trust who was helping with what everyone now called the nature reserve. There were paths and undergrowth to be cleared during the winter months, and Adrian was involved too, making new gates to replace the stiles, and extending the bird hide with a ramp for wheelchair access.

He still had bad dreams, Marcus had told Grace, and often went quiet, retreating inside himself where no one could reach. But he had a mentor to talk to at such times, or just to be with.

'It's good you're staying on,' Adrian said to her once, while she and Marcus were helping him hang a gate. 'Especially as it turns out we're relations. Fourth cousins or whatever. Who'd have guessed it?'

She was beginning to see what the old Adrian had been like – relaxed, capable, taking pride in his work.

'It's great to be back,' he said, with his rare, dazzling smile that made Grace think she knew how Christina's Mark must have looked.

He'd only stayed away a few nights. But she knew he meant more than that. He was coming back from wherever he'd been.

It bothered her that she had kicked him hard, painfully, and never apologized. But how could she raise the subject? She wasn't even sure she really *was* sorry. What else could she have done?

'No, I don't think you should say anything,' Roger said, when she asked what he thought best. 'It'll only remind him of something he's ashamed of. It's not as if you're likely to kick him again, or anyone else, is it? I hope you'll never need to.' He thought for a moment. 'But if anyone tries to mug you on a dark night – it's good to know you've got a secret weapon.'

Roger and Jamie were already in the barn for the reading rehearsal. Jamie and Grace were to read pieces chosen by Roger and Grace's mum respectively: Grace's *Testament of Youth* extract and Jamie's piece from *All Quiet on the Western Front*, a story told by a young German soldier. Marcus, though, had chosen his own poem.

'It's a Siegfried Sassoon one we read at school.'

'Who Cat Siggy's named after,' Grace said. She knew Roger particularly liked Sassoon's poems.

'"Aftermath",' Roger said, looking at the printed sheet Marcus handed him. 'Yes, I know it. Mmm – excellent choice. That must come at the end. But you can go first now.'

Marcus stood at the end of the barn where they were imagining a stage, and read the poem aloud, his voice lifting to the barn's high spaces.

'*Have you forgotten yet?* . . .

For the world's events have rumbled on since those gagged days,

Like traffic checked a while at the crossing of city ways:

And the haunted gap in your mind has filled with thoughts that flow

Like clouds in the lit heavens of life; and you're a man reprieved to go,

Taking your peaceful share of Time, with joy to spare.

But the past is just the same – and War's a bloody game . . .

Have you forgotten yet? . . .

Look down, and swear by the slain of the War that you'll never forget.

Do you remember the dark months you held the sector at Mametz –

The nights you watched and wired and dug and piled sandbags on parapets?

Do you remember the rats; and the stench

Of corpses rotting in front of the front-line trench –

And dawn coming, dirty-white, and chill with a hopeless rain?

Do you ever stop and ask, 'Is it all going to happen again?'

Do you remember that hour of din before the attack –

And the anger, the blind compassion that seized and shook you then

As you peered at the doomed and haggard faces of your men?

Do you remember the stretcher-cases lurching back

With dying eyes and lolling heads, those ashen-grey

Masks of the lads who once were keen and kind and gay?

Have you forgotten yet? . . .

Look up, and swear by the green of the Spring that you'll never forget.'

There was a husky note in Marcus's voice as he reached the end, and Grace knew, as she was sure they all did, that it wasn't only the First World War he was thinking of.

'That's perfect, Marcus,' Roger said. 'Thank you. And Siegfried.'

Five days later, looking out of the window as the car approached Thiepval, Grace was thinking of this. Mametz was no longer just a word in the poem but a real place with signposts pointing the way; she had seen one a few moments ago.

They had driven out from Paris – Grace, her mother, Marie-Louise and her parents – in search of Will's grave. This final day of their visit was being devoted to their personal First World War pilgrimage.

'So *many* cemeteries!' Mum kept exclaiming, as another one came into view. 'My goodness!'

There were more and more, on both sides of the road: some with massive arches and walls, others only a few graves clustered around a stark, simple stone cross.

Grace looked out at stubble fields and grazing cattle, small villages, a roadside shrine, a stall at a crossroads selling vegetables and flowers. Only by the place names and the hundreds and hundreds of graves could anyone tell that some of the fiercest fighting of the war had been here, and the heaviest losses. Grace thought of the ghost soldiers Marcus and Jamie had seen at Liverpool Street, and the real owners of those names who'd headed here to die, all unknowing.

'So this is where the Somme fighting took place,' said Marie-Louise's father, at the wheel. 'Before the war the Somme was just a slow-flowing river that gave its name to the *département*. Now that one word has come to mean slaughter on a vast scale.'

Through Will and Christina and Mark, Grace felt a personal connection to the war, but now registered that a dull-witted part of her brain had expected the fighting to take place on something called a battlefield, marked out like a football pitch. Of course it hadn't. The war had been fought over fields and woods like those around Flambards.

It was as if enemy troops had camped by the lake in their wood, set up machine-gun posts at the edge of the trees and fired shells into the meadow, turning it into no-man's land. The ground between the two armies had been churned and ravaged, as in the photographs she'd seen; the front line had shifted in one direction or the other, at terrible human cost. It was oddly familiar from the poems and photos, but also distant. The unthinkable numbers of dead were tidied into respectful neatness and measured now by these lines of gravestones.

Their first destination, the Thiepval Memorial to the Missing, was a huge structure of brick and stone, set on a ridge and visible for miles around. Grace thought of a Lego giant bestriding the high ground, massive feet squarely planted. They left the parked car, walked up and stood dwarfed beneath the monument, and she saw its complicated structure, arches within arches that made many stone-panelled sides. Each of these faces was carved with thousands of names: the names of soldiers with no known grave, who had simply been lost in the slaughter.

They all stood silent and awed. When they spoke, it was in respectful whispers. A line from the poem sounded in Grace's head: *Look up, and swear by the green of the Spring that you'll never forget . . .*

Except that it was autumn now, not spring. The sky was grey and overcast, the trees wind-tossed, fallen leaves strewing the grass like copper coins.

Do you remember? The words, repeated through the

poem, tingled through her, as they had when Marcus read them aloud. In front of the huge memorial were a large number of gravestones with lettering that said simply, *A soldier of the Great War* or *Known Unto God*.

'Graves without names,' Mum said, 'and names without graves. Imagine losing someone and never knowing what happened to them!'

Marie-Louise's father took a great many photographs, and Grace took several too; Marie-Louise sniffed, dabbing at her eyes with a tissue. Grace did not cry. She felt a weight of solemnity too heavy for tears.

They returned to the car for the next stage of their journey.

Will's grave was not in a place of stern grandeur like the Thiepval memorial park. Grace's mother had found it on the Commonwealth War Graves website, and the sat nav took them northwards for more than an hour, then to a large village near Béthune, past a Super-U store and signs for *école maternelle* and *Bricolage*. Their destination this time was an ordinary cemetery, a large and sprawling one with an assortment of styles, grave after grave bedecked with urns, statues, photographs, real flowers, plastic flowers, even a teddy bear for a child – the bric-a-brac of mourning. By a wall at the back was a line of five war graves identical to the ones they'd seen at Thiepval and in every roadside cemetery on the way. Their simplicity was set against the clutter and fussiness of the rest: pale stone, cross and inscription, the headstones fronted by a neat strip of earth and closely mown grass.

'Here. Here he is.'

They had found him.

There was Will's name, on the middle headstone of five: beneath the regimental emblem with its soaring eagle and *Per Ardua ad Astra*.

CAPTAIN WILLIAM RUSSELL
ROYAL FLYING CORPS
28TH JUNE 1916 AGE 22

'Hello, Will,' Grace's mother said softly. Grace's throat was too tight to say anything at all.

Will Russell. Only twenty-two when he was shot down – just a few years older than Marcus and Jamie. The boy who had grown up at Flambards and found wings to fly had ended up here in the earth. Whatever plans or dreams he'd had for his future had been cut short. He'd died without knowing he had fathered a daughter, Isobel, continuing the line of Russells that led to Grace and her mother standing here.

'He doesn't know about us, does he?' Grace said.

It sounded silly, but her mother understood, and put an arm round her. Grace had the swimmy sense of double-vision she had felt before. Will came from four generations back; he was her great-great-grandfather from another century, and *Captain* made him sound grown-up and important. But he was also Will from Flambards: the boy with the wonky leg, the smiling face of the photograph, ambitious, clever

299

and bold; the young man who had loved Christina, and who she'd said was the love of her life, so soon lost.

If I were Christina, Grace thought, I'd have loved him too. He was so brave, so bold, and so frail.

She thought of Christina's name carved on Mark's gravestone, not Will's, as Mark's *beloved wife*. But she'd been Will's beloved wife first, and they lay in their graves hundreds of miles apart, separated by the English Channel and by Christina's long years of life. It felt as if Will was abandoned here. *This* version of Will.

'What would he think of us?'

'I think he'd be proud,' her mother said, and gave her a squeeze. 'And pleased we've come all this way.'

The village church bell sounded the hour with its resonant, distinctively French chime. Grace had brought a handful of conkers from the trees that lined the drive to the stables. It had been her mother's idea to bring something from Flambards: but what, they had wondered. Flowers wouldn't have lasted the five days since they left; berries would fade and wrinkle. Then Grace thought of the conkers, from the same trees Will would have known, walking past them many a time, maybe stooping to pick up a particularly shiny new conker from its split case – because who could resist doing that? And it was under those trees that she liked to imagine his ghost, almost-visible, as if he would have appeared if he possibly could.

He'd be there when she got back.

Carefully she placed the conkers on the well-tended strip of earth in front of the grave.

They took photographs; then Marie-Louise took several of Grace and her mother standing behind the grave, each with a hand resting on the curved top.

'The three of you!'

'The three of us. Three Russells.'

It was difficult to leave, but Grace knew she could bring herself back here in her thoughts whenever she wanted.

On this last evening they had dinner in a bistro, Grace's mother's thank you to Marie-Louise's parents for their hospitality. Grace had been showing her photographs of Flambards and its people and animals to Marie-Louise. She flicked through pictures of Plum, Jamie and his family, Mum and Roger in the garden; some of herself, in athletics shorts, with the new activity limb that meant she could run again. Run *fast*, like she used to.

'One of the boys in my form asked to try it on and have a go . . . Well yeah, only you'll have to cut your leg off first.' Flick, flick: Flash, Cat Siggy. 'And here's Sirius, Charlie's horse, with Marcus riding. Look – isn't he gorgeous!'

'Mmmm.' Marie-Louise took the phone and gazed, deeply appreciative. 'Yes, for sure. And the horse is also a beauty.'

Grace giggled, having set that up for her. 'And this one's of Skye. She's my friend at school.'

'She looks nice. *Géniale.*'

'Oh yes, she is. You'll meet her when you come to stay.'

Skye would never be a replacement for Marie-Louise,

Grace knew that. Their friendship was special, and would last – for ever, she hoped – whereas sunny Skye was the sort of open-hearted, confident person who seemed to like everyone equally and was popular in return. Skye was going out with another boy now, while Jamie was keen on a girl in Grace's year called Mia, but they were still on good terms.

'And this . . .' Grace found what she was looking for, and held out her phone to Marie-Louise, suddenly self-conscious. 'I drew this for Marcus. It's his birthday today.'

It was the ink drawing of Flash, the one she'd worked and worked on and at last perfected, or at least made as good as she could possibly manage. Flash in all his Flash-ness stared out of the drawing, smiley-faced, prick-eared, rough-haired, caught in a moment of eager alertness.

Grace had given it to Marcus after the rehearsal.

'An early birthday present,' she told him. He looked at her, then down at the card protected by two sheets of thin paper. He lifted the top sheet and made a small sound of surprise, gazing at the picture.

'You did this?'

She nodded.

'Oh, Grace,' was all he said. But the way he said her name, and looked at her, was more than enough.

Grace smiled, remembering.

'That's fantastic!' Marie-Louise exclaimed. 'You and Marcus are spending a lot of time together, yes?'

'Mm. We're good friends.'

'Not more than that?'

Marie-Louise had a boyfriend now, Fabien, and was keen for Grace to have one too. There *was* a boy she liked, Patrick in Year Eleven, who seemed to like her in return . . . but that was too tentative even to tell Marie-Louise, just yet. And they were talking about Marcus.

'Very good friends. But not the way you mean.'

'No? But you like him very much, I think? Please don't tell me he's got a girlfriend?'

'Nope.'

'Boyfriend?' Marie-Louise raised her eyebrows.

'Got it. Someone in the sixth form.'

'Aaaah. So you guessed right after all. That is just too unfair to girls.'

But Grace was content – more than content. It was odd now to remember her first days at Flambards, when Jamie had been her ally, Marcus distant and unapproachable, someone she'd never expected to get to know. Now both were important to her. Jamie was always around, at Marsh House and at school and at Flambards; his latest text was full of excitement about seeing marsh harriers in flight and a bittern in the reeds.

Grace had sent Marcus a happy birthday message earlier, but now she sent another, with photos of the Thiepval Memorial and Will's grave. An answer pinged straight back.

Must be amazing seeing it all. Wish I was there.

How's your day going? she asked. **Has the Big Moment happened yet?**

Not so big after all. Mum had already guessed.

Clever Sally! And your dad?

OK with it. Mega relief. (He'd added a whole row of grinning faces.) **I'm even bringing Liam home to meet them.**

Well done you! Grace returned, with a smiley face of her own. **I want to meet him properly too. Home tomorrow. See you then. Gx**

'For goodness' sake, Grace, put your phone away!' her mother called across the table – as if she didn't spend every spare moment texting Roger. 'Typical teenager! Come on, Gracey, we ought to be practising our French. It's our last chance. *Parlons français*,' she added: so unmistakably English and self-conscious that Grace couldn't help laughing.

Their remaining time ran out fast. At Paris Nord next morning they all said their goodbyes, exchanged hugs and thanks, made promises; Marie-Louise and her parents stood waving as Grace and her mother rode up the escalator to Eurostar departures.

Settling into her seat on the train, Grace felt a tearful mingling of sadness and happiness.

They'd be at Flambards this evening. Roger would meet them at the little station and drive them home.

It would be dark by then, but tomorrow was Sunday. She'd wake up with Cat Siggy on her bed (Mum disapproved, but Grace found ways of getting round that), and she'd look out of her window at the view she loved: meadow, autumn trees, sky in changing moods. She would cycle to Marsh House with carrots for Plum; she would ride across the fields, and maybe Marcus and Flash would run with her as they often did.

She thought of a phrase from Marcus's poem: *joy to spare*. Yes. So much; enough to make her giddy.

Her mother was looking at her phone. 'Roger says he's making a special meal for us tonight. A surprise.'

'Well, duh! How can it be a surprise now he's told you?'

'He hasn't said *what*.'

Grace reached for her own phone, thinking that she'd text Marie-Louise – **missing you already** – and maybe Skye. Rummaging in the front pocket of her rucksack, her fingers closed on the keyring Roger had given her. She pulled it out and held it in the palm of her hand.

He'd had a fob made with Jamie's otter photo on one side and Grace riding Plum on the other. On the ring, as well as the small keys for her school locker and bike padlock, there were two house keys. One was for Roger's flat, though he said she'd better stop calling it that now that she and Mum lived there too. The other was for the main door.

'The key to Flambards,' he said. 'Front door. You need your own key, now that you properly live here.'

In the window, her reflection smiled.

She was going home. Home to Flambards.

ACKNOWLEDGEMENTS

As always, I'm deeply grateful to David Fickling, Hannah Featherstone, Anthony Hinton, Bella Pearson and Linda Sargent for their editorial suggestions and encouragement and to Trevor Arrowsmith for being my first reader. I'd also like to thank Yvonne Coppard and Sue Hendra for their insights, and Gillian McBain, ambassador to Ottobock, for her specialist advice on adapting to a prosthetic limb. Thanks, too, to Katie Hartnett for her beautiful cover design.

Of course, my biggest thanks are to Kathy (K. M.) Peyton, whose captivating Flambards books inspired me, long ago in my student days, to make a serious effort to write for young readers. I couldn't have guessed then that I'd one day have the cheek to suggest this project to Kathy, or that she'd so kindly give me permission to use her characters and settings. I still can't quite believe that this book is here and finished, as well as I *can* finish it.

It's been a joy and a privilege to revisit the Flambards quartet and to imagine what happened to those unforgettable characters after the end of *Flambards Divided*, the final part. (Yes, it was tempting to call my book *Flambards Revisited*.) I hope admirers of *Flambards* will either approve or forgive. If, as I hope, *The Key to Flambards* brings new readers to K M Peyton's wonderful stories, I shall be delighted.

Linda Newbery, February 2018

NOTES

The Flambards quartet is published by Oxford University Press:

Flambards
The Edge of the Cloud
Flambards in Summer
Flambards Divided

Set before, during and after the First World War, the stories follow Christina from her arrival at Flambards at the age of twelve as far as young adulthood, leaving her in her twenties and about to marry Mark, with whom she's always had a tempestuous relationship. The only one of these books not set at Flambards is *The Edge of the Cloud,* in which Christina supports Will through his ambitions as a pilot, confronting many tests of her own bravery.

The Oxford Companion to Children's Literature describes the Flambards books as 'one of the major achievements of modern British fiction for younger readers.' K. M. Peyton was awarded the Carnegie Medal in 1969 for *The Edge of the Cloud,* and the Guardian Children's Fiction Prize in 1970 for the Flambards trilogy (as it was then). In the 2014 New Year Honours List she was appointed MBE for services to children's literature.

To find out more about the 'ghost soldiers' Marcus and

Jamie talk about on page 138, and to see them for yourself, visit https://www.1418now.org.uk/commissions/were-here-because-were-here/

On 1st July 2016, thousands of volunteers took part in 'we're here because we're here' – a UK-wide event marking the centenary of the Battle of the Somme. It was commissioned by 14-18 NOW and created by Turner Prize-winning artist Jeremy Deller and Rufus Norris, Director of the National Theatre. It was a strikingly clever and poignant way of remembering the huge losses of the Somme campaign and of reaching large numbers of the public.

The poet Marcus refers to on page 140 is Edward Thomas. Asked by his friend Eleanor Farjeon if he knew what he was fighting for, Thomas picked up a pinch of earth and crumbled it in his hand before letting it fall, saying, 'Literally, for this.' Edward Thomas was killed at Arras in April 1917.

The Patrick Ness book Grace and Marie-Louise have been reading is *Release,* published by Walker, 2017.

The readings by Grace, Jamie and Marcus for the Armistice weekend are from:

Testament of Youth by Vera Brittain, published by Virago

All Quiet on the Western Front by Erich Maria Remarque, published by Vintage.

'Aftermath' by Siegfried Sassoon, copyright Siegfried Sassoon, reproduced by kind permission of the Estate of George Sassoon. Widely anthologized. For more of Sassoon's war poetry, see *Poets of the Great War: Siegfried Sasson,* published by Faber.

Afterword, by K.M. Peyton
Author of Flambards

I wrote the first *Flambards* book fifty years ago, and the two sequels immediately afterwards. The fourth, *Flambards Divided*, was written twelve years later, after the first three books had been made into the TV series and been so successful that the actors (who had a whale of a time making it) wanted some more. Unfortunately their enthusiasm was not matched by Yorkshire Television (who had made the films) and no more was made, in spite of its popularity. So *Flambards Divided* stayed unfilmed. After that I thought enough was enough, although I sometimes toyed with yet more *Flambards*. I told Linda once how I thought the story would have continued, but I had since gone into pastures new with my series of *Pennington* books and did not want to go back to *Flambards*.

So it was quite a pleasant surprise to read how Linda has used my original story to base her own story on. She had asked me if she could do this and of course I didn't mind, not wanting to write any more myself. Funnily enough the real Flambards is a house near where I live, but although I filched the name my imagination over time changed the appearance of the house quite substantially. It is usually the way with writing: real places or incidents become the base for the writer's embroidery, usually straying so far from the original that the writer forgets where it all came from in the first place. 'Where do you get your ideas from?' is the most common question a writer is asked, and usually most writers can't answer it. 'Out of the blue' is no answer but mostly the one that springs immediately to mind. It is quite often that only years later the writer realises where a certain book was born. The same with the characters: we all say they are totally figments of our imagination, but is this true? How can they be? Amalgams of all the people we meet in some way, a bit of him, a bit of her. I only once totally wrote about a character who was a straight lift from my life, and when the book was published this character – the most real character I ever put into words – was dismissed in criticism as a complete stereotype. One critic said she was completely unbelievable. *Ho ho* I smiled: *come and meet her, she would love it. She would make mincemeat of you.* She is still one of my best friends as we both approach our nineties.

K.M. Peyton, May 2018